CONCERTO

Book One of the
Alexis Brooks Series

SANDRA MILLER

Concerto

Concerto
Published by Onda Mountain Books

Cover Art
Musical vignette LXVIII © Odyssei|Dreamstime.com
Crosshair sight © Blojfo | Dreamstime.com
Violin player violinist © Alenavlad | Dreamstime.com

Cover Design and Text © 2013 by Sandra Miller.

Copyright © 2010 by Sandra Miller

This is a work of fiction. Names, characters, places and incidents either are the product of the author's imagination or are used fictitiously, and any resemblance to any actual persons, living or dead, events, or locales is entirely coincidental.

Discover other titles by Sandra Miller at
www.sandra-miller.com

RITORNELLO:
The Nightmare

The dream was always the same.

I was running, running as fast as I could, running for my life--and for someone else's. Cold sweat pasted my clothes to me, and my feet screamed in painful protest. My throat made ragged choking sounds as I struggled to pull in air.

But I knew it didn't matter. I knew I was too late. A building loomed up ahead, a brick building with climbing ivy, a building I had to get inside. It was so close, and yet so impossibly far away. Still, it was in sight. I felt a doomed hope rush through me, and I did what I would have sworn couldn't be done--I ran even faster.

I was holding nothing back now, my muscles working so frantically there was no time for pain. One of my blood-spattered canvas tennis shoes worked itself completely off my foot on the stairs. I didn't slow down, really didn't even notice. My attention was fixed on the third-floor landing, coming into view. Just around the corner now....I had to go faster....

I heard a woman scream, but I couldn't have told you if it was me or her.

The door was cracked open. But even as I pushed it open I knew I was too late; even as I first saw her lying bleeding on the living room floor I knew I couldn't save her....

And then I heard the footsteps, and I knew I couldn't save myself.

MOVEMENT ONE:
The Nightmare Continues

I've got to tell you, there's nothing like a recurring nightmare about a brutal murder to really screw up your sleep.

Who am I? My name is Chrispen Marnett. I am a violinist, part-time artist and until this nightmare thing started, grounded realist.

This nightmare had been plaguing me for about a week. When I woke up screaming from the latest recurrence, it was three o'clock in the morning.

Now it was six-thirty that same morning, and I walked into the Green Room of the Newton Concert Hall. Rehearsal didn't start until eight, but what was the difference? I hadn't been able to sleep any more, and I was driving myself crazy pacing around my little house.

So I threw my violin in the car, picked up a big cup of steaming coffee from a convenience store, and went to rehearsal early.

I didn't really expect anyone else to be there so early. I

figured I was just lucky the building was open at all. The Green Room--which wasn't green at all, performer's lingo is weird sometimes--had wide counters along two walls, and sofas and chairs clustered around low tables around the room. Usually the room was crowded with people, and I would avoid the groups at the tables, standing by a counter to warm up. But today, the room was empty and I was tired. I left my violin case on the counter and sank into one of the chairs.

The quiet of the large room was very soothing. The only sound was the low hum of the air conditioning fans. I leaned my head back against the chair. Sleep at home was out of the question, but I was surprised to find I could drift off to sleep here, no problem. It would be sort of embarrassing when people started coming in, though...

The sound of a door opening jolted me fully awake. I could hear faint voices approaching. The hallway nearest to me led to the dressing rooms and soloist lounge, but this seemed to be coming from the far hall, which led to the restrooms and the conductor's office.

Nobody was likely to be in the Green Room restrooms at six-thirty in the morning. It had to be the conductor then--Darren Johnson must have been having a meeting.

"I'm sorry, Darren, I cannot discuss this any further."

Well, now I knew who Darren was meeting so early. That particular voice always made my knees a little weak. Alexis Brooks, international superstar, accused murderer, and concertmaster of the Newton Philharmonic Symphony Orchestra.

And an ongoing fangirl crush of mine since I was sixteen, but I was pretty sure this was not a good time to be thinking about that. The voices were getting louder now, and I was about to be involved in a confrontation between the conductor and the concertmaster of the symphony I worked for.

Not a pretty place to be. Pacing the house was not looking

so bad right now.

"Alexis, stop." I couldn't tell if Darren was trying to plead or command. "You aren't being reasonable, you have to see that."

"I don't care, I--" Alexis came around the corner and stopped short, staring at me. I could feel my face start burning. Terrific.

I tried to think of something to say to him, anything that wouldn't make me look like a psycho eavesdropper. But I was drawing a total blank, and so I was still standing there like a red-faced idiot when Darren came barreling around the corner after Alexis and nearly ran right into him.

"Alexis, I--oh, look, Chrispen is here!" Darren sounded like this was an unexpected gift. Whatever this argument was, he must really have been losing it. "Surely she will help us sort out this little difficulty. Won't you, Chrispen?"

I darted a glance at Alexis. He didn't say a word, just regarded me in silence. "I--you know I'm always happy to help when I can."

"There now," Darren said, as if this solved everything, "we'll soon have this settled. Let me bring you up to speed, dear girl. You are aware of our situation regarding the mid-May performance?"

Oh, boy. Mid-May--he was talking about the tribute concert. Alexis's birthday was May sixteenth, and we were featuring the Mendelssohn Violin Concerto in his honor.

This was not a disagreement I wanted any part of. I bit my lip and nodded.

"Naturally," Darren said. He put his arm around my shoulders as if we were old buddies. "Here's the rub, though--we can't find a soloist willing to play the Mendelssohn with us."

"Not one?" This was a surprise--with a concertmaster the caliber of Alexis Brooks, we had no problems lining up any soloist we wanted.

"Not one." Darren was emphatic. "It's his signature piece, you see? He defined it--it brought him international fame. No one is willing to play it with Alexis in the orchestra--would you sing 'Over the Rainbow' with Judy Garland in the chorus?"

I made some non-committal noise of understanding. I glanced at Alexis again, but he seemed content for now to listen, arms folded, regarding us both with what appeared to be amusement.

"So there we are," Darren continued. "A heavily advertised concert in two weeks, well on its way to selling out, with no soloist! It's untenable, you must agree. So the Board of Trustees thought, quite reasonably, that--"

"I won't do it," Alexis interjected. His tone was warning.

"Hush, dear boy. They thought, quite reasonably, that Alexis could play the solo himself. His trademark piece! First time in five years! Just think of the media stir!"

Alexis's glare could have cut stone. Whatever he was about to say, I could only assume it wasn't going to improve relations between him and Darren.

"I don't think that's such a good idea," I put in quickly, before whatever was behind that glare could find its way into words. Alexis looked at me in surprise.

Darren looked surprised too, and thoroughly deflated. "What?"

I shrugged uncomfortably. "Alexis obviously doesn't want to solo on that piece. I don't think you should force him."

Darren's eyes narrowed. "Don't think I should-- now look here, does he work for this symphony or not?"

"Darren!" I protested. "You're not being fair."

Alexis threw up his hands. "That's what I said. You want to honor my birthday by torturing me? No, thank you. It doesn't matter to me whether we have the damn concert or not. I'm not playing the Mendelssohn. Period." He shook his head and made a beeline for the door.

"I can still catch him," Darren said. "I can--"

I grabbed his arm. "Darren, wait. Maybe you should let him go. Are you sure you want to push this?"

He sat down and ran a hand through his graying hair. "No. I'm not sure at all. Alexis could be anywhere, anywhere in the world he chose to go--but he's here, and we are lucky to have him. I know that. You must think I'm a heartless old man. But what can I do? The Board specifically demanded that Alexis play this performance."

I sat down across from him. "Then they aren't being reasonable, either, however you try to justify it. I'm sorry, Darren, but I wonder if the lot of you aren't blinded by dollar signs. What's the real purpose of the mid-May concert? To honor Alexis, or to make a lot of money and publicity for the symphony?"

"To honor Alexis, of course." He sounded offended.

I shook my head. "Then how can you even ask that of him? The last time he played that concerto with this symphony, his wife died. He's never played it again since he played it at her funeral. He obviously isn't ready to play it now."

Darren looked at me bleakly. He probably regretted bringing me into the conversation at all. "Then what do you suggest we do?"

I couldn't detect any sarcasm in the remark. "For now, nothing. If you try to force him on this--I don't know, he seemed pretty upset. I think he might leave the symphony before he'd agree. We'll find someone else, anyone else."

He sighed. "But the Board--they want Alexis to play..."

I considered a moment. "The Board doesn't want to lose him any more than you do. Did I hear Dmitri Kast had to cancel his appearance with us next week?"

"News certainly travels fast. Yes, he's been hospitalized with pneumonia. There's no way he'll be able to play. Another problem the Board will want an answer for..."

"Well, what if you ask Alexis to fill that hole instead? Not with the Mendelssohn, but something else."

Darren suddenly seemed to be looking right through me to something on the other side. "I think you're onto something there. Not the Mendelssohn, but something he knows just as well. Something that provides some cover in case he cracks after so many years without solo performances...maybe not a solo, then, but--how about the Bach Double?"

"That's perfect. We've all played it so many times-- we'll have it ready, no problem. Dwight can play the second violin solo."

"Yes... " He stood up abruptly. "I'm going to call Alexis right now. If he doesn't show for rehearsal, you'll know it didn't go well."

He disappeared down the hall towards his office, whistling. He obviously expected it to go very well indeed.

I got up and went back to the counter. I was way too awake to nap now. May as well get some practice in, I decided.

My coffee was cold and my fingers were pleasantly warm and tingly from playing by the time other people started showing up for rehearsal. I laid my violin in its case and shook out my hands.

Alexis came back in and headed straight back to Darren Johnson's office.

A few minutes later, Dwight Richards came in. For some reason I couldn't quite put my finger on, I always felt tense when he was around. Dwight was the symphony's principal second violinist. He was dark-haired and dark-eyed and really a handsome man. He'd been asking me out pretty consistently since I came to town six months ago, but I just couldn't feel comfortable enough around him to say yes. We were pretty good friends though. He dumped his violin case in a chair, stretched, looked around, and saw me.

Uh-oh. I knew that look, and I didn't feel like having the same conversation, ending with the same no, this early this morning. I picked up my styrofoam coffee cup and headed for the sink farther down the counter, hoping to discourage him.

No such luck. "And how is Ms. Assistant-Concertmaster today?" demanded a cheerful, deep voice at my shoulder as I turned the water on.

"Oh, you know, could be better, could be worse," I said evasively, rinsing the cup and lid. "I didn't sleep well. But I'm still here, which is a plus. And you?"

He didn't answer. He stood there silently at my shoulder until I threw away the cup and turned around, and I saw he was frowning.

"What?" His scrutiny unnerved me. I looked away and saw principal violist Daniella Lewis walk in, scowl at us, and cross the room to sit down.

"I knew it," he said quietly. "You look terrible. What happened?"

I sighed. I didn't really want to talk about this with Dwight--he was insanely jealous of Alexis Brooks. Just the mention of our concertmaster's name could sour a conversation. But it wasn't like this one had been going so well anyway. "There was some excitement this morning. Alexis was pretty upset. But I think it all worked out all right in the end--it sounds like you're going to play the Bach Double with him next week. Pretty cool, right?"

Dwight didn't appear to think so. He stared at me a moment longer, like he was trying to hear everything I hadn't said. "That's it? Our high-and-mighty concertmaster was upset?" He paused. "And that upset you?"

"Well, he sounded to me like he might leave the symphony for awhile there."

Dwight snorted. "And that would be a Terrible, Bad Thing, right?" He looked like he was thinking about stomping off. "Look, there was a Newton Philharmonic Symphony Orchestra before Alexis Brooks came here. I'm sure we'd survive if he left."

I shook my head. "It wasn't the same, Dwight. You were here before Alexis came, you must know that. I just got here six months ago and I can tell. Newton's too small a town, and the symphony is too new to compete with the big East Coast orchestras. You'd never get the talent you have now without him. People don't go to Juilliard to play in little mid-west symphonies."

"People don't...wait, Ms. I-Went-To-Juilliard, why did you move out here, then?"

I could feel my face turn red. "For the opportunity to work with Alexis Brooks, of course. The greatest violinist of our age-- some say the greatest violinist who ever lived. And I get to share the first stand of the symphony with him. I'd have to be crazy to pass that up, right?"

Dwight was staring at me like I was sprouting horns. "And the fact that he was the prime suspect in his wife's murder--that he stood trial for it, and only got off on a technicality--that doesn't bother you at all?"

"No. I don't know how to put it but bluntly. I don't believe Alexis killed Madeleine Brooks."

Dwight's eyes narrowed. If the conversation had soured before, it was about to turn absolutely rancid.

Alexis leaned around the corner behind me, out of the hallway. "Oh, Dwight, there you are. Can you come back to Darren's office, please?" His eyes cut to me, and I swear he winked.

If it was possible, my face turned even redder. What was that about?

Alexis disappeared back down the hallway. Dwight stood looking at the corner with an unpleasant expression on his face.

Then he turned back to me.

"Chris, I..." He glanced back at the hall and shook his head. "Just take care of yourself, okay? I'll talk to you later." He went down the hall after Alexis.

The room wasn't cold at all, but I shivered anyway.

♫

I gathered up my violin and music folder and made my way out onto the stage before Dwight and Alexis came back. Tossing out my coffee was beginning to seem like a bad decision, even if it had been cold. Now that the drama was over, my lack of sleep settled over me like a feather comforter, and I didn't see how I would stay awake through rehearsal. I hoped the bright stage lights would help.

Quite a few others had come onstage too, and the hall was filling with the sound of an orchestra warming up, a distinctive cacophony of sound that is always unique, and yet somehow fundamentally the same. That sound always quickened my pulse, no matter how many times I heard it.

I had only come to Newton six months ago, so there were still a lot of people here I didn't know. I left my music on the stand and went over to one of the few friends I had made, my best friend, Kolbi Edwards.

Kolbi was a pianist, one of the best I had ever heard. But she also played several other instruments, so though she was technically part-time with the symphony, she was involved in almost every concert. For next week's concert, she was playing the harp solo in Bizet's *L'Arlesienne Suite #2*.

"Funny instrument, the harp," she said as I approached. "Popular culture says that angels play them. I wonder if the angels have blistered fingers and carpal tunnel syndrome like I do?"

I laughed. "I wonder if they complain as much as you do."

Kolbi laughed too. "Maybe, but not as much as you. Because the violin is the devil's instrument. So we know where all the real complainers are."

I shook my head. "Guilty as charged. How are things in the harpist's corner today?"

Her grin turned wicked. "In the harpist's corner, things are great. Out there where you are--maybe not so much. I hear we're deep diving today."

I tried not to groan, and was mostly successful. "Really?"

"Yup--and it can't be L'Arlesienne, because I've been released to solo practice today. So....watch yourself, Chris, Alexis hasn't been in a very good mood lately."

I nodded grimly. "That's par for the course, though, isn't it?"

Kolbi's short bark of laughter didn't have much humor in it. "Oh, if only you knew. Why do you suppose Jack Duncan left?"

Jack Duncan had been the assistant concertmaster before me. I glanced over my shoulder--over half of the seats were still empty. Plenty of time. "I have no idea. Why did he leave?" I pulled up the page-turner's chair and sat down.

"Jack was the concertmaster of this symphony after Alexei Brooks retired back, oh, ten or fifteen years ago. As soon as Alexis graduated from high school, Darren was after him to take his father's old job, but you can guess how that went."

I nodded. Alexis's rise to international fame touring the world immediately after high school was a well-known story.

"He came back five years ago to perform the Mendelssohn Violin Concerto for a benefit concert, but I don't think he ever intended it to be more than a guest solo appearance. He and Madeleine rented a little house, planned to stay a couple months visiting family, and have a real vacation.

"Only Madeleine--Madeleine died, and--part of Alexis seemed to die with her. He canceled all his engagements, bought the house they were renting, and just parked his life right there."

"And then the police accused him of the murder," I said, remembering the coverage, how gleefully the media had turned on their darling.

"Yes." Kolbi looked unhappy. "They....well, they did. There was never really any evidence for that. And then at the trial it came out that the prosecution had falsified the evidence they did have. The case was thrown out. Alexis, though--he was never the same. He crawled into his grief and locked the door behind him. If he had business cards, they'd say 'Alexis Brooks, Widower.'" She shook her head. "He took Darren up on his offer of the concertmaster position. So Jack was bumped to assistant-concertmaster."

"And then he left?"

"No, he didn't. He wasn't happy, but he knew what an opportunity it was for the symphony. And Alexis, he was here, but he wasn't, if you know what I mean. He played the music they gave him, and went home. Jack was still handling all the responsibilities of concertmaster.

"After a few years, though, Alexis changed. I think he got lonely. So he tried to fill that hole, the only way he knew--with music. He started the Madeleine Brooks Foundation, with the recital series and the music scholarship fund. And he started being the concertmaster, with a vengeance. The first violins had a brutal section rehearsal schedule, still do. He's always critical and pushing for more from everybody. He took over the second violins, and was even getting in the viola's business. That's when Jack left. He just couldn't take Alexis anymore."

"But you have to cut the man some slack," I objected. "Look what he's been through--how can anyone fault him for doing the best he can?"

"I agree with you," Kolbi said, plucking out a little melody on her harp. She still looked sad. "I guess what I'm getting at is-- keep the faith. Don't be a Jack Duncan. Alexis needs his friends around him."

"Am I his friend?" I said, surprised by the idea. For all my fangirl leanings, I had hardly spoken to Alexis in the months I'd been here.

"You could be. You know, I really think you could be."

For some reason, Kolbi didn't look so sad anymore.

♫

The stage was nearly full, so I figured I had better go ahead to my seat. Dwight came out to the stage, followed closely by Daniella. She was doing her best to talk to him, and he was doing his best to ignore her. It was funny, in a mean-spirited way. I pretended not to see the dirty look she gave me as she took her seat.

Dwight seemed to be in a good mood as he sat down on my left at the head of the second violins. He shot me a thumbs-up as he reached for his music. Darren must have propositioned him about that solo, then--which meant that Alexis must have accepted the arrangement. I couldn't say why that should make me feel so relieved, but it did.

Alexis and Darren were the last ones out, and both seemed in higher spirits than I had seen them that day. It seemed to raise the mood of the whole symphony.

And then Darren took the podium and said, "Today we'll deep dive into the Symphony in G-minor." The good vibe sailed right out the window, and a few people gave voice to the groan I had restrained earlier.

It was true, a deep dive on a symphony was going to take awhile. First we'd play through the symphony, then all the sections of the orchestra would split up and rehearse it individually. Finally, we'd all come back together and play it through again, presumably to show how much better we'd gotten. My theory was that a deep dive was a good way for Darren to have a rehearsal when he had other things to attend to. But I'd heard a rumor that Alexis had come up with it, which fit pretty well with Kolbi's story.

Either way, deep dives were not a favorite with the members of the orchestra. But it could have been worse. Mozart's Symphony Number 40 in G-minor was one of my favorite pieces--had been since college--and I always welcomed the chance to play it.

Our first play through was a bit rusty. To be expected, really, on the first piece of the day, but I think we were all glad to break out into sections, knowing we'd have a chance to redeem ourselves later.

I was ready for the worst. Really, Kolbi hadn't been kidding, Alexis had a habit of pushing everybody too hard. And I didn't think he'd be thrilled about my interference that morning, even if it had been Darren who really caused it.

No, I figured this section rehearsal was going to be a painful slog, so I buckled down and prepared to suffer through it.

He didn't waste any time. He spread his music out on the podium while we got ourselves settled, then perched on the stool in front of it. We sat there quietly, expectantly, waiting for instructions.

"From the top," he said, counted us in, and we were off.

We made it farther than I really expected to before he lowered his violin and called out, "Wait, wait! That B-flat--I don't think we're quite flat enough on that."

I reached for my pencil to mark the offending note on my part. A moment later, he counted us back in. There was a time, not too distant, when he would have called out the offending player by name, and made them replay the phrase until he was happy with it. More than once, each of us had taken a turn playing a particular phrase over and over, seeking his approval.

Come to think of it, I supposed I did understand why none of the other sections welcomed his interference.

So this mellowness was a pleasant surprise, but I knew it wouldn't last. The other shoe would drop.

I played along with the rest, and waited for that shoe. We were all taking our places back out onstage before I finally realized that it wasn't coming.

Wow. I thought about it as the section leads conferred with Darren in the wings. That was probably the least stressful section rehearsal we'd ever had, at least since I had been there. Was it just coincidence that we played so much better today?

The last play through was awesome. I couldn't speak for the rest of the symphony, but the first violins were on fire. Darren seemed to notice as well.

"Alexis, my boy," he said as we packed up our things, "whatever you did today, bottle it and bring it for our next deep dive. Your section was amazing today."

He patted my shoulder as he walked by. "And Chrispen, thank you for your help today. I know the Board of Trustees will be pleased with this arrangement."

What I said was, "Anytime."

But I watched Alexis pack up his violin, and what I thought was, "Hang the Board of Trustees."

Kolbi grinned at me knowingly, and I stuck my tongue out at her.

About an hour after I went to bed, the phone rang. Late night phone calls are always scary. Nobody calls late without a reason, and the reason is usually bad. I rolled over and reached for the handset on the nightstand. What had happened? Was someone sick? Or--dear Lord, had someone died? My father had passed away when I was in high school, but my mother still lived back in Carolina, and I hadn't talked to her since last weekend. What if--

The caller ID screen said "Private."

Private? Really? Someone called me at that hour and blocked their number? I punched the talk button. If a telemarketer answered, they were never going to know what hit them.

"Hello?"

Nobody answered. "Hello? Hello?" Nothing.

I frowned. There was silence, but not dead air--it sure seemed like this call was connected to something.

I was out of patience, though. I hung up the phone and rolled over to go back to sleep. If it was important, they'd call back. If not, well, that would be even better. I was really tired.

Ten minutes later, the phone rang again. I swore under my breath as I grabbed the handset. It still said, "Private."

I attempted to be reasonable--it wasn't easy, given my current mood. Maybe something had gone wonky with the first connection, so I just hadn't been able to hear what they had said. Maybe they'd dumped hot coffee in their lap, and had to hang up and tend to it before they could call me back.

"Hello?"

Or maybe it was just some kid making prank calls. I hung up. I'd always heard those kind of people did it for the reaction--a total lack of response was generally the best way to handle them. I hoped my particular lack of response would encourage this particular punk to find a better hobby.

When the phone had not rung again after fifteen minutes, I started to breathe normally again. The excitement was over, so maybe I could finally get some sleep. At the rate I was going, I wasn't going to be worth anything the next day. I rolled over on my back and stared up at the ceiling fan, making lazy slow circles above me. It made me even sleepier, and without meaning to I closed my eyes.

The damned phone rang again.

At this point I was out of reasonable excuses. I also was

beginning to doubt this was an ordinary prankster. The timing of these calls was too deliberate. And not once had I been asked if my refrigerator was running, or if I had Prince Albert in a can.

Silence did not discourage this caller.

Well, whatever his deal was, I was done with him. The answering machine could get it, and then it and he could make silence at each other for as long as he wanted. Maybe that would settle him.

After a few rings, the machine did pick up. I could hear my voice inform the caller that I was not available, and the obligatory beep. With quiet thus restored, I rolled over to make another attempt at sleep.

"I see you."

Oh, man. I wish I had words to tell you how totally, completely freaked out I was right then. If I lived a thousand years I would never forget that voice--rough, gravelly, and very male. He said his few words, then there was a soft click as he hung up the phone.

My skin crawled all over. This was no kid, no casual prankster. A line had just been crossed here, and I didn't see any reason to believe he would quit now.

First I unplugged the phone. Let him call all night if he felt like it. Maybe that kind of silence would discourage him.

Then I erased his message. Just seeing that red number 1 flashing in the darkness, knowing what was behind it--well, it severely creeped me out.

There was no way I was getting to sleep under my own steam now. None. I went into the bathroom and slugged down a couple of Tylenol PM with half a glass of water.

Carefully keeping my mind away from what I most wanted to think about, I made my way back to bed.

Knowing that the telephone was unplugged made the silence seem unnatural.

I curled up on my side, staring at the numbers on my alarm clock and waiting for sleep to find me.

♪

It felt like only a few minutes later when something forced me awake--doggedly, insistently nagging at the back of my mind until I couldn't ignore it. I lay still in the quiet a moment, then rubbed at my eyes, resisting an urge to cry. I couldn't remember a time when I'd felt so bone-tired.

What on earth had woken me? As tired as I was, there was no way I'd have awakened on my own. Even now, I could feel the Tylenol PM pulling me toward sleep.

It took me a moment to identify the ringing, drifting in from another room. That utterly dumbfounded me, because even with the drug clouding my brain I clearly remembered unplugging the phone. So just how did it manage to be ringing now? And why did it sound so weird?

Oh, right--the fax machine in my office. I worked that out about the time the ringing stopped and the machine picked up. This was why I hated sleeping pills. My brain felt wrapped in cotton, my wits were addled. Figuring out the fax machine was ringing felt like solving a real puzzle.

I pushed myself out of bed and trudged down the hall to the office, sleep weighing on me like a physical force.

Sure enough, the fax machine in the corner was printing away. There were probably ten or twelve pages stacked up in the tray already. I raised my hand to cover a yawn. Someone was apparently trying to fax me a novel.

Someone--

I froze mid-yawn, creeping horror prickling my scalp. This couldn't be connected to the phone calls, right? Because some random caller wouldn't have my fax number. And I so wanted this to be random. If it was random, this was likely to be the only night like this I'd suffer. If not-- well, I didn't even want to consider that.

My hand was shaking as I reached for the stack of papers. One glance told me that this was far from random.

I SEE YOU

I felt faint. And I seemed to have tunnel vision--all I could see were those creepy, ransom-note letters, wavering in front of my eyes as my hands trembled. The room was suddenly very cold.

Every paper in my hands had the same message. The damn fax machine was still printing, too; another stack of messages was quickly forming.

I felt like screaming and tearing my hair. Instead, I jerked the fax machine plug out of the wall.

I gathered up all the faxes and went to the kitchen. I grabbed a box of matches, and burned each page to ashes over the kitchen sink, one at a time. Then I ran the ashes down the garbage disposal.

I couldn't have said why, but that little ritual did make me feel better. I poured myself a small measure of blueberry wine. Between that and the medicine, I figured I'd have no trouble sleeping.

At least, I hoped not.

I was up early the next morning, whether I liked it or not. I slept only as long as the medication could hold me there, then I was too freaked out to sleep more. The memories were surprisingly vivid, given the state I'd been in.

And now, in the cold light of morning, I discovered I wasn't just spooked by my strange phone friend. I also felt the first flickering of anger.

I reckoned that this was probably healthy. I was coming to recognize this type of harassment as a violation, in a way I had not understood before it happened to me. Fear was fine; fear would keep me safe, but only anger would find a way to stop this from happening again, if anything would.

So before I even gave in to the inevitable and got out of bed, I was kicking around the idea of blocking the caller.

I was pretty frustrated to find that you had to know the phone number you wanted to block. Allowing the caller to block sending their number, which was required if you wanted to block them...at that moment it felt like the system was designed to protect him, not me. Those flickers of anger were growing into crackling flames, and that didn't feel healthy at all.

So I grabbed a bagel from the kitchen and headed into my office for my morning practice, perhaps a little early today, but sorely needed if my blood pressure was any indication.

I threw a towel over the fax machine so I wouldn't have to look at it. I lifted my violin out of its case and looked it over carefully, wiping away a spot of rosin dust I had missed after yesterday's rehearsal. These older instruments could be temperamental, and a sudden change in temperature or humidity could sprout a crack or open a seam. Mine was a 1610 Maggini I called Matteo--it was the perfect shade of brown, with delicate shaping and striking grain. The purfling at the top and bottom of the back was wound into beautiful, elaborate designs. The violin was my prized possession. It was currently insured for $1,750,000, but no amount of money could really replace it.

Today's inspection revealed no flaws, so I tightened and rosined my bow, shook my hands, and started playing long, slow three-octave major scales, loosening up my fingers and warming up my vibrato.

It is one of the joys of a really fine violin that even chores like scales become a pleasure to play. I never tired of the sweet, rich voice of a violin under my ear, even if it was only playing a G major scale.

As my hands limbered up I moved to scales in thirds, and octaves, with more complex bowing patterns. I played through a few fast arpeggios to get my fingerwork up to speed.

This practice had been the perfect call, I already felt so much better. I could always count on playing the violin to even out my mood, no matter what was wrong. I spread out my parts for next week's concert and started working through those.

But all too soon, I was done with them. I folded everything shut and tucked all the music back into my black symphony folder, frowning. When I had moved here from North Carolina, I had driven here in my little Toyota, only the barest essentials with me. My music library had stayed at my mother's house--it had to, I didn't have room for it in the car. We figured she could ship it out later, when I had gotten settled, only I had never asked her for it. I couldn't say I had ever really missed it until now.

I wiped my violin down, loosened the bow and put them back in the case. Clearly it was time to ask.

I left the office, considering. I would call her--but I was going to wait awhile longer. My mother was a notoriously late sleeper, and I had no desire to disturb her if she was having better luck than me in that regard. First, I'd grab the morning paper and give it a read-through. After that, it should be late enough to call Mom and ask her to ship out my music.

I pulled open the front door, and my jaw dropped. I stared around the front yard a moment, trying to make sense of what I was seeing. The image was pretty clear, but my brain flatly refused to accept it.

Copies of last night's fax plastered my lawn. The grass was strewn with them. They had been taped all over my mailbox, to my car, to the front door, across all the windows....the trunk of the big tree was wrapped with them. I even thought I could see a few caught way up in the branches.

I just stood there, trying really hard to maintain my composure. My throat was making little choking sounds.

The anger that had been smoldering all morning erupted into white-hot flames that threatened to consume me. My temples pounded, and I could hear my pulse thumping in my ears.

A neighbor walking his dog down the sidewalk looked curiously from my littered lawn to me. I couldn't blame him, but it did nothing to improve my mood. I slammed the front door shut and leaned against it, trying my best to think.

Okay, so my place was trashed. That was not cool. But standing here in the foyer hiding from the neighbors wasn't helping the situation at all. I sighed and went to get the big trashcan out of the carport.

It took forever, gathering up all those papers, prying some of them loose from whatever they had been attached to, and stuffing them into the trash can. When I pulled all the papers off the windshield of my car, I found a message in white paint on the glass.

I SEE YOU

After the trash can was finally full, and the windshield scraped and cleaned, I stood in the carport and looked around the yard again. It was hardly recognizable as the wreck that had greeted me that morning.

But in my mind's eye, I saw the same man who had made all those calls running off all those copies of that fax, the light from the photocopier casting a faint green glow on the smirking face whose features I could not imagine. I saw him creeping around the outside of my house while I tried vainly to sleep inside, taping those awful messages all over everything.

All of the sudden I had to get away from the house. Forget calling Mom--I would go out and buy a whole new library. It would take me awhile. With any luck, it would take me all day.

I locked up, grabbed my purse, and headed for the car.

An hour later I was at the House of Violins music shop, raiding their music bins. I wasn't overly concerned with what exactly I bought, as long as there was a lot of it. I wanted enough music to keep me busy for months. I wanted so much music to work on that my mind would have no time to dwell on this twisted man currently disrupting my life.

Maybe it wasn't the best coping strategy, but it was all I had.

Vivaldi's *Four Seasons?* Absolutely.

Paganini's *Twenty-four Caprices?* Bring it on.

The Devil's Trill? Yes.

Sibelius *Violin Concerto?* My favorite--throw it on the pile.

Brahms *Violin Sonatas?* Sure, why not?

I had a substantial pile of music. Not much I hadn't played before, but that didn't matter. I could still work them back up.

I pulled out a nice edition of the Mendelssohn Violin Concerto and regarded it thoughtfully. That would be fun--I hadn't played that one since my freshman year of college. I thought I would really enjoy working on it again. I flipped through it, checking out the arrangement.

All at once, Alexis Brooks was standing beside me. It gave me a start--I hadn't even realized he was in the shop and I sure didn't remember him walking up to me.

"Hello," I said lamely, trying to cover my surprise.

"Hello yourself," he returned, seeming to all purposes very casual. But I frowned--in spite of his easy words he was projecting an intensity that made me nervous. "I see you're stocking your music library."

I nodded. There wasn't really much I could add to that.

"You'll like the Mendelssohn Concerto," Alexis said suddenly, looking directly into my eyes, which sort of stopped my brain, "although the included fingering-- especially for the second half-- is less than ideal. I think my substitutions will suit you better."

I stared at him blankly, confused. Substitutions? Now what was he talking about? Did he ever say anything that wasn't cryptic?

His smile was funny, like he'd laugh if he didn't think it would hurt my feelings. He gave me a small, controlled bow, picked up a new violin case he'd evidently just purchased, and left.

I shook my head and put my music on the counter, still confused. "What was that all about?"

The cashier shrugged and handed me a copy of the Mendelssohn, an older edition than the one I had looked at. "Maestro Brooks bought it, wrote in some fingerings, and left it for you," she said, like that explained everything. And maybe for her, it did. A gift of music--surely a usual thing for musicians. How could she have known just how strange it really was? Fingerings for solo pieces were something every musician worked out on their own; they weren't generally shared, except from teacher to pupil, or perhaps between close friends. But neither situation applied here, and it was an emotionally sensitive piece, to boot. It just didn't make sense, from any angle.

The girl shook her head and smiled, revealing a pair of dimples. "Isn't he something?"

"Yes," I agreed, watched Alexis drive out of the parking lot in his white Jaguar. "Yes, he certainly is."

♪

The first and second violins had a combined section rehearsal that evening. I put my case on the counter and got out my violin to warm up, but no sooner did I put bow to strings than Dwight appeared in front of me. He was grinning like something great had happened.

I kept my violin and bow up a moment longer just to annoy him, then lowered them. "All right, I'll bite. What's got you in such a good mood?"

"So, are you going?" he answered, which to my mind wasn't much of an answer at all. "You are going, right?"

"Dwight, you have got to know I have no idea what you're on about."

He looked honestly surprised. "You haven't heard about the recital? But it was the front page of the entertainment section!"

"Oh," I said, remembering. "Yeah, I didn't read the paper this morning because--well, I just didn't."

"I can't believe you haven't heard! Of course, I can't believe they managed to keep it under wraps until today--I suppose he must have wanted it that way, but--"

"*Dwight,* what are you talking about?"

"Alexis! He's giving a recital tomorrow night! Here!"

I stared at him. It felt like my brain had missed a shift. "Alexis? But he hasn't done a single solo performance in..."

"Five years, I know!" he crowed. "It'll sell out, you watch. I'm going--do you want to go with me?"

"Gee, Dwight, thanks for asking, but I'd better pass."

He stepped in uncomfortably close to me. I wanted to take a step back, but I was already against the counter. "Come on, Chrispen, don't be like that. Would it kill you to go out with me just once?"

I blinked at him in stupid surprise.

He shifted his stance. "I'm sorry. I'm a bit desperate--see, I already have two tickets. If you won't go with me I'll have no excuse not to take Daniella, and Chris, I really, *really* don't want to do that."

I started to say no. I took a breath to say no, I was *going* to say no--but then I happened to glance over Dwight's shoulder and saw Daniella on one of the sofas, fists clenched, staring daggers at me.

I smiled weakly, swallowing my planned response. "Sure, Dwight. Okay."

So it was childish. I admit that. But I hadn't spoken two words to that woman, and she hated me. That seemed pretty childish, too. Might as well give her a reason. And it gave me a petty kind of pleasure to deliberately aggravate her.

And I'd made Dwight happy, too. He beamed at me, and for a moment I could see what Daniella saw in him. "Great! I'll pick you up about six?"

I nodded, but before I could speak, he glanced at the door and his expression crumpled and became sullen. The moment, it seemed, was over.

I turned to follow his gaze and found Alexis, about to walk by us.

"Alexis!" I called out, a little louder than I had intended. I couldn't let him get by--he was the only escape I could see from the corner Dwight had me backed into. "I wanted to thank you for--"

"Hush!" He grabbed my arm and hauled me out of the corner, right past Dwight. He didn't slow down though, and so we crossed the room quickly in an awkward lockstep.

"But I only--"

"Kindly," he cut me off between clenched teeth, "keep your mouth shut."

Well, that was pretty clear. Wasn't I the one always telling everyone they had to cut Alexis some slack? Turned out it wasn't as easy as I thought. I bit my tongue and stumbled along beside him, trying not to think the word *jerk*.

We rounded the corner into the far hallway, and he threw open a rehearsal room door. I don't think he expected to find a couple of cellists in there making out.

Alexis made a small sound of impatience. "Wrong kind of warming up," he informed them dryly, and they scattered out the door toward the Green Room in considerable embarrassment.

Alexis gave me a push into the recently vacated room, and shut the door behind us.

"Fancy a little warming up?" I quipped when he turned back around. It wasn't nice, but I was low on patience.

He rolled his eyes. "Ha, ha. You're quite a wit." He lowered his violin case into a chair gingerly, as if it had made his shoulder sore.

"So I'm allowed to speak now?"

"I'm sorry, Chrispen. I know that was rude..."

"Psycho, even," I interjected helpfully.

"...but I couldn't think of any other way. I don't think the whole symphony needs to know about the Mendelssohn."

I stared at him. I was pretty sure one of us wasn't making sense, and I hoped it wasn't me. "I wasn't planning to make a general announcement, Alexis. I was only talking to you."

He sighed and sat down heavily in a chair next to his violin. "It would be better if Dwight didn't know. He was standing with you."

As if I could have missed that. Still....it occurred to me that Dwight's problem with Alexis maybe wasn't an isolated thing. Maybe Alexis had issues of his own.

He didn't seem inclined to discuss it further, though. He sat quiet in the chair, hands on his knees, and regarded me calmly.

"So...what I wanted to say was thank you. You know, for the

Mendelssohn. You were right--your way is better."

He smiled at me, and the room lit up. "I'm glad." He reached for his violin case and started digging around in the music pocket. "It gets better, though."

"It...does?" How could a person be so difficult to have a normal conversation with?

"Sure. See, you've only got half." He pulled a couple sheets of paper out of his case and handed them to me. "Here's the other half."

Honestly, I had no idea what he was talking about.

The two sheets of music in my hand were utterly unfamiliar. This could have been anything. And it wasn't even labeled.

But--it was in E-minor. I looked closer, followed the melody...and all at once I could hear this in my head. I *knew* this. It had been on Alexis's first CD, the one he made while he was still in high school, the one that made him famous.

"This is your cadenza!" I blurted in sudden understanding. "Your cadenza to the Mendelssohn Violin Concerto. The cadenza you wrote yourself."

He grinned at me. "Yes. I hope you like it."

"Like it? I *adore* that cadenza! But are you sure you want to share it?" I had known a couple other violinists who liked to write their own cadenzas; a cadenza was tailor-made for displaying personal strengths, and showcasing your mastery of your instrument. But I had never known a violinist who had written their own cadenza and given it to anyone else.

"I've kept this to myself for far too long," he said soberly. "I think it's high time I shared it with someone else."

I couldn't place the tone in his voice. But it felt like things had taken a left turn somewhere, and I wasn't sure how to bring the conversation back on track.

As it turned out, I didn't have to. There was a small click from the doorknob, and a second later the door was open and

Dwight was standing in the doorway.

"There you two are," he said flatly. "It's about time to start, everyone's heading for the stage."

He gave me an accusing look, and for some stupid reason my face turned red.

Alexis looked at my face and laughed. "I'm running this rehearsal," he told Dwight, "it's time to start when I say it is." He turned to pick up his violin case, effectively shutting Dwight out of the conversation.

It was a move I would never have gotten away with, but it worked for Alexis. Dwight left with no further comment. None we could hear, anyway.

Alexis pulled the violin case strap over his shoulder, and motioned me toward the door. As I passed him, he leaned closer to me.

"Blushing easily isn't a crime," he said quietly, "but it sure can make you look guilty."

I looked at him in surprise, and I could feel my face burning again. Alexis laughed, and we walked out of the room.

But I couldn't stop wondering--what was I guilty of this time?

♫

When I got home after rehearsal late that night, the phone was ringing and the answering machine light was blinking 3. I grabbed the phone.

"Hello?"

"Hi, Chrispen, it's Kolbi."

"Oh, hey, Kolbi." I hit the playback button, and tried to keep one ear on her and the other one on the machine, while I poured myself a glass of iced tea. Multitasking: it's not just for computers anymore.

"Message One," the synthesized voice on my machine announced, and the recording began to play. "The House of

Violins would like to announce their new selection of fine bows!
Come in today and--"

"--and then I heard about Alexis's recital," Kolbi said, "and of
course--"

"Message Two: Hi Chrispen, my girl, it's Darren. I wanted to
let you know we're canceling rehearsal tomorrow to allow
everyone to attend the recital, and--"

"--naturally, but *five years?* Seriously? I wonder--"

"I see you."

I spit tea all over the counter. The message had my full
attention.

"Nice Alexis Brooks poster." My eyes cut fearfully to the
collage on my living room wall--how could he know? *How?* "I
hope your tea is just as nice. I made it just for you."

I must have repeated "oh, my God" half a dozen times before
I realized I was doing it.

"Chrispen!" Kolbi's voice cut through my rising panic. I had
sort of forgotten her. "What is it?"

"I have to go, Kolbi. I think--I think I need to call the
police."

"Okay." She must have heard some of what had happened.
"Call me as soon as you can. I'm worried about you."

I agreed and hung up the phone, but my mind was still
repeating, *oh, my God.* This madman was in my *house!*

And might still be in my house...

I breathed deep, trying not to pass out. I grabbed a kitchen
knife out of the butcher block and edged out into the living room,
my heart crashing in my ears.

"What do you want?" My voice sounded hoarse, like a rough
whisper. Like one of those dreams where you want to scream,
but can't make the sound come out.

The only reply was the fluttering of the drapes hanging out of
the open front window.

I felt faint. I closed my eyes and forced myself to keep breathing. Steeling myself, I pushed the playback button on the answering machine.

Nothing happened.

Someone had erased my messages.

So I called the police. I mean, this lunacy had gone on long enough, right? This guy was a nutter. He had my phone number, my fax number, and had evidently broken into my house. It made me feel ill.

Time to call in Johnny Law to put the smack down on this guy.

The police officer arrived at my house at 12:30 that morning. He introduced himself as Officer Parker, and sat quietly on the couch and listened to me tell the story of my night so far, the creepy message and the iced tea and the open window.

He brushed for fingerprints on the answering machine, but the only prints there were mine. He checked the front window, from the inside and outside. He walked through the kitchen and the living room, and spent several long minutes examining my collage poster of Alexis.

"You made this poster?" he asked, backing away a few steps to see it all at once.

"Yes." Really, poster wasn't a good word for the things I made, but I didn't have a better one. It was something like a large scrapbook style display, laid out on fabric covered plywood and coated with lacquer to protect it. This one had photos, programs, ticket stubs, newspaper clippings, and all kinds of laces and trims to make it pretty. I was very proud of it--it was beautiful--but for some reason this cop's attention was bothering me.

"I work with Alexis Brooks," I told him, perhaps a bit defensively.

"That so." He moved closer to examine individual photos. "Know him very well?"

I shrugged. "Well enough." He sounded like he wanted me to think he was just shooting the breeze. But I didn't think that, and he was making me uncomfortable. Really uncomfortable--I felt almost nauseous.

Officer Parker sat back down on the couch and looked at me with a guarded expression that did not bode well.

"Miss Marnett, I don't know any other way to say it. There isn't much we can do for you."

If I hadn't felt so awful, I'd have protested. He seemed almost to expect it, pausing before he went on.

"You say a man broke in through your front window. There are no signs of forced entry, and there is no damage at all to the window. You say he left a message. There is no message. You say he erased it. There are no fingerprints on the machine. There are no fingerprints anywhere. You say he made iced tea." He made a face. "He made iced tea? A man broke into your house to make *iced tea*? I don't even know what to do with that one. I don't have any evidence of a crime here, and there isn't much I can do. I can file a report for you, but that's about it."

I rubbed at my pounding temples. "I see."

He looked at me and sighed. "Look, I wish I had better news for you. If you want some free advice though-- stay away from that character." He jerked his chin in the direction of my collage.

"What, Alexis?"

"He's bad news. I expect you're new in town, or you would already know that. You seem like a nice lady, and you don't want to get mixed up with that Alexis Brooks."

I just stared at him. I didn't even know how to answer that.

Officer Parker looked away. "If there's nothing else...?"

"No." I felt like I might be sick. "No, there's nothing else. Thank you for your time, officer."

He picked up his hat and left.

♪

"He didn't believe me," I said flatly, rinsing the tea down the kitchen sink. I was discouraged, and I felt terrible.

There was a short silence on the phone. "What?" Kolbi managed to pack a lot of outrage into one short word.

I sighed. "He couldn't find any proof of anything I told him. He'll file a report, nothing else."

"Damn. Did you tell him how this man has been harassing you?"

"Honestly, no, I didn't. I'm really not feeling very well at all right now, Kolbi, and I don't have any evidence, since I threw out his faxes."

Kolbi sighed. "I still think there ought to be something more they can do for you."

My throat closed up all at once, and I couldn't breathe. I was panicking, trying to say something, to ask Kolbi for help, *anything,* but the only sound I made was a sort of strangled gasp I was pretty sure she couldn't even hear.

"Chris? Are you there?"

I tried again. The room was spinning like mad, and things were starting to look kind of speckled and sparkly.

"Chris?" Kolbi's voice rang with alarm, even over the roaring in my ears. "Are you okay? Chrispen! *Are you all right?*"

I wanted to answer her, I really did. But I couldn't breathe and the phone slipped from my hand, and everything went black.

♪

Falling.

I was falling, endlessly falling, tumbling over and over in a bottomless black void. I fell faster and faster, the wind rushing in my ears....

"I think she's coming around."

The words floated by me, nagged at my attention for a moment, and were gone. The black void swallowed me again, unrelenting.

"Nah, false alarm. Should I try to wake her?"

"If you can wake her, I think you should."

Two voices, one male, one female. Beyond that--well, the pounding pain increased every time I tried to consider who they were, or where I was. Better not to think about it. I sank unresisting into the blackness.

Someone was trying to drive away my comforting blackness. Short slaps, rhythmic and sharp, stung my cheeks, forcing me to awareness.

"Come on, Chris, wake up. Don't leave us."

The female voice was pleading, and naggingly familiar.

Was she the one slapping me? Why did I hang around with people who treated me like that?

Nothing made sense, and apparently I was not going to be allowed to rest in peace. I groaned and cracked an eye open a sliver.

My eye, dry and crusty, protested this vehemently until I closed it again. But I had managed to make out a Jaguar emblem embedded into the tan leather of the thing I was slumped against.

That's when it all came together, like the flip of a light switch. Alexis drove the Jaguar. Why I was there, I had no idea. But I had heard his voice earlier--his and Kolbi's. She was the one who had slapped me to awaken me.

I scrubbed at my eyes with the heels of my hands. I felt like hammered hell.

The Jaguar took a sharp left and I was pitched away from the door into Kolbi, who caught me and tried to stabilize me.

"Could you drive a little slower?" she asked. She didn't sound angry, just worried.

"No," Alexis said shortly. "We're almost there. How is she?"

"I think she's waking up. She's having a hard time of it, though. Something's wrong."

"We knew that. Hang on."

The car whipped around a sharp turn and stopped hard. I forced my eyes open--I swear, I could hear them creaking--and found the world to be a dark, blurry mess. I rubbed my eyes again. I could see Kolbi's pale, strained face peering at me in the uneven darkness. "How do you feel?"

"Bad." My voice was creaky too.

The door next to me opened, and Alexis leaned in, as pale and worried as Kolbi. "Can you walk?"

"I--I think so." Actually I wouldn't have bet money on it. But since Alexis had asked, I was going to try.

He took my hand and helped me gingerly out of the car. "Kolbi, come around here and take her other arm in case she stumbles."

We were in a parking lot, in front of a large, bright building.

"Is that a hospital?" The words seemed to come from somewhere else.

Alexis nodded. "Yes. And we are taking you in there."

I didn't really have an answer for that. "Why?"

Before he could reply, before Kolbi even made it around the car, I fell onto my hands and knees and vomited on the pavement.

"Um, yeah," Kolbi said, "that's why."

"Take it easy, Kolbi." Alexis's voice was close. Was he holding my hair back? Oh, man--if there had ever been a moment in my life as mortifying as that one, I had forgotten it.

He handed me a handkerchief and helped me to my feet. My head was pounding. I ached in every muscle I had, and a few I hadn't known about. My brain was too fuzzy to sort out what had happened to me, why I felt so terrible, why I needed a hospital. I couldn't even frame the questions coherently. I just stood in the dark parking lot, shivering uncontrollably, waiting for whatever happened to me next.

Alexis took my left arm, and Kolbi took my right, and we moved toward the hospital in an awkward shaky hobble. That shaking--I didn't know what to make of it. It wasn't cold outside. But I couldn't make it stop.

We made it into the emergency room, where I discovered the bright lights made my headache orders of magnitude worse as my eyes wrenched themselves trying to adjust to the sudden change. I had a vague impression of light, of shiny floors and plastic chairs, but I couldn't seem to focus on anything. I was in a tunnel, and that gleaming room was way down at the other end. The sounds of the place were tinny and faint, hard to hear over the rumbling noise in my ears.

"I think I need to sit down," I said, but I never heard the words. I saw Alexis turn to me in alarm, then the blackness swallowed me and the silence was complete.

♫

Any concept of time I ever had was completely gone. It could have been minutes or hours later when I opened my eyes to find myself staring up at a bright fluorescent light fixture.

I tried to move, to sit up a little and adjust my position, then gave up on that notion before someone got hurt. This was unmistakably a hospital bed. Hospital beds did not make sitting up unassisted an easy thing. I was also unpleasantly surprised to discover an I.V. inserted into the crook of my right elbow-- another thing that made sitting up in the bed a uniquely painful proposition.

I leaned back against the pillows. A heavy fabric curtain on a metal rail separated my bed and a wooden chair from the rest of the room.

In the chair I found Alexis, watching me and looking worried.

"Where's Kolbi?" My voice sounded like gravel under hard shoes.

"She stepped out to call your mother. Are you awake?"

I frowned, trying to make sense of that. "I think so. Why is she calling my mother?"

Alexis leaned forward and took my hand. "Honestly, you haven't been doing very well. You've been talking, but nothing that made sense. Hallucinating. You stopped breathing once, and gave us all a scare." He shook his head. "We just thought she should know. They drew blood to try to find out what caused this, but...." He shrugged, looking away uncomfortably.

I shivered. That sounded horrific, and I was glad I didn't remember any of it.

The curtain slid back, and a doctor in green scrubs stepped in, pulling it shut behind her. She gave Alexis a stern look over the top of her reading glasses, then turned to me.

"Miss Marnett, I'm Dr. James. How long have you been taking Valium?"

I goggled at her. "Valium? I've only ever taken it once, years ago."

She frowned and made a note on her clipboard. "And tonight?"

I shook my head, but Alexis cut me off before I could speak, squeezing my hand. "Once before tonight, obviously."

Dr. James favored Alexis with that sharp look again. "Is this true, Miss Marnett? Did you take Valium this evening?"

All at once I saw where Alexis was going with this. I didn't want to admit I that I had a drug in my system I did not voluntarily ingest either. A wild story about drugged tea might get me pegged as an abuser. "Yes. Yes, I did."

She looked at me a moment. "May I ask where you obtained this drug?" She obviously could tell something was up. In my condition, quick thinking seemed beyond me.

"She just moved here a few months ago," Alexis said, covering my loss for words, "and--"

This time Dr. James sent some sharp words along with the look. "Mr. Brooks, can the lady speak for herself, do you suppose?"

Her cutting tone would have sent me looking for cover, but Alexis regarded her evenly. "I don't know. She seems very ill to me."

"It's all right," I put in quickly. "Alexis is right. I did just move. My old doctor prescribed me some Valium before I left, in case moving away from my family alone proved too stressful. Tonight I couldn't sleep, so I took one."

She made another note on her clipboard. "I see. Well, don't take any more. You are allergic to Valium, Miss Marnett."

"That's what all this was?" I blurted. "Just an allergic reaction?" I thought of an allergic reaction as itching, maybe some hives. This--well, I figured my tea must have been laced with rat poison or something.

"Yes, and it could have been fatal. You have been very lucky." She wrote something else, and turned toward Alexis. "Mr. Brooks, I want you to know that we are not unaware of your history. We will be keeping our records on this matter, and if you are ever discovered to be involved in administering this drug, we will use these records to assist in your prosecution."

"Naturally," Alexis said coolly, unfazed.

She clicked her pen shut and left.

I stared after her, floored. "Did she--did she just--" I couldn't seem to speak coherently.

Alexis smiled at my outrage. "Try not to be too upset with her. She's only trying to look after your safety."

I tried to think about it that way. After all, she clearly believed Alexis to be dangerous. And his prompting me with answers--he could have been helping me not to look like a druggie. Or, to a more suspicious mind, he could have been concealing his hand in slipping me a drug I had not meant to take. It was, I supposed, a question of how suspicious your mind was.

I shivered in a sudden chill, my hand tightening convulsively around his.

How suspicious was my mind?

♫

I kept telling them it wasn't necessary, but both Kolbi and Alexis insisted on helping me into my house. In truth, it was probably best that they did. I couldn't remember ever being so shaky and weak before.

They helped me back to my bedroom, and got me settled in bed. Kolbi brought me a glass of water, and leaned over to pat my shoulder. "I'm going to head home," she said quietly.

"Thank you, Kolbi. I think you saved my life," I said seriously. "But can I ask you something?"

She looked surprised. "Sure, anything."

He wasn't even in the room, but I lowered my voice anyway. "Why did you bring Alexis?"

Kolbi appeared to consider it. "I couldn't come over here alone, not knowing what had happened to you. There aren't many people you know you can call at one-thirty in the morning. Besides--I knew he'd take good care of you." She winked at me.

I was still picking my jaw up off the floor when she laughed and left the room. I had just gotten settled back against the pillows and gotten the burning in my face under control when Alexis leaned around the door jamb, saw I was awake, and came into the room. "How are you feeling?"

"I'll live. I do wish I hadn't run that tea down the sink, though. I wonder if the police would have believed me if they had tested it."

Alexis shook his head. "I don't know. I haven't had good

experiences with the police around here, though."

I nodded. We sat in an awkward silence for a moment, then I cleared my throat. "I guess you'll have to be leaving then?" I didn't really enjoy the prospect; I couldn't say I looked forward to the rest of the night alone in the dark, after everything that had happened.

He looked surprised. "No. I came to ask if you have an extra blanket I can borrow. I'm bunking on your couch."

I pushed myself up from the pillows. "What?"

"There's only one reason to put Valium in someone's drink, Chrispen. Whoever did this wanted you to sleep-- *really* sleep." His expression was sober, and it scared me. "He intended to come back here. And I intend to be here if he does."

I hoped I didn't look as pale as I felt. "But you have to get some sleep--you have your recital tomorrow."

"I do," he said, looking at me evenly. "And I'd like you to be alive to see it."

On that, I could agree.

It felt inhumanly early when I opened my eyes, but light was coming in around the curtains. I groaned and put my feet on the floor. May as well greet the day. Maybe it would be nicer to me than yesterday.

I padded over to the window on feet that felt swollen and sore. I put my hands at the base of my back and stretched backwards--it sounded like someone stepping on bubble wrap. Yes, certainly today would be nicer to me than yesterday had been. It could hardly be meaner.

I pulled the curtain open and realized there was something stuck to the outside of the window glass.

I SEE YOU

I let out an unlovely shriek and dropped the curtains back over the window.

Alexis burst into the room, his shirt and hair rumpled. "What is it? What happened?"

He raked over the room in one wild glance, found nothing to justify my outburst, and looked to me for answers. And all at once the last two days crashed down on me--the terror, the sleeplessness, and the physical collapse-- and I was sitting on the floor with my face in my hands, bawling like a little girl.

"Oh--no," Alexis said helplessly, running a hand through his hair. "I didn't mean to upset you, I just--I'm sorry..."

"No--it's not--your fault." I gave up trying to be coherent through my tears and waved a hand at the window.

Alexis stepped over me, and flipped a curtain back with a twitch of his hand. His face stiffened, and he dropped the curtain back into place.

"It's all right," he said, kneeling in front of me. "I know it doesn't feel like it right now, but it's going to be okay. Let's get you off that floor."

He held out his hands and helped me to my feet. I sniffled and grabbed a tissue from the box on my nightstand.

"Better already, right?" Alexis smiled at me, and I tried to smile back, but it felt a little shaky.

"Sure," I said. I sounded a little shaky, too.

"I'm going to go get that thing off your window. I'll be in the living room if you want to talk." He turned and went back out into the hallway.

I sighed and went into the bathroom to get cleaned up. It looked like today was going to be a mean one after all.

When I walked into the living room, I found Alexis standing over near the wall, looking over the big collage. My face turned immediately red--this particular possibility had never, ever occurred to me.

"Chrispen," he said, though I would have bet money he hadn't known I was there. "What makes you believe I did not murder my wife?"

A chill crept up the back of my neck. Alexis always seemed to be coming out of left field at me. It was difficult to keep up with him.

Still, I tried. I walked farther into the room and tried to keep my tone light. "What makes you believe I don't?"

He turned and regarded me solemnly. "I don't believe you would have let a murderer sleep in your living room last night. You were outraged when Dr. James hinted that I may have drugged you." He smiled faintly. "And I heard you say so to Dwight."

Belatedly I remembered that conversation.

He seemed serious about this, so I put my joking aside and attempted to answer him. "That seems like a simple question," I told him, sitting down on the couch. "But the answer isn't really easy at all."

Alexis said nothing, but turned back to examine the collage again, taking the pressure off, giving me a moment to collect my thoughts.

"When I was a freshman in college," I began slowly, "I dated a pianist named Robin Woods. He was, all taken, a good guy. He was so talented....his rendition of Beethoven's *Pathetique Sonata* always made me cry. But he was also very headstrong, sort of obsessive, and a bit controlling." I shook my head, remembering, deliberately not looking at Alexis as he turned back around to face me.

"One day Robin got the idea in his head that we should get

married." I sighed. "I tried to explain to him, Alexis, I tried to make him understand all the reasons why a marriage between us would never have worked. But I never could talk him out of anything he was set on." I took a shaky breath, and realized with a little shock that I had tears on my face. "They found him in his closet. He'd hung himself with one of his own ties. A tie I'd given him, actually."

Alexis's face was tight and pale. "I'm very sorry."

I shook my head. "My loss pales next to yours, Alexis. You can imagine, his family blamed me for his death. And so did I. But I played at his funeral. He had--he had left instructions requesting that I play, and so they tolerated it."

My hands were shaking when I raised them to wipe my face. "I know that you know now what that was like. But I also knew when it happened to you."

"I had no idea," Alexis breathed. "What did you play at Robin's funeral?"

I winced, the irony was painful. "Guess."

"No--it can't be."

I sighed. "Yes. I played the first movement of the Mendelssohn Violin Concerto, at Robin's specific request."

I stood up suddenly, unable to sit still any longer, and paced up and down the living room. "I heard people afterwards, say that you were attention-mongering, playing your signature piece at your wife's funeral. Those people were morons. They had no clue, no idea, how it killed you to do that.

"But I know, Alexis. And I listened to the broadcast of your performance...and the Mendelssohn you played that day did not come from a man who murdered his wife. I'd stake my life on it."

Alexis stared at me, stricken. "You may have done just that," he finally said. "You may have. Do you realize that?"

He was staring at the collage. I followed his gaze; he was focused on a picture of himself playing the violin, a picture that had been taken at that very funeral service.

"I admit I had not thought of it quite that way," I said, "but it doesn't matter. I can't change my belief on that--you'll have to prove me wrong. You're no murderer, Alexis."

Alexis stared for a moment in silence at the massive poster, running his fingers lightly over the funeral picture. "I--I don't know what to say, Chrispen."

My face was glowing red. The moment was almost painful, and in something like self-defense I changed the subject. "Me either. I really did not expect you would ever see that collage. I used to be--something of a fangirl."

He looked at me in surprise, and I thought I had lost him. Then all at once he grinned. "Used to be? Not anymore?"

Incredibly, my face managed an even deeper red. "No! No, I--of course, I still am. I would never have auditioned for the NPSO if you hadn't been here, after all."

Alexis laughed, and it was good to hear it. "Please don't be embarrassed. That wasn't nice of me, to put you on the spot like that." He turned back to the collage, shaking his head. "This is the most beautiful thing I have ever seen."

"Me, too," I agreed.

But I wasn't looking at the poster when I said it.

♪

It was maybe an hour after Alexis left that a sharp rap at the front door startled me. I had made use of that hour relaxing in my armchair, dozing--at least, until that knock at the door.

I pushed myself out of the chair with a heavy sigh. No rest for the wicked, it seemed.

Officer Parker stood on the porch, holding his hat in his hands. He carefully inspected my face as he spoke, probably noting the dark circles and pale complexion. I definitely looked worse than the last time he had seen me. "Miss Marnett, good morning."

I leaned on the edge of the door. "Officer Parker. Please, come in."

We stepped into the living room, and I sank back into the armchair. "What brings you here this morning?"

He turned over his hat in his hands, as if he was dreading the conversation he was about to start. Or maybe I was dreading it for him. "Miss Marnett, we received a tip early this morning we feel is relevant to your complaint."

I sat up a little straighter. "So you've decided to investigate?"

He looked uncomfortable. "We need to check out this tip, anyway. Last night you mentioned an intruder and iced tea. May I see the tea, please?"

Right then it clicked for me--all at once I understood. This wasn't about some anonymous tip concerning suspicious activity in my neighborhood. This was about my hospital visit. Dr. James had done more than issue rather vague threats. She had called the police with her suspicions.

And if Dr. James had made the call, then in the end this officer's visit was about Alexis.

I sat back. "I'm sorry, Officer Parker. I don't have the tea anymore. I rinsed it down the sink after you left last night."

He looked surprised. "But--why would you do that?"

"Why wouldn't I? You indicated that the police couldn't do anything, and I certainly didn't want it. Besides, the tea didn't have anything to do with the call you got. I took a Valium last night so I could sleep. I was in the hospital with an allergic reaction to Valium, as I'm sure Dr. James must have told you."

His face registered no surprise. "Dr. James did not discuss the particulars of your case, Miss Marnett. That would have been a privacy violation as I understand it." He paused. "May I see the Valium, please?"

I stared at him. "You want to see my bottle of Valium?"

He nodded, revealing nothing. He didn't have to--just the fact that he had asked the question told me pretty clearly that he did not believe me. Clearly he understood that the tea had been drugged.

I could not admit that, though, because he wanted to put it on Alexis. Double jeopardy protected Alexis from standing trial again for Madeleine's murder, since the first trial had ended in a mistrial for prosecutorial misconduct. But this officer clearly believed Alexis was guilty. He would be happy to take any criminal charges he could find.

I shook my head. "I don't have it. I got rid of it after I got back home from the hospital last night."

His eyebrows shot up. "Really?"

"Well, sure--I mean, the stuff nearly killed me, Officer Parker. Would you want something like that hanging around your house?"

"I suppose not," he said grudgingly, obviously trying to see my side of it. He shook his head and glanced at the collage. "It is frustrating, though, the way you keep discarding evidence."

"Evidence? Last night you told me there was no evidence. Now you believe there has been a crime?"

He twisted his hat. "Dr. James indicated that Alexis Brooks was with you at the emergency room. Is that accurate?"

Ah-ha. I knew this would come back to Alexis eventually. Patient privacy was protected, but Alexis had not been a patient.

"Yes, that is accurate. Alexis drove me to the hospital. He saved my life. If you're looking for someone to badmouth him, you're in the wrong place."

"Miss Marnett, please calm down. How did Mr. Brooks know you would be needing a ride to the hospital? It is my understanding that you were unconscious upon arrival."

I took a deep breath. "I am trying to be calm. But it is difficult for me to do that while you conduct this witch hunt in my living room."

"Witch hunt? Witch hunt? Do you know what this man did? Thirty-seven stab wounds from your beloved husband, how is that for a way to die? And now he walks free and his friends are getting mysterious intruders and turning up in hospitals with deadly drug reactions, and you stand here talking to me about witch hunts! Perhaps you'd care to answer the question?"

I folded my hands tightly in my lap so he couldn't see them shaking. "I was on the phone with my best friend when I collapsed. She called Alexis and they took me to the hospital."

"Hmph. And why didn't Dr. James mention her?"

I shrugged. "I was not conscious for most of it. But Alexis told me that she went outside to call my mother."

"Miss Marnett, you seem like a nice enough lady. But you're either astoundingly naive, or you are just determined to protect Alexis Brooks, even at your own expense." He headed for the door. "The police are not your enemies. We want to protect you. But we can't do that if you won't help protect yourself. I implore you, for your own sake and safety, please reconsider your relationship with Alexis Brooks. I don't want to be investigating your homicide one day."

He closed the front door behind him, but a cold draft blew through the room anyway.

CADENZA

The lights came back up in the Newton Concert Hall for intermission, and Dwight stretched lazily in his seat, sneaking an arm around my shoulders. "Have I told you that you look ravishing?"

"Twice, I think," I replied, "and I still don't believe you."

Dwight laughed, but it sounded a little weak. "You do look a bit tired," he said, brushing a finger against the purple bags under my eyes.

I shied away from the touch. "Yes--I'm sorry I'm not the best company tonight. There was a bit of excitement last night, and I didn't get much sleep."

"A bit of excitement," he repeated. "That's what you said at rehearsal, too. Did it have to do with Alexis again?"

It was my turn to fake a laugh, and it sounded just as weak when I did it. "Only peripherally."

Dwight frowned. "What happened?"

So I told him. I told him about the creepy message, the tea, the police, and my near-death experience in the kitchen. I told him about my visit with Dr. James. I told him about my newly discovered allergy to Valium. And I told him about Dr. James's coldly professional threat.

He was still frowning when I finished. "You know, you could have called me to take you to the hospital. I would be happy to help, anytime."

"I didn't call Alexis," I pointed out, glossing over the fact that I would not have called Dwight anyway. "Kolbi did."

"Ah, Kolbi," he sighed. "That explains it."

Something in his tone caught my attention. "Why? What's wrong with Kolbi?"

"Nothing, nothing. It's just--there's some bad blood there, if you catch my drift."

"No way! You and Kolbi *dated?*"

He shrugged, uncomfortable. "For awhile. It was years ago, but I'm afraid she doesn't think much of me now."

"That can happen," I said, turning this new information over in my mind.

Dwight squeezed my shoulders. "Weren't you scared to be home alone, after all that happened?"

"Oh, I wasn't alone," I blurted like an idiot. "Alexis was there."

Dwight's eyebrows shot up, and he stared at me unabashedly.

My face felt hot. "No, no, not like that! He slept out on the couch. He thought it would be safer if he was there."

Dwight pulled his arm back into his own seat. "I swear, Chrispen, you really must have no instinct for self- preservation at all."

"What on earth are you talking about?"

"Letting a homicidal maniac camp out on your couch can't be one of your brightest moves." He shook his head. "Kolbi should never have called him. I suppose she's probably carrying a torch for him, too."

I stared at him. "You're talking crazy."

He laughed. Dwight laughed crazy, too, when he was upset. "Always happens. Alexis steals anyone I'm ever interested in--Madeleine, even you--so why not Kolbi, too? Why not make a full run of it?"

"Wait, wait, wait. You knew Madeleine Brooks?"

"Knew her? Madeleine *Avery* was my girlfriend in high school, way before she ever met Alexis. That was my fault--I took her to a recital of his, I wanted her to see for herself this prodigy I'd been complaining about, and..."

"Hold on," I interrupted. It felt like the world had just turned sideways. "You knew Madeleine in high school--and Alexis?"

He laughed his crazy laugh again. "Sure did. We all went to the same high school. But Madeleine and I went to different schools than Alexis before high school. I started playing the violin when I was in the third grade. As soon as I touched the instrument I was hooked. I was the best around. My teacher used to say I must have been a violinist in a previous life, that's how easy it was for me. I always sat first chair, first violin. I always won all the awards, all the solos. Always. I planned out my future when I was in the sixth grade. I would go to Juilliard. I knew which teachers I would study with, which competitions I would win. I was an unstoppable force."

He looked so sad. "What happened?" I asked.

"Hmph. I got to high school, and my unstoppable force ran into the immovable object that was Alexis Brooks. And from that moment on, I never sat first chair again. Alexis was concertmaster in the school orchestra, in the youth symphony--Darren was asking him to be concertmaster of the NPSO before he even graduated high school. Alexis got all the solos, won all of the competitions. And then Madeleine heard him play the

Mendelssohn, and he won her, too."

I stared at him in silence. I had known Dwight didn't like Alexis. I never dreamed the extent of it.

"Alexis Brooks stole my entire life." His voice was hard with emotion. "I never followed my plans, never went to Juilliard--what was the point? Even if everything went right, it wouldn't have beaten Alexis. It wouldn't have brought Madeleine back. I auditioned into the symphony right out of high school, and I've been here ever since. Then he comes back, like the prodigal son, and it's the same story all over again."

"But he's been so quiet for so long after Madeleine died," I said. "Why do you suppose he suddenly decided to perform again now?"

Dwight looked over at me--suspiciously? "I haven't the faintest idea."

♪

The Green Room was jam-packed full of people after the recital. It seemed everyone had rushed back to congratulate Alexis on his performance. I stood near the door, trying to figure a way through the mass of well-wishers.

A hand grabbed my arm, and I turned to face Dwight. His face was a little red, and he was short of breath. Had I really made it back to the Green Room that fast?

"There you are," I said. "Get lost?"

He ignored the quip. "What are we doing back here?"

"Isn't it obvious? We are going to congratulate Alexis and tell him how wonderful his performance was."

Dwight looked around the crowded room dubiously. "Every person in this room is telling him the same thing. You think he needs to hear it from us?"

"Of course he needs to hear it from us. We're his friends, Dwight."

"Speak for yourself," Dwight muttered, but he plowed into the crowd right behind me. Before long, though, we were separated.

Alexis stood in the center of a tight knot of people, shaking hands all around and smiling as if his face was stuck that way.

He suddenly turned around and saw me approaching, and this time when he smiled the whole room lit up. He excused himself to those around him, and made his way over to me. "Chrispen! What a pleasant surprise. I didn't think you would be up to making it tonight."

"How could I stay away? I--"

"Hold that thought, my dear, it's much too noisy out here to talk." Alexis threaded my arm through his and led me through the crowded room, down the hallway to the soloist's lounge.

When the door was safely closed behind us, he turned and eyed me critically. "How are you feeling tonight?"

"Much better now," I assured him. "I have never heard anything like the way you played tonight. You were absolutely amazing."

"Thank you," he said, and laughed. "You know, it's a good thing you showed up. I was just--"

The door creaked open, and Dwight leaned in. "Chris? I need to call my mother--I promised to have dinner with her, and it looks like I'm going to be late. I'll be right back."

He ducked back out of the room, and eased the door shut behind him.

"Sorry about that," I said, turning back to Alexis. "What were you saying?"

Alexis was glaring at me like I'd just drowned his puppy. "You came here with him, didn't you?" He threw the words at me as if they were stones.

I took a step back from him. "Well, yes, but--"

He slammed his fist down on the counter. "Chrispen, do you

realize what you are doing? Do you have any *idea?"*

No, I did not. And I did not understand where this sudden anger had come from--he had been in such a good mood a moment before, and why should it matter to him who I came with? But the last thing I wanted to do was antagonize him further. "I don't understand what you are trying to tell me," I said, keeping my tone carefully even, determined not to fight with him.

Alexis sighed in audible exasperation. "No, of course you don't. How could you? I'll make it very plain for you," he said, as if he was giving me a gift. "Get away from Dwight Richards."

"What?"

"I haven't got time to explain. Just don't leave with him. I'll give you a ride home, and I swear to you I will explain it all on the way. But don't leave here with Dwight. And *do not* go anywhere else with that man."

I couldn't believe what I was hearing. I just could not. Never mind that I had only gone out with Dwight at all to spite someone else. And never mind that he'd been kind of creeping me out all evening. I still maintained that I had a perfect right to date him if I wanted to, and for anyone-- even Alexis Brooks--to stand here and tell me otherwise raised every hackle I had. "Of all the nerve! Are you actually *ordering* me to stay away from Dwight?"

Alexis sighed, as if he were dealing with a particularly dull-witted child. "I suppose if an order is what it takes, then yes, I am. We don't have time for bruised vanity, Chrispen-- yours or mine. He'll be back any moment. Will you leave with me?"

"No!" The single word burst with outrage. "I can't believe-- the arrogance--the *audacity*--"

"Fine, then," Alexis cut me off shortly. I thought I might explode from sheer pique. I turned away from him, staring darkly at the wall.

"I'm sure he will be back in a minute," Alexis continued, and suddenly grabbed me by the shoulders and spun me around to face him. His eyes burned mine, and even in my anger I had to look away. "But whatever happens, now or later, don't you ever, *ever* say I didn't warn you."

His words gave me an ominous chill, and I wondered if I had done the right thing. Maybe he had reasons for this after all. Alexis grabbed his violin case and stomped towards the door.

"Alexis, wait," I said in sudden, irrational fear, "where are you going?"

"I have to make a phone call," he snapped.

He slammed the door behind him when he left.

The light on my answering machine was blinking 1 when I got home. I could see it as soon as I stepped in the door, flashing red in the dark, mocking me as I put my things away; blinking, blinking, blinking...

I couldn't suppress a sense of deja vu. I was growing to dread checking my messages. I sighed and pushed the playback button.

I could feel the hair stand up on the back of my neck. That peculiar dead-air sound--it was unmistakable and I recognized it at once.

"Stay away from him."

I hated that voice. Hated it, and hated its unseen owner. I erased the message.

I didn't know what to make of it, though. Stay away from who, exactly? It seemed like everyone thought I should stay away from someone; Dwight wanted me to stay away from Alexis, and Alexis wanted me to stay away from Dwight. The police voted against Alexis, too. Now a nameless jerk offered the helpful opinion that I should stay away from a nameless him.

It all hacked me off, now that I thought about it. What gave any of those people the right to tell me how I should conduct my relationships?

The phone rang.

Did the outrage never end? Was I never to have a moment's peace, a moment's quiet, ever again? Shaking with impotent anger, I snatched up the phone.

"What?" I shouted. "You got me, what the hell do you want from me?"

My mother sounded very taken aback. "Chrispen, dear, is everything all right? You--don't sound so good."

"Oh, my gosh. I'm sorry, Mom. I thought you were someone else."

She made a little clucking sound. "Kolbi told me about that horrible man who has been bothering you. Are you feeling better?"

"Much better." It wasn't really a lie. Maybe an exaggeration.

Okay, maybe it really was a lie. But who wants to make their mother worry?

"That's good. I do hope you'll consider calling the police. This man has to be stopped."

I sighed. "I did, Mom. They've been out here twice. There isn't anything they can do."

"Nothing? Nothing at all? But--surely they have some ideas about how to protect you?"

I laughed. "Not that I can tell. The only advice they've had so far is to stay away from Alexis."

There was a short silence. "Why would they tell you that? What have you been doing?"

"Nothing, Mom."

"I can hear you rolling your eyes at me, Chrispen! I'm serious--why would the police warn you to stay away from him, unless you haven't been?"

"Mom, I *work* with him!"

She wasn't listening. "I knew this was a bad idea. You should have gone to that symphony in New York. Or you could have stayed here. There was no need to run off to Ohio and get yourself tangled up with a murderer!"

"Mother!"

Her rant ended abruptly. "I'm sorry, dear. I know you've always looked up to him. It's nice to see someone your own age succeed so wildly. But Chrispen, just because people are famous and talented, doesn't mean they don't sometimes do horrible things. I really think--"

"I'm sorry, Mom," I cut her off. "I really have to go."

"All right, dear." I could tell from her tone that I hadn't fooled her. "I know you believe he's innocent. And faith is a good thing. Just--just be careful, okay? Be very, very careful."

"I will, Mom. Love you."

I hung up the phone, wondering how hard it was going to be to keep that promise.

MOVEMENT TWO:
On the Trail of a Madman

I was running, running as fast as I could, running for my life--
and for someone else's. Someone who had suffered enough,
someone I had to save. Cold sweat pasted my clothes to me, and
my feet screamed in painful protest. How had things gone so
wrong? How had we screwed up so badly? My throat made
ragged choking sounds as I struggled to pull in air.

But I knew it didn't matter. I knew I was too late. A building
loomed up ahead, a brick building with climbing ivy, a building I
had to get inside.

A building I'd vowed never to enter again.

It was so close, and yet so impossibly far away. Still, it was in
sight. I felt a doomed hope rush through me, and I did what I
would have sworn couldn't be done--I ran even faster.

It couldn't be done, I knew that. We had miscalculated, and
badly, and no power on earth could stop him now.

I was holding nothing back now, my muscles working so frantically there was no time for pain. One of my blood-spattered canvas tennis shoes worked itself completely off my foot on the stairs. I didn't slow down, really didn't even notice. My attention was fixed on the third-floor landing, coming into view. Just around the corner now...I had to go faster...

I heard a woman scream, but I couldn't have told you if it was me or her. Had Madeleine screamed like that? Did he also think of Madeleine now? Did he even care?

The door was cracked open. But even as I pushed it open I knew I was too late; even as I first saw her lying bleeding on the living room floor I knew I couldn't save her.

I fell on my knees beside her, crying hot tears. "No, no, no," I whispered, a desperate, hopeless plea, "please don't die, you can't die!"

She turned her head my direction and with her last breath managed to gasp a single word.

A name.

And then I heard the footsteps, and I knew I couldn't save myself.

♫

I had unplugged the phone and the fax machine, and I was so tired I finally got some sleep. The nightmare came, and woke me screaming as always, but it was six-thirty in the morning when it did.

So all in all, I felt better than I had in awhile.

Maybe because it happened so late in the morning, I could remember more of the dream this time. It was frustrating to me that I understood everything when I was dreaming, but as soon as I woke up that understanding slipped away, like trying to hold sand in my hands.

I couldn't even remember whose murder I had just witnessed.

I thought about it a lot that day, while I went about my usual business. Who was murdered? What was the name she said with her dying breath?

I couldn't really say why it should matter so much. I knew it was just a dream. But it kept coming back, and it bothered me. I picked at it like a scab.

No matter. By rehearsal time I was no closer to any answers than I had been when I woke up that morning.

I had, however, gained myself a whopper of a headache.

I didn't show up for rehearsal as early as I might have, and I was not in as good a mood as I might have been. When I walked in the Green Room, almost everyone was there already.

"Chrispen! How are you feeling?" Kolbi's voice came from a group of chairs off to my right somewhere. I turned towards the sound, and saw her bouncing my direction, smiling and happy, and in that instant my brain exploded into flames.

I knew, all at once, whose murder I had witnessed. The color drained from my face, and I couldn't seem to stand. I fell on my knees, right there in front of everybody in the Green Room.

Kolbi grabbed my arm before I could topple onto my face. "Something's wrong with you," she said, which seemed pretty obvious to me. "Alexis!"

Alexis was at my side in an instant, grabbing my other arm and helping me to a chair. "What happened?" he demanded. "You were doing so much better last night. Are you sick? Did something hurt you?"

I couldn't answer him. There didn't seem to be any air in the room. I thought I'd had a shock when I first saw Kolbi, but that was evidently only the beginning.

In my mind I could still hear her calling for Alexis. And I knew whose name she had said with her dying breath.

Talk about an eventful way to start a rehearsal! Thankfully, once Alexis and Kolbi helped me to a chair, people began to head out onstage. I suppose we must have stopped being interesting.

I finally started breathing again.

"What was that?" Alexis asked, watching me anxiously. "What happened?"

I glanced at him, and looked quickly away. Why would Kolbi's final word be his name?

Was she naming her killer?

"There isn't time to talk about it," I said hastily. "Rehearsal is starting."

"So what?" Alexis returned. "Look at you, you are in no condition to play. You need to go home and rest."

"No--I'll be fine. Really. I just need a minute to catch my breath."

"Okay," Alexis said, but he looked dubious. "I'll go out and let Darren know you're on your way." He went down the stairs to the stage.

"Chrispen, are you sure about this?" Kolbi sounded worried. "You really look terrible."

"I'm fine," I insisted.

"Well...okay, if you're sure. Are you ready to head out that way, then?"

No. But sitting here freaking out was not the answer. I swallowed hard and nodded.

I picked up my violin case and lurched to my feet. I didn't normally take the case to the stage, but right now I wasn't willing to risk falling with my unprotected violin. Kolbi eyed me doubtfully, but she put her hand under my elbow and walked with me toward the stage.

"Have you ever noticed those pictures?" I said suddenly, stopping on the stairs to look at them. I was always so focused on getting from the Green Room quickly to the stage, I had never seen the handful of framed photographs hanging in the stairwell.

"Hmm. Yes, but I don't really look at them anymore. Always in a hurry."

"Is--is that one Alexis?" Even as I said the words, I knew it couldn't be right, this man was too old.

"No, that's Alexei Brooks--Alexis's father."

"Alexei?"

"Yes. He's Russian. Alexei Bruskalov, I believe. When he immigrated to the United States, he changed the name to Brooks--you know, to make it more American. He married Victoria Fleming, a well to-do pianist in Philadelphia, but they moved out here because the social elite out there never would really accept that she married a foreigner."

"Wow, I never knew that," I said. "And he was in the symphony?"

"In the symphony? Alexei Brooks *started* the symphony. Darren was an assistant conductor with a big symphony in Boston, until Alexei asked him to come help with the NPSO. They both dreamed of making this a world- class symphony."

"Wow," I said again. "I bet Alexei would have been proud to see his son take over concertmaster. What happened to him?"

Kolbi wouldn't look at me. "Alexei retired from the symphony about twelve years ago. He served on the Board of Trustees for awhile."

"And?"

"And he walked out in protest the day they hired me, and hasn't spoken to any of us since," Alexis said.

Every other blush I'd ever had was just a warm-up for this one. He was standing at the bottom of the stairs, looking up at us, bemused. "Any other questions?"

"You have to try to see it Alexei's way," Kolbi said quickly. "He came here with high ideas about America. He has great faith in American justice. He really can't believe that the police would say that Alexis is guilty if he isn't."

"Really?" I said. "Because from everything I've ever heard about the Russian police..."

"That's just it," Alexis said. "America has to be different, doesn't it? If it isn't, then everything he did--that dangerous emigration, losing his entire family--was done for nothing. So they have to be right. And who wants to see a murderer in charge of the symphony they've spent their life building?"

"You're no murderer, Alexis," I said.

But in my mind, I could hear Kolbi gasp his name as she died, and I couldn't look at him when I said it.

Needless to say, everyone was waiting for us when we got out onstage. If everyone hadn't seen me collapse, if it hadn't been so obvious that I was not well, there would have been hell to pay.

I sat down in my usual chair and fumbled my violin out of its case, clumsy in my haste. The music for Bach's *Concerto for Two Violins* had been distributed onto our stands, and I reached for my part so we could get started.

But something was wrong. The part I held was not a first violin orchestra part, but the second violin solo. I turned to give it to Dwight, but before I could open my mouth Alexis was there beside me.

"Ready to start?" he asked.

"Are you sure she can handle it?" Daniella snickered from the viola section. "I mean, she might faint."

"Chrispen," Alexis said, as if he hadn't heard anything, "what's the definition of perfect pitch?"

"I--what?"

"Tossing a viola into the toilet without hitting the rim."

Daniella and I both stared at him, and then her face suddenly turned red.

Alexis winked at me. "Are you ready?"

"There must have been some mistake," I told him, holding out the part, but he took hold of my arm and pulled my out of my chair.

"I'm sorry to put you on the spot like this," he said, leading me to the front of the stage, "but there's no mistake."

"Shall we begin?" Darren said, and raised his baton.

What could I do? In the Bach Double the second violins start, and Darren was already counting us in. I put my part on the stand and played the familiar opening D-minor run with the orchestra.

I was sight-reading a piece that I hadn't played in years, but I thought I was doing pretty well--until Alexis came in on his part. It was like playing with a force of nature, I swear--he just blew me away. I'd played next to him on orchestral pieces for months, but that was nothing like playing with him in solo mode. I couldn't remember the last time I'd been so thoroughly humbled.

Poor Dwight! I had cheerfully set him up for this, never realizing what it would be like. *Pretty cool*, I had said. Little did I know!

After rehearsal was over, I went to Darren while everyone else headed for the Green Room and packed up.

"I am so sorry about rehearsal today," I told him.

"Don't give it another thought, dear girl. I'm just glad you were able to stay and play with us."

"About that...I thought we had discussed giving that second violin solo to Dwight? I don't want to seem ungrateful, because I'm very pleased--but wasn't he supposed to get that part?"

Darren had been putting his scores in his briefcase, but now he stopped. "We did discuss that, you're right. I'm sorry we put you up there with no warning like that."

"Oh, please don't misunderstand me. I'm not complaining at all. I just--what about Dwight?"

Darren sighed. "I know how much he wanted this. But Alexis called last night after his concert and specifically asked that you be given the part. You. Specifically."

I stared at him. "Me?" I didn't know what to make of that. When Alexis stormed from the lounge to make a phone call, I would have expected doing me favors to be the last thing on his mind.

Darren did look at me then, and his eyes were bleak and helpless. "What else was I to do? You know as well as I do what an asset he is to this symphony. He brought us where we are today, no one can deny that. And his recital last night was absolutely sold out. He's beginning to act like himself again, Chrispen. I don't want to give him any reason to leave." He clicked the latches on his briefcase shut. "Was there anything else?"

"No--no, thank you," I said, trying to seem unfazed. "I'll have my bowings ready for next rehearsal."

He smiled. "Thank you. I knew I could count on you, dear girl."

He was whistling the opening to the concerto when he walked offstage.

When I finally made it up the stairs with my violin over my shoulder, the Green Room was deserted. I deliberately avoided looking at the pictures on my way up the stairs. If Alexis did leave the symphony, would Alexei come back to the Board?

I hoped I didn't have to find out. I hurried as much as I was able to get away from the pictures.

Did I say the Green Room was deserted? My mistake. It was almost deserted.

Dwight leaned back against the counter, waiting for me.

"Oh, Dwight," I said, "I'm so sorry. I had no idea they were going to change the solo like that."

Dwight's smile was a little weak, but at least he was trying. "I figured that much out from your face. Neither Darren or Alexis will speak to me today--I was hoping you could tell me what happened."

I shifted my violin case so the strap wasn't digging into my neck. "I wondered the same thing, Dwight--I spoke to Darren after rehearsal. He said Alexis called last night and told him to give the part to me."

"You mean after I left you in the lounge? What on earth happened in there? Things must have gone better than you let on." He eyed me suspiciously.

Of course, I blushed. "You know better than that! I really have no idea what possessed him to do that."

"You really don't, do you? Do you ever listen to anything I say to you? Alexis always steals anyone I'm interested in, ever. If I agreed to go out with Daniella, he'd be after her, too."

I don't know why, but that comment stung. "That doesn't even make sense."

"Doesn't it? Giving you a solo you otherwise never would have gotten is just what I'm talking about--making you feel indebted to him, showing off the resources he knows I don't have. And it's only the beginning."

I shook my head. I could hear his temper rising in his words, and I didn't want to make things worse, but I couldn't agree with his assessment.

He pushed himself away from the counter. "Don't you get it? Don't you see the symbolic separation here--Alexis pulls you to the front of the stage with him, while I'm stuck buried in the background?"

"Dwight," I said, "it isn't like that. Really, I think you're reading too much into this. Alexis--"

"He's afraid!" Dwight crowed. "This was it--this was my

chance to show the world I could hold my own against the great Alexis Brooks. He's afraid to let that happen!"

I couldn't help it, I laughed out loud. "Alexis has nothing to fear from any of us," I said bluntly. "Did you miss how totally he kicked my butt today? None of us are honest competition for him, Dwight. Not one."

Dwight grabbed his violin and looked at me blackly. "I am," he said. "You can count me out if you want, but I intend to give him a run for his money." He gave me a dirty look and left.

And belatedly I wondered--was he even talking about playing the violin?

The note was taped to my front door.

**i see you
i know you'll
like the pictures**

Pictures? What the devil was he talking about? I turned the note over, but there were no pictures on the back, either.

I wondered if Officer Parker would listen to me if I showed him this. I toyed with the idea of calling him, then dismissed it. He would only be interested in comparing the handwriting to Alexis's, anyway.

The pictures, I discovered, were everywhere, without at first appearing to be anywhere. The house looked completely normal when I stepped in; I couldn't find a single thing out of place.

But when I opened my copy of the Mendelssohn Concerto, a picture of me gaping at a lawn covered with faxes fluttered to the floor. There was a picture of the inside of my closet tucked inside my address book.

In my desk drawer I encountered a picture of the inside of the cabinet under my bathroom sink. A picture of me talking on the phone and pouring iced tea had been carefully placed under my pillow, and it chilled me to the bone to think about when that had been taken.

I couldn't look anywhere, do anything, without discovering one of the blasted things. I was ill at ease in my own house.

It didn't make me feel any better to know that this was the whole point.

The next day I had all my locks changed. I called the phone company and had my phone number changed, and kept it unlisted. I canceled the fax line; I had never really used it anyway. If somebody had something to send me, they usually used email.

And thinking of email reminded me, it had been a couple of days since I had checked mine--I figured I had better get on the computer and do it. What if a Nigerian prince needed to wire me ten million dollars? How would I know?

There was quite a bit of junk in there, but not nearly as bad as I feared. And it looked like I had emails from Dwight, Alexis, and Darren--several from each of them.

That was odd. None of them had mentioned emailing me when I saw them at rehearsal.

Looking on down the list, I also had emails from Kolbi--and the principal cellist--and Daniella?

Okay, so something wasn't right. Sure, Daniella and the cellist could have gotten my email address from the symphony directory, but why would they?

I picked the one from Daniella first, since it was the most likely to explode when I opened it.

It seemed to take longer than usual. I drummed my fingers on the desk--then froze.

I SEE YOU

Holy cow. I had a sudden, awful suspicion.

I opened email after email. Sure enough, all of these emails that seemed to be from my friends and co-workers were the same.

How was this even possible?

I clicked from one email to the next, trying to find something that explained why everyone I knew was suddenly sending me this creepy note, but I found nothing, and I was getting frustrated.

It took me a minute to realize my cell phone was ringing. That didn't happen very often. I dug it out of my purse, and glanced at the incoming call notification.

Richards, Dwight.

Completely against my better judgment, I answered it. "Hey Dwight, what's up?"

"Hi, Chris. Did you know your regular phone isn't working?"

"Oh--right, I just changed my number. Here, I'll get the new one for you." I dug out my notes from the phone company, and read the new number off to him. "Got it?"

There was a short pause. "You don't sound so good-- what's wrong?"

I laughed. "Can't hide anything from you, Dwight."

"You're learning! So, what is it?"

"Well, here's the thing. I'm checking my email, right? And there's all these emails here, like here are a few that say they're from you. But I just don't think they are."

"Hmm--are they love letters?"

This time my laugh sounded more like a bark. "No. No, not by any stretch of the imagination."

"Then I didn't send them. What do you think is going on?"

"Your guess is as good as mine."

"Well..." Dwight hesitated. "Actually my guess might be slightly better."

"What?"

"I used to run a little computer consulting business, you know, on the side. You mind if I take a look?"

"Wow--if you think you might be able to help, have at it. I'd love to hear what you make of it."

"Sure thing. I'm on my way."

I disconnected the call, but before I dropped the cell phone back in my purse, an icon on the display caught my eye. I had text messages? When had that happened?

Okay, so maybe I was paranoid, but I had a bad feeling about this.

There were five new messages, from two cell phone numbers I did not recognize. The area code was local, though. I pulled up one of the text messages.

STAY AWAY FROM HIM

The doorbell rang, so I snapped the phone shut and went to answer it.

"Hey, Chris," Dwight said when I opened the door. "Boy, you don't look so good, either."

I rolled my eyes. "Gee, thanks, Dwight." I stepped aside and let him in the house.

"No, seriously, you look like you've just seen a ghost. Are you okay?"

"I think so. Dwight, if I give you a cell phone number, can you tell me whose it is?"

He laced his fingers together and flexed his hands out, cracking his knuckles. "Let me at your computer. I have a few tricks I can try."

I pulled up a web browser window and got him settled at the computer, then read him off the two cell phone numbers who had sent me the mysterious text messages.

Dwight's fingers moved so fast across the keyboard I couldn't see them clearly. I had never seen anyone type so fast before; it was mesmerizing to watch.

I couldn't make sense of the stuff scrolling up the screen, either, but it seemed to mean something to him. He frowned at the display, and his hands went off on another wild flurry across the keyboard.

He inspected the results, and shook his head. "I'm sorry, Chrispen, it's a no-go. These are disposable phones."

"Disposable?"

He twisted around to face me, draping an arm over the back of the chair. "Yeah--you know, one of those prepaid phones you can buy from the supermarket for twenty bucks? They draw numbers out of a pool when they are activated. And unless someone used a credit card, there's no way to tell who has it."

I clicked my cell phone shut. "I bet that was deliberate. Can you take a look at these emails for me?" I leaned over him and pulled up my email program.

"Sure, sure." He clicked on one that had his name on it. "Whoa, Chris, that's creepy!" He sat back and looked at the message a moment, then regarded me sternly. "You been getting a lot of these?"

"No, these are the first." I didn't tell him about the phone calls, or the faxes....I just wasn't going to go there.

"Alrighty." Dwight turned back to the computer. "Let's see if we can track down this psycho." He started typing and talking at the same time, another trick I could never pull off. "See, the thing most people don't understand about email is that a lot of the information in them can be faked. You can send an email and make it look like it has my name on it, even spoof my email address. But with the message headers, you can find out where it really came from. And...here's where we run into the same problem." He stopped typing. "These are throwaway email addresses."

"Okay, clue me in," I said. "Why would I want to throw away my email address?"

He smiled at me. "Well, obviously, you wouldn't. But say you decided to send a bunch of creepy emails to someone and didn't want to get caught--then you might want to. You go to one of those free email sites, and you sign up using a fake name. Don't put any of your real contact information. Then email away."

I frowned. "Yeah, but--at least I can block the email address, right?"

He shrugged. "You could, but it won't help if he just keeps creating new ones. Look, he's already gone through four of them." He shook his head. "Whoever this guy is, he knows what he's doing."

My shoulders slumped--that was not the news I'd been hoping for. Blocked numbers, throwaway emails, disposable cell phones--so far I hadn't found a single way to strike back at this bastard.

The phone rang.

Dwight gave it a sharp, irritated glance. "I thought you said you changed your number."

"I did. Some people have it already." I looked quickly at the caller ID, and answered the phone. "Hello, Alexis." I turned away from Dwight, but I could still feel his eyes boring into my back.

"Hello, yourself," he returned. "Where are you?"

"What? I'm at home, obviously, I--oh, man. Oh, Alexis--I am so sorry. I got busy and totally forgot about our rehearsal. I'm turning into a total flake!"

Alexis laughed. "Nah, I wouldn't say that. Just hurry over here. I'll be waiting for you."

I turned around and found Dwight looking at me the way he might look at something on the bottom of his shoe. "What?" I asked defensively.

"You gave *Alexis* your new phone number?"

I replaced the handset in the cradle. "Dwight, we have to rehearse together for the concerto. How do you suggest we do that if we can't call each other?"

Dwight shook his head. "Change your number and then give it to Alexis Brooks? It's like giving the fox the key to the hen-house."

"I am so not having this argument. I'm late." I threw my violin case over my shoulder and grabbed my music folder, heading for the door.

Dwight followed me out. "Look, just be careful, okay?"

I dug in my purse for my keys to lock up, and made a small sound of impatience. "Honestly, Dwight, it's a rehearsal. What do you think is going to happen?"

"I don't know," he said seriously. "All I know is, that solo was a favor. You owe him now, and you don't know what he wants as payment. Don't you see the way he looks at you? Just watch yourself. I'm serious about that fox thing."

I stared at him, frozen. Was he crazy for talking like that, or was I crazy for dismissing him out of hand?

Dwight shook his head and took the keys from my hand. "Here, let me show you something." He pulled a single hair from his head and closed it between the door and the frame. Then he locked the front door, and folded my hand around the keys again. "When you get home, look for that. If it isn't there, you'll know someone has been through here."

I blinked in surprise. "That's pretty clever, Dwight. Thank you. I'll remember that."

"You do that," he said, shaking his head as he walked toward his car. "With the friends you keep, you're going to need all the help you can get."

♫

All told, I was over an hour late. I apologized over and over, but Alexis just laughed it off.

We had lost the stage, though; there was a woodwind sectional scheduled onstage by the time I showed up. There were vacant rehearsal rooms, though, so we moved into one of those. As fate would have it, it was the same room we had kicked the frisky cellists out of before. It made me think of Dwight's comments, and I was uncomfortable as I unpacked my instrument.

Alexis, however, seemed perfectly at ease. "You mentioned you were busy with something," he said, rosining his bow. "If you don't mind me asking, what were you up to?"

I unzipped my violin case and reached for the latch. "Oh-- well, I had some weird emails and text messages--like that thing on my window the other morning. Dwight was helping me try to trace them on the computer."

"Dwight? On your computer? Isn't that kind of putting the fox in the hen-house?"

I put my hands on my hips. "That's exactly what he said about you."

Alexis didn't seem so comfortable anymore. He looked away. "Shall we start, then?"

We tuned up quickly, neither of us eager to continue that conversation. I started in playing immediately, my nervousness pushing the tempo a bit faster than I had meant to go.

Alexis looked over at me in surprise. It was too fast, but what could I do? I couldn't slow down. It was a pride thing now.

My hands limbered up after a few measures, and the tempo didn't feel so unreasonable. I was rocking along, doing really well--or so I thought until Alexis made his entrance.

He was an explosion of perfect sound next to me, casting glittering, crystalline notes around us I could almost reach out and touch. I could easily have just sat down and listened to him play, and I would have been happy, any other time.

But right now, well, this was my solo too, and I was getting sand kicked in my face. I kicked it up a notch, vibrato stinging the notes I wanted to make shine, my bow work clean and precise, enunciating each note with a little bite. This was more like it; this was a performance I could be happy with.

And then Alexis did the same thing, reaching farther and outdistancing me again.

What could I do? I opened it up farther, poured on the technique, pushing it higher. Alexis pushed back, and we were both whaling on it for all we were worth when we reached the end.

It was the most competitive Bach Double I had ever played, and also the most exhausting. I collapsed into a chair, short of breath.

"We can't do that at the concert," I panted. "We'll both die."

Alexis laughed. "That's why I like playing with you. You always push me to do better."

I examined the tip of my bow, like I was only paying half attention to the conversation. "Is that why you gave me this solo?"

My attempt at nonchalance didn't work. Alexis frowned. "Gave you this solo?"

I squirmed in my chair. "Well, it was supposed to go to Dwight, you know. He says you gave me a solo I'd never have gotten on my own."

He snorted derisively. "He's just jealous. Really, that part should have been yours from the beginning. Darren only offered it to Dwight because you suggested it."

"Really?" This was a different take on things than I'd had.

"Of course. I should have argued against it from the start, but I was just so relieved not to be badgered about the Mendelssohn anymore, I didn't question it. I--wasn't thinking too clearly."

I eyed him speculatively. "Yes...I noticed you've been doing better lately."

He looked suddenly away. "Ready for another play-through?"

We went back to the music stands. This time we took a more reasonable tempo, and stopped several times to make sure we were matching bowings, fingerings, and phrasing where it seemed like we should.

"Was Dwight able to help you with your problem?" Alexis asked me when we finished, while I marked in some bowings on my part.

"No, not really. It seems like whoever is doing this is taking all the precautions."

"Hmm." He pulled a cloth out of his case and wiped the rosin dust off of his violin. "Have the police turned up anything else?"

I sighed. "No. Officer Parker came by to investigate a tip, but it turned out Dr. James had convinced him you drugged me. He wanted to remind me what a risk I'm taking in just knowing such a terrible, horrible person."

He shrugged it off. "You can't really blame them for wanting justice. They're only trying to look out for you."

I shook my head, watching him strap his violin back into the case. "I'm sorry, I just can't see it. You saved my life, Alexis."

He turned away from me. "You make too much of that. It's

what anyone would have done."

"Is it?" I couldn't seem to make anyone understand-- not Dwight, not the police, not Dr. James. But Alexis--he had to understand. I moved closer to him, frustrated. "I don't think so. You drove me to the hospital, knowing what you were going to face. You could have let Kolbi take me in alone. I don't believe just anyone would have done what you did. What you don't even want to take credit for."

"How can you be so sure?" He latched his violin case and leaned forward on it, keeping his back to me. "Maybe I hadn't counted on an allergic reaction and just didn't want you to die yet. Maybe I was just covering my own tracks. Maybe you're being hopelessly naive, and everything they are saying is true."

I stared at him in shock, but I shook my head. "No," I breathed.

He spun suddenly around to face me, and he looked just as frustrated as I felt. "But you don't know that for sure. You can't know that for sure. You don't believe I'm dangerous because you don't *want* to believe I'm dangerous."

He took a slow, measured step toward me, watching me steadily, and I have to admit he was kind of scary. At least, my pulse raced.

But I couldn't back down, not now. This was a threshold, even I could sense that, and if I doubted him now I would never have another chance.

So I tried to ignore the beats my heart was skipping. "Do you have a better reason?"

"No," he said, and dipped his face toward mine.

I think he meant to kiss me. I know I meant to kiss him. But at that exact moment the door to the rehearsal room flew open, and we each took a reflexive step back.

"Oh, I should have known Alexis had his super-special snowflake in here," Daniella said from the doorway. "It's not like we haven't heard the showing-off for the past hour." She shook her head dramatically, bouncing her curly hair off her shoulders. "With all this sparking going on, I wonder where the violas can have their sectional?"

"Daniella," Alexis said conversationally, "why did the chicken cross the road?"

"What?" She seemed as surprised as I was.

He turned around and picked up his violin case. "To get away from the viola recital."

♫

So I admit I didn't leave immediately. Daniella huffed away to rehearse somewhere else, and Alexis said goodbye to me and headed out the door.

And me, I sat there in a sort of stupor with my violin in my lap. What had just happened here--or almost happened? Was I ready for this? My heart was pounding, my hands were shaking, and I couldn't decide if I should be angry with Daniella for ruining the moment, or grateful to her.

Alexis, I think, was embarrassed. So was I. I could imagine Kolbi, grinning and clapping me on the back. But I could also imagine my mother asking me if I had really lost my mind, or just wanted her hair to turn completely gray.

My good friend Officer Parker would have a conniption fit.

And Dwight--I just couldn't even go there.

I was being pulled in so many different directions, I had no idea what I was supposed to feel. But what I did feel was...well, sort of thrilled.

Eventually, I did manage to get packed up and out of the building. But I was sort of distracted. I put my violin on the floor in front of the backseat of my car, and slid into the driver's seat. I put the key into the ignition, and froze.

My instinct was to jump out of the car, screaming, and run as far as I could, as fast as I could.

Instead, I slowly turned to regard the passenger seat of my car.

A squarish, short, crystal vase was resting on the seat. A fabulous display of flowers burst from it; roses, sunflowers, tulips and carnations, plus some I couldn't even identify. It should have been gorgeous.

But they were dead. Every flower, every spray, was black and shriveled.

Dead flowers aren't usually scary, but finding this in my car was sort of horrifying. It felt sort of unreal.

There was a card on the thing.

Did I really want to read it? I debated that, staring at it in dull horror. No, I didn't really care to read anything this nutter had to say. But there could be a clue there, something I could finally use against him.

So in the end I gingerly pulled the card free and flipped it over. There were only a few short lines, scrawled in heavy blue ink.

Roses are red,

Violets are blue,

Smile for the camera,

I'm watching you.

♫

It felt good to get home, after all the emotional upheaval. I even remembered to check Dwight's strand of hair in the door, and found it undisturbed, which was great. I was in a good mood again before I even opened the door.

There were long-stemmed roses scattered all over my living room, and they were all dead. Black, crunchy flowers with their brown withered stems littered the floor, the couch, the computer desk...

And attached to each fragile stem was a little card that said:

Roses are red,

Violets are blue,

Smile for the camera,

I'm watching you.

All of the sudden it didn't feel so good to be home anymore. Either my visitor was too clever for Dwight's trick, or he wasn't using the front door. But if I trapped every door and window on my house every time I left, I'd be bald before the week was out.

I shook open a heavy trash bag, and started shoveling flowers in. They crumbled when they were handled. Everything they were scattered on would need to be vacuumed, which did not improve my mood.

Dead flowers still had thorns, too. Also not good for my mood.

I managed to give myself a paper cut on one of the little cards. *Great*, I thought, sucking my injured finger, *just great*. I glared at the card.

...smile for the camera, I'm watching you...

Maybe the creepy little rhyme wouldn't have bothered me so much, if I hadn't known it was true.

I went to bed a little early. After the day I'd had, I was ready to concede defeat. All I wanted was to be left alone for a few hours to recover, so maybe I would feel normal again in the morning.

As soon as I turned off the light, the phone rang.

When I checked the handset, the caller ID showed "Private."

Seriously? Changing my number hadn't even held this guy off

for a day? Nothing was ever easy, I knew that, but even so...wow.

I let the machine get it. The last thing I felt like doing was playing this guy's games...he would get one message, in the hope he might reveal some clue that would help me stop him. After that, I was unplugging the phone.

"I don't want to be investigating your homicide one day."

The voice was Officer Parker's. For a wild moment I thought he was messing with me now, too, but the sound wasn't right--he sounded tinny. "I implore you, for your own sake and safety, please reconsider...don't want to be investigating your homicide..."

No. No, no, no--that was a recording, a recording someone had edited, and looped.

I jerked the phone line out of the wall and tried to think. No one had been in the house but Officer Parker and I when we had that conversation. I was certain of it. Officer Parker had nothing to do with this recording. Which meant...

No way. No *way* this guy had bugged my house.

One thing was for sure--I was not going to be able to sleep not knowing.

I turned on all the lights in the living room and started trashing the place. Well, not deliberately, of course, but that's sure what it looked like. I tore the cushions off the sofa, I pulled pictures off the wall, dumped the books out of my bookshelf.

It looked like someone had picked up the room, turned it over a few times, and then put it back down. It looked like a yard sale that had been ransacked by goblin hordes.

But I found it. Carefully mounted on the wall behind my collage, where I never would have found it if I hadn't been specifically looking.

I flushed it down the toilet.

I suppose I could have just gone to bed at that point. But actually *finding* the transmitter in my house creeped me out even more than just thinking it was there, and I had a feeling they were like roaches.

For every one you see, there are more that you don't.

So I went from room to room, destroying my house, and then I went back through putting it together again. I found a transmitter in my bedroom, and in my music room. Night had moved to the wee hours of the morning before I went to sleep.

But I slept well, knowing I'd thwarted him. I hadn't yet found a way to keep him out of the house entirely. But I had made sure he would no longer eavesdrop on what happened when he wasn't there.

And for tonight, that was enough.

The symphony had a rehearsal late the next evening. I slept till almost lunchtime, catching up for the last few nights.

I showed up to the Green Room half an hour early, so I was already well warmed up by the time Daniella came in at T minus ten minutes. She parked herself in a chair near the door--much closer to my spot than she usually chose--and spent the next few minutes trying to glare a hole into me.

I dug a pencil out of my violin case and marked a few more bowings on my Bach Double part, ignoring her. I couldn't figure out what she was up to.

Until Dwight walked in the room. He saw me and started my direction, but Daniella launched herself out of that chair and grabbed his arm, stopping him in his tracks. I laughed out loud, then tried to pass it off as a coughing fit. Unfortunately when I stopped I could still hear her.

"...just needed a place to rehearse, Dwight," Daniella was saying, gesticulating wildly, "and they were in there *making out!* I mean, no shame at all! In a rehearsal room!"

Uh-oh, that didn't sound so good. I hadn't counted on Daniella ratting me out with a grossly exaggerated version of events.

Dwight's face darkened and he looked my way with a frown that did not bode well. I didn't think much of my chances of making him listen to my side of the story right then, and I decided to beat a hasty retreat. Live to fight another day and all that.

I gathered up all my things and hopped down the stairs to the wings of the big stage.

A Green Room has a culture and atmosphere all its own. Green Rooms are fabulous places to be. But nothing quite compares to the stage, and the wings hold all of the anticipation. It's an environment that's electric with excitement, where people tiptoe and whisper and take one last hard gulp before facing fate under the bright lights.

There is, frankly, nothing else like it.

The stage was pretty sparsely populated. Most people were still in the Green Room, warming up and chatting, and getting first violinists into trouble for things they didn't even do.

An exception was Kolbi--that harp was too big to move around easily. Mostly it stayed on the stage, and so mostly she did, too.

She saw me take my seat and she came to me, but slowly, like she feared another fit. "You okay?"

I smiled, but I had to look away. "Yeah, I'm all right."

She sat down in Alexis's chair. "What was that the other day, anyway?"

I darted a glance around the stage. There was no one else around us, but I knew the sound monitors in the Green Room were usually on. I dropped my voice, relying on the noodling of the other musicians to cover us. "Nothing, really. I mean, it was just a dream."

"All that because of a dream? It must have been a humdinger!"

"Yeah..." I looked down at my hands on my violin. "I keep having the same nightmare over and over. It's about a murder...a murder I'm always too late to stop."

Kolbi's eyes were wide and round. "That's a real downer right there. No wonder you always look so tired. Who gets offed?"

I swallowed hard. "Well, actually--you do, Kolbi."

There was a long silence. When I finally dared to look at her, her color was funny, but she tried to laugh it off. It sounded a little hollow. "Wow. No biggie, I guess--I mean, it's just a crazy dream, right?"

"Right," I said, too quickly. "Just a crazy dream."

"There you are," boomed a voice behind me, the last voice in the world I wanted to hear right then. "I've been looking all over for you."

"Oh, gee," Kolbi said, as if she hadn't noticed Dwight, "look how late it's gotten. Rehearsal is about to begin. I think you had better head up front with Alexis, Chris."

It was wonderful to have a friend as good as Kolbi, willing to rescue me from Dwight even at the risk of a glare as combustible as the one he was aiming at her now.

"Thank you," I mouthed at her.

Then I grabbed my music and scooted.

Alas, rehearsal couldn't save me forever. Eventually it had to end.

When it did, I made record time back to the Green Room, and I was packed up and headed for the door while most people were still out on the stage.

Still, though, when I reached the door I found Dwight standing in front of it, arms folded. He looked like a thundercloud, standing there in my way.

"Hello, Dwight. Care to let me by?"

The thundercloud shifted stance. I swear I heard him rumble. "Nothing to say for yourself at all?"

I sighed. "I don't know what you're talking about."

"The hell you don't!"

I stepped back and crossed my arms. "I don't appreciate your tone, Dwight. And anything I choose to do--and who I choose to do it with--is my business. I don't owe you any explanations."

He looked pained. "I know. But Chris..."

I shook my head. "None of your business. But what Daniella told you wasn't true."

"Really?"

"Really."

"Nothing happened?"

"Nothing at all. Dwight, you can't keep this up." My temper was kicking in now. "Anything that did happen would be my business. Anything that may yet happen will be my business. I'll go have sex in the middle of the parking lot if I want to, and *it's my business!*"

Dwight stared at me.

Belatedly I realized everyone else in the Green Room was staring at me, too. And by this time, most people had made it in from the stage.

"Sing it, sister," Kolbi said from across the room.

So, pretty much, crap. I stood there, face glowing like a heat lamp, at a total loss. Dwight was still in front of the door, totally thunderstruck.

"Eh--I hate to interrupt, dear girl," said Darren from behind me, "but did you say you would have bowings ready today?"

"Yes. Yes, I have them here." I couldn't quite look at either of them.

"Wonderful. Come back to my office and you can copy those for me--I'm sure Dwight will want to distribute them at his next sectional."

"Oh, indubitably." Dwight looked sullen. My rant had evidently not pleased him.

I followed Darren back to his office, grateful for the escape. I intended to copy bowings slowly, so that everyone would be gone by the time I left. Even Dwight couldn't wait for me all night.

At least, I hoped not.

♫

By the time I finished, I think even Darren was tired of me. But I did accomplish my goal; by the time I left the Green Room was absolutely empty.

So I finally relaxed as I drove away from the concert hall. I wasn't sure what to do about Dwight--I knew he disapproved of any involvement I had with Alexis, but I also knew it wasn't up to him. How did I get him to see that?

I sort of zoned out while I drove, navigating the familiar route from memory, not really paying full attention.

Then I saw the flashing blue lights on the street in front of my house. There was a white Jaguar in my driveway.

I whipped into my driveway behind the Jaguar, and was out of my car before it completely stopped running. The blue lights flashing in the darkness gave me a surreal feeling.

There were two cops in my front yard. One was my old friend Officer Parker, crossing the yard toward me.

The other was putting handcuffs on Alexis Brooks.

"Good evening, Miss Marnett," Officer Parker said.

"Is it?" I tore my eyes away from Alexis and saw the front window of my house--shattered, jagged glass teeth left hanging in the frame. "What happened here?"

He shook his head and started back towards Alexis and the other cop. "We're still figuring that out. We got a call from your neighbor; he reported an individual prowling around your house.

When we got here we found the window broken. There is a flowerpot inside; Mr. Brooks admits that is what he used to break the window. We found this caught on one of the pieces of glass still in the window."

He showed me a burgundy piece of fabric in a little plastic bag. We stopped in front of Alexis, and I could see the place the fabric came from; the sleeve of his burgundy shirt.

"It's pretty clear," Officer Parker said, "that we've found your intruder."

"Chrispen," Alexis said impatiently, "this is ridiculous. Tell them I didn't do this!"

I stared at the scene--the jagged hole in his shirt, the front window with its toothy, broken grin, the flashing blue lights reflecting off the handcuffs on his wrists--and my first impulse in that moment was not to assert his innocence.

"Chrispen?" Alexis sounded stricken.

I couldn't say a word. What if this was how the story ended? What if Dwight, my mother, Officer Parker--what if all of them were right?

I turned away, in a numb sort of shock.

I heard the officer behind me hustling Alexis into the squad car, but it didn't seem real.

Officer Parker walked me to my front door, talking about statements and pressing charges and paperwork I would need to sign at the station, but that didn't seem real, either.

I stood in my living room alone, in the cold draft through the broken window, looking at a clay flowerpot that had scattered dirt and plant parts and shards of glass all over my carpet and my furniture. It didn't seem real.

I sat down numbly on the edge of the armchair. I looked at my collage of Alexis on the wall and something in me snapped and I cried and cried.

That felt real.

♪

When I thought I had it all out of system, I picked up the phone. The police thought they had their resolution--the harassing phone calls, the pictures, the faxes, emails, all of it--they thought it was done. All tied up with a neat little bow on top. All that was left now was for me to fill out some paperwork to press charges.

Somehow, I couldn't feel the resolution.

It was late, but I called Kolbi anyway. I listened to the phone ring, and looked at the disaster that was my living room, wondering why it didn't feel like it had anything at all to do with me.

"Hello?"

"Alexis is going to jail." The words sounded like I felt hollowed-out, flat.

"What? What on earth happened?"

"The police caught him trying to break into my house. He said he threw a flowerpot through the front window. Part of his shirt was caught on the glass."

"Oh, Chrispen." Kolbi paused. "It just doesn't seem right, does it?"

I instantly felt defensive, like she was questioning my judgment. "I should have expected that--you always support him. What would it take to get you to doubt him?"

There was a little silence. "You always supported him, too, until now. I don't think you are thinking this through. Alexis wouldn't do something like that."

I sighed. "I didn't think so either, but he was in the yard, the flowerpot was through the window, and he admitted putting it there. What could I say?"

"Are you going to press charges?"

I shivered in the cold breeze from the window. "I don't see

how I could. If I put him in jail, there goes my job when Darren finds out."

"Now you're starting to sound like you're thinking again," Kolbi said. "I'll be right over. You sound like you could use some help cleaning up. I'll be there in ten minutes."

I put the phone back in the cradle with a heavy sigh, and turned to survey my living room. It was such a mess it was hard to know where to look first, but for some reason I zeroed in on the flowerpot, lying cracked on the floor. A flowerpot that had for the last six months sat out on my little patio, happily housing a growing fern.

And all at once I had a revelation like lightning across my brain.

The flowerpot.

That was it, wasn't it? That one last straw of hope I'd been grasping for--it was laying in the middle of my living room floor all along.

I felt like dancing, but instead I dug out a trash bag and the vacuum cleaner and started cleaning up the living room.

The dancing would wait until later. I had more important fish to fry first.

♫

Right at ten minutes later, a knock sounded on my door. It was Kolbi, and she was frowning.

"Chrispen," she said by way of greeting. "Get out here and take a look at this."

I frowned back. What was this about?

She waved a flashlight at me. "Come on!"

I followed her outside and into the yard, to the jagged hole where my front window should have been. It still seemed creepy to see it like that.

Kolbi suddenly turned her flashlight on the ground,

examining the grass and mud in front of the window. "Did Alexis say there was anyone else here with him?"

"No. Why?"

"Have you looked at your front lawn?"

"No." I was starting to lose my patience. What was all the mystery about? Why was Kolbi answering my questions with questions?

"Did you or the police walk through this part of the yard?" Kolbi seemed exasperated, too, as though she expected me to have some idea where this was going.

I did not. "No. We came up the driveway. What does my front lawn have to do with anything?"

"Well, it proves that unless Alexis was dancing the jitterbug when he put that pot through your window, he wasn't alone."

I gaped at her a moment, my mind refusing to make sense of the words I had just heard. Wasn't alone? I snatched the flashlight from Kolbi and stared at the ground.

Kolbi was right. The footprints were scattered, and looking in the mud it was easy to see one set of feet was a different size, with different tread patterns on the shoes.

"Why didn't the police see this?" I wondered aloud.

Kolbi shrugged. "Why would they look? They had their criminal."

"They will never believe this," I pointed out. "They might even think I faked this to free Alexis. I think Officer Parker already thinks I'm half crazy."

"You don't have to convince them of anything," Kolbi said. "Only one person decides whether she wants to help them prosecute."

Of course, she was right.

Kolbi helped me board up my broken window. We brought

the keys to the Jaguar inside the house, then she drove us to the police station.

A receptionist glanced up at us as we walked into the bright, cold lobby. "Name?"

"Chrispen Marnett."

"Ooh, right." She pressed a button on the large desk telephone in front of her. "Parker, Marnett is here for you."

She smiled at me. It looked like she wanted me to think the smile was sincere. "You've made his day," she informed me, and popped her gum.

I smiled, but I didn't really care if she thought it was sincere or not.

"Miss Marnett!" Officer Parker bounded around the counter and pumped my hand. "I'm so glad you could make it. I was just working on some reports."

"Officer Parker, hello."

"Call me Bob, call me Bob. And this is?" He turned to Kolbi.

"Kolbi Edwards," she said, shaking his hand.

"Wonderful. Come back with me to my office and we'll get started."

We followed him down a narrow hallway into a small room just big enough for a desk with one chair behind it and three in front of it.

Officer Parker sat down at the chair behind the desk and began shuffling through papers. I hovered in the doorway uneasily. I was pretty sure he wasn't going to like the direction I was about to take.

He glanced up at me. "Come in, come in!" He waved me forward with one hand, gathering papers with the other.

Kolbi sat down in the far chair. I took the closest one, and perched myself uncomfortably on the edge of it.

"I've got everything all ready for you," said Officer Parker, handing me a heavy rollerball pen. He took a sheet of paper off the top of the little stack he had made, turned it around, and slid it toward me across the desk. "First we'll need your John Hancock on this form."

I turned the pen end over end in my hand. "Actually, Officer Parker...I'm not interested in pressing charges against Alexis."

He gaped at me, then sat back in his chair. "I see. Could you tell me why?"

"Alexis is not the one who has been harassing me."

"But we caught him breaking into your house."

"I'm sorry, Officer, but I just disagree. You caught him at my house, but I don't think he was breaking in. Did you find any evidence he ever entered the house?"

He sighed. "No."

"Whoever has been doing this has been in my house several times with no sign of forced entry. Why would he suddenly shatter a window?'

"Miss Marnett, I don't have an answer for that. But I don't think you should give up on this so easily."

"I'm sorry, Officer. My mind is made up--I don't want to have anything to do with prosecuting Alexis."

Officer Parker leaned back in his chair and laced his fingers behind his head. "You know that this case could be prosecuted without you."

I stared at him.

"But the truth is that you are right. I've already spoken with the D.A., and he doesn't feel like we have much of a case without your testimony--maybe vandalism, but without your support, we're liable to spend a lot of effort and taxpayer money only to lose him again."

"Will you be releasing him, then?" The question was Kolbi's first contribution to the conversation.

Officer Parker glanced at her like he had forgotten she was

there. "I suppose we will, since Miss Marnett has declined to move forward with the case. But let me be abundantly clear here--we do not share your view. I'm not looking to get Alexis Brooks in here on a vandalism change-- he'll do more than that. I am good with letting him go now because I am certain he will be back soon. Give him enough rope and all that."

"I see." I stood up abruptly out of my chair. "I'm afraid we will have to agree to disagree. I don't believe Alexis is harassing me. I don't believe Alexis murdered his wife. I can't support your vendetta against him."

"Vendetta?" He looked surprised. "Miss Marnett, all I want is to see a man brought to justice for a horrendous act. Right now all the evidence I have indicates that Alexis Brooks is that man. If you have evidence that indicates otherwise, I would love to see it."

I had no answer for that--I just stood there, uncomfortable.

Officer Parker stood up. "From your silence, I am guessing that you have no such evidence. I want justice, ladies, not vendetta, for whoever is guilty. You may wait in the lobby. Mr. Brooks will be out shortly."

♪

I felt a little giddy, standing in the lobby waiting for Alexis. I knew things could easily have been so much worse, but I couldn't help feeling like I had made it out of the lion's den. I had gone to bat for Alexis, and won! I imagined how happy he would be while I paced the lobby, waiting.

But when he did come out, *happy* was not the word I would have chosen to describe him. In fact, it wouldn't even have made the top ten.

I had a cold, sick feeling in my stomach. This Alexis was familiar. Isolated, cold, shut-off--an Alexis with no twinkle in his eye, no spark in his smile, who never told viola jokes. I had not seen this Alexis in at least a week, and I had hoped I never would again.

I looked uncertainly at Kolbi, but she looked just as confused as me. "Um--are you ready to go, Alexis?" I tried to sound normal, but I can't say it really worked.

He didn't even look at me, just nodded once and stood there, staring at nothing.

Something was wrong, all right, but I couldn't even hazard a guess as to what.

Kolbi shrugged, grabbed my arm, and started walking. We went out to her car, with the blank Alexis-zombie following behind us.

"I think," Kolbi said, so quietly I wasn't at first sure I had actually heard her, "that you had better ride in the back. See if you can get him to talk."

I nodded, but I felt oddly nervous about the prospect. Alexis held the door while I slid across the back seat, then sat down woodenly next to me.

What could I do? I had no idea what was wrong, no clue how to get through to him. But I watched his face, stony and impassive, under the dim lights of the street lights passing outside, and I knew I had to try.

"So," I said conversationally, as though anything like conversation was possible under the circumstances, "are you glad to be out of there?"

"Hmm. I suppose."

Kolbi gave me an urgent look in the rearview mirror. I looked back helplessly and shrugged. If I'd had any better lines, I would have led with them.

"Ready for rehearsal tomorrow?"

His gaze slid over me without pausing. "Yes."

I gave up. If Kolbi wanted him talking, she would have to do it herself.

Apparently Kolbi had seen the futility of it as well, because she didn't go there either, and the three of us finished our ride to my house in an uncomfortable silence.

Kolbi pulled to a stop in front of my house, and Alexis and I piled out of the car. "Good luck," she told me, nodding sharply in his direction, and she drove away.

Alexis was already headed for the Jaguar. He was just going to leave, after all that, not even a word?

I decided I didn't give up after all. I caught up with him and tapped his arm. "I locked up your car and put your keys in the house, Alexis. Come in with me and I'll get them for you."

"Thank you." Perfectly polite, even though he sounded distant. And then he turned to face me, and I could have cried. His face was passive, disinterested, but his eyes-- his eyes were haunted with sadness.

I unlocked the front door, went inside, and grabbed his keys off the kitchen counter. I never heard a sound behind me, but when I turned around he was right there.

I put my hands behind my back and stood there, offering nothing.

Alexis regarded me a moment. "May I have my keys, please?"

"Oh, absolutely." I stepped past him and closed the front door. "But first, you are going to talk to me."

His face turned wary, but he said nothing.

"What's wrong, Alexis?" I went back into the kitchen, and put his keys on the counter in plain sight. He made no move toward them, though.

Maybe he did want to talk after all.

Except, of course, that he wasn't actually talking. I sighed. "Look at you. You're blank, shut off, like you're not even there. I haven't seen you like this in awhile. What happened? Are you upset that the police arrested you?"

"Damn the police," he said, and his voice shook. "I don't

care about what they think, or the rest of the town, or the rest of the world. They gave up on me years ago." He looked at me accusingly. *"You* thought that I did these things to you."

Things clicked right then, though I probably should have understood long before. I knew why Alexis had spent the last five years as a lonely, isolated, broken shell of a man. It wasn't the loss of his wife--people lost loved ones and grieved, without becoming what he had become. It wasn't even the fact that the police had blamed him.

It was the way the press, his fans, his friends and especially his own family had turned on him like rabid dogs, immediately, that had wounded him so deeply. No faith, no support, even though the case against him was circumstance and speculation.

And now I had done the same thing.

"If you really believe I tried to break into your house," he said, "if you really think I did any of the rest of this, you should have left me in police custody. I'd rather be in jail than be out here, with you thinking that way of me."

"No." I shook my head. It all made sense now--the improvement I had seen in Alexis in the last week wasn't spontaneous healing--it was because he had one person at last who really believed in him. "No, Alexis, stop. Listen to me, if I really thought any of that I would have left you there. I don't believe you did any of that."

"You don't believe it *now.*"

I sighed. "You're right, I did doubt you at the time. I shouldn't have, but I wasn't thinking straight. I'm sorry."

He eyed me doubtfully.

"You are no murderer. You're no burglar, no vandal, no stalker. You are the kindest, most generous, most talented person I've ever met. I believe in you, Alexis. But do you believe me?"

He stared at me, and before I was ready he caught me up into a bone-crushing hug. "I'm sorry," he said, his voice muffled in my hair.

"I'm sorry too," I told him. "You were right, I should have told the police right away that you couldn't have been doing this."

The world felt right again. Alexis was vital, and warm, and the shell that had encased him was gone.

He was still wounded, though. Now I knew that, and understood it. My faith helped; it was a start, it allowed him to function as a normal man. But he was only improved, not healed. I knew there was only one way to heal him, and I knew the only one who could do it was me.

I had to clear Alexis's name. I had to do what the police had been unable to do.

I had to solve Madeleine's murder.

♪

The goal was mine; I didn't choose it, it owned me. As soon as the thought had formed in my mind, I knew it to be true. Madeleine's murder had to be solved, and I had to do it.

How, though, I had no idea.

The dress rehearsal for our concert was early the next afternoon. "Dress rehearsal" for an orchestra is a bit of a misleading term; we don't actually wear concert dress. We do set the stage up and play the program exactly as if it was the real performance. It's a very important rehearsal, early in the afternoon on the same day as the concert.

Because it is such an important rehearsal, the stress level tends to be high at dress rehearsal, and tempers can be short. Maybe that's why Dwight was all over me, barely letting me step inside the door before he was on the attack.

"Chris, I saw what happened in the news this morning. After everything that he did to you, they finally catch him, and you let him go? Why didn't you press charges against that son of a bitch?"

I pushed past Dwight to my usual spot by the counter. If I was going to have this conversation at all--which was certainly not my intent--I did not want to have it with him. I put my violin case on the counter, turning my back on Dwight. "I didn't see any reason to." There. That kind of short answer should encourage anyone to mind their own business.

Anyone but Dwight. He pushed right in next to me at the counter. "Didn't see any reason to? They found him at the broken window, his fingerprints on the weapon, his shirt on the glass--what more do you want, a signed letter of confession? Jesus, I can't believe you're standing here defending him!"

I sighed. "This is my decision, Dwight, to handle how I choose. My business, not yours. I would need a whole lot more than circumstantial evidence to believe that Alexis was trying to break into my house."

He gaped at me. "You really don't believe he was breaking in?"

"No. I really don't. And you may as well quit wasting your breath on it, because nothing you say will convince me."

"Do you realize you are crazy?"

I folded my arms. "Do you realize you are very mouthy for someone who wasn't even there?" Subtle hints, I decided, did not get far with Dwight.

He looked honestly surprised. "But Chris, I was there. Didn't Alexis tell you that?"

It was my turn to gape, and I did staggeringly well at it. It was one of those moments where you're going along your happy way and suddenly discover reality has lurched about three yards to your left and everything around you, while it is still the same, feels fundamentally different than it was before.

Dwight leaned back against the counter. "I'm guessing from your face that he didn't. No wonder you let him off, you never got the whole story, did you?" He shook his head. "I saw Alexis lurking around outside your house, and I knew you were staying late with Darren, so I stopped to see what he was up to."

"And?"

"And he threw a flowerpot through your front window when I tried to stop him. He's completely mental, Chris. And frankly, so are you for letting him go when you had a chance to stop him."

"Maybe you're right," I said. Somebody here was certainly mental.

But then, Kolbi and I had seen already that there were two people at my house that evening. I just never imagined Dwight as the other person.

"Are you ready for the concert tonight?" Dwight had said his piece, it seemed, and was ready to let the matter drop.

"Ready as I'll ever be, I suppose."

He made a face. "You don't sound very excited. Aren't you ready to show the world Alexis can't outshine you?"

"But he can, Dwight. Without even trying." I shook my head. "But I know this inside and out, and I'm going to do my best. It's going to be a good show."

He grinned at me. "You'll be great."

Daniella walked by us, suspiciously close, and with suspiciously good timing. "With all the one-on-one time she's had with our concertmaster, she should be *fabulous*. And I bet the solo isn't half bad, either."

Dwight's face clouded. Mine, of course, turned a bright, glowing red.

The concertmaster in question chose that moment to come through the door. He took one look at my face and his smile disappeared. "Chrispen, are you all right?"

I tried to smile at him, but it felt sort of sickly. I didn't know if Daniella's primary goal was to embarrass me or aggravate Dwight, but being the butt of her crude jokes was no fun for me, and she caused me no end of trouble with Dwight. "I'm fine," I said.

Alexis looked from me to Daniella, and frowned. "Daniella, why don't you toddle along and play with the other children now?"

She snickered and patted Dwight's arm. "Careful, Dwight, Alexis doesn't like to share."

"Seriously," Dwight told her, "get lost."

She opened her mouth, but before more snark could come out, Alexis cut her off. "Daniella, did you hear about the violist who played in tune?"

She stared at him.

"Yeah," he said, "neither did I."

Dwight laughed out loud, and Daniella turned up her nose and left.

"Just out of curiosity," I said, "how many of those jokes do you know?"

Alexis winked at me. "If she keeps picking on you, I guess you'll find out." He put his violin case on the counter next to mine. "What was going on over here, anyway?" He glanced at Dwight. "Two against one?"

Dwight snorted. "I don't side with anyone against Chrispen-- you should know that. I didn't do anything to her but tell her the truth. You may want to give it a try yourself sometime."

He gave us a sour look and left.

Alexis watched him thoughtfully. "What was that all about?"

"Dwight wanted to tell me his version of last night's big event. He says he was there."

"Yes, he was."

I goggled at him. "How come you didn't tell me?"

"How come you didn't ask? Seriously, there never seemed to be an appropriate time. We never did really discuss what happened."

"You're right." I unzipped my case and started unpacking for rehearsal. "What did happen?"

Alexis leaned back against the counter and folded his arms, watching the activity in the rest of the room. "You wouldn't know this, but your house is on my way home from here. Since you've been having this--trouble, it's become sort of a habit of mine to check things out as I pass, make sure everything looks okay."

He shrugged. "It always has--until last night. As I came around the corner I thought I saw someone duck behind the bushes in front of your porch to hide. So I pulled into your driveway to see what was going on."

"It was Dwight?"

"It was. I guess he thought he'd seen something too, which should have been the end of it. He was acting weird though--he had been drinking and he was in a really foul mood. He said some things, and I said some things back, and you know how that goes. I'm afraid I ended up losing my temper. The flowerpot was the nearest thing to hand, so I threw it at him. Of course, I missed."

"You look really embarrassed."

He laughed, and turned around to unpack his own violin. "I am really embarrassed."

"Because you threw it, or because you missed?"

That made him laugh again. "Both, I suppose. I really am sorry, Chrispen. None of that should have happened. I don't know what kind of story Dwight made out of it, but I only wanted to stop something bad from happening, if I could."

"You don't need to apologize, Alexis--I understand completely."

And I thought I finally did. I had two friends, both trying to look out for me, but whose personal differences were just too great. If you could take their mutual dislike out of the picture, you really just had two guys trying to help keep me safe. It sort of made me teary-eyed.

Then I saw Daniella, hanging on Dwight's arm and laughing too loudly at something he had said. She stuck her tongue out at me, and I shook my head as I gathered up my things to go onstage.

Not everybody was my friend, I knew that. But Daniella had a long way to go if she wanted to turn Dwight against me, and her constant jibes at me did not endear her to him.

Alexis took my free arm and we headed for the stage. I paid more attention to his handsome profile than to my feet, trusting him not to let me fall.

Not everyone was my friend, but everyone who mattered to me was.

Dress rehearsals at the Newton Philharmonic were a more serious affair than at other orchestras I had been with. Backstage, Darren gave us any remarks he felt necessary; particular passages he needed to hear certain sections louder on, things he wanted us to watch for, and other business of that nature.

But after he said, "All right, let's hit the stage," that was it--no more talking for the rest of the rehearsal. We filed silently out onto the stage in the proper order, as if this were the real performance.

"Proper order" meant that after the rest of the orchestra was seated, Alexis came out alone and took a bow before taking his seat next to me. It was a protocol formality he claimed to despise, but I thought he secretly got a kick out of it. Who wouldn't? It was one of the perks of being concertmaster.

Only after Alexis sat down did Darren come out and take his bow. He raised his baton, and we all snapped to position like a group of well-trained soldiers.

There was no talking between pieces, either--no questions, no criticism. Darren lowered his arms, we all shifted our music around to the next piece, then returned to concert rest position. A moment of still silence for imaginary applause, then Darren raised his arms and we were off again.

The Bach Double was our closing piece. I'll tell you, that big concert hall had never seemed quite so big as when I stepped out to the front of the stage with Alexis, even though it was only a rehearsal. I had only ever played in the orchestra here--until that moment I don't think it quite hit me, what playing a solo here was going to be like. It was a good thing this was just a rehearsal, because I could feel a case of the nerves coming on.

As I moved in the silence to the edge of the stage, I could have sworn I saw something move in the shadows, way out in the back of the orchestra level seating. It gave me a turn, and I missed a step and stumbled.

Alexis caught my arm, and leaned close to me. "Are you okay?" His voice was a mere murmur against my ear; in the tense silence of the empty house a regular voice would have carried through the whole place.

I nodded, and tried to lower my voice to match his. "I'm fine. I'm sorry, I--I thought I saw someone out in the house."

He frowned, and squinted out into the darkness, shading his eyes against the stage lights with his hand. "There's nobody there."

"I know." I smoothed my clothes down and stood at the ready, trying to look like a capable soloist, not someone who had just freaked out over shadows. "I'm sorry."

Alexis grinned at me and winked, and then Darren raised his baton again and we were off.

It sounded brilliant, it really did. The rest of the program had given us plenty of warm-up, so we were in fine form, and we were playing to make beautiful music, not to one-up each other.

We finished, Darren lowered his baton, and the entire orchestra broke into spontaneous applause. I gave Alexis a high-five, and he swept me into an intense, one-armed hug. We laughed till we were almost crying.

And then the noise of the orchestra died down, and we could hear another sound in the sudden quiet. A single person clapping, loudly, and so slowly it was almost rude.

And it was coming from out in the seats.

"Bravo, my friends," said a heavily accented voice. "Bravo."

Alexis stiffened. I peered out into the house, but I still couldn't see anyone there.

"Dismissed, everyone!" Darren called loudly. "Great rehearsal--go back to the Green Room, please, and pack up, if you will. Move along, now, and I will see you all at tonight's performance."

A few people seemed inclined to hang around and see what happened, but at Darren's urging the orchestra cleared out. I would have gone with them, but Alexis held me firmly where I was with an arm around my shoulders. His face was carved from stone.

Darren came to stand with us, facing calmly out into the darkness. "Hello, Alexei."

I did a double-take, and tightened my arm around Alexis. No wonder he looked so awful. And yet, I had hope. Maybe he'd had a change of heart--maybe this would be their long overdue reconciliation; he had come to see the rehearsal, after all.

He came down the center aisle, an older, grayer version of Alexis, with deep lines around his eyes and mouth that had not been there when the pictures in the stairwell were taken. "Darren, my old friend, that was wonderful. You have done an excellent job here."

Darren gave a small, stiff bow. "I'm very glad to hear you say that."

But before Alexei even spoke again I knew it wasn't going to be that easy. The compliment was the appetizer, not the meal, and *congratulations* was not what he had come to say. I stood there unmoving beside Alexis, waiting for it.

Alexei stopped in front of the stage, and darted a quick glance at us before addressing Darren. "So you are really going on with it, then?"

Darren's face was the picture of innocence. "Going on with what, Alexei?"

Alexei's face hardened. "Putting this--this *ubiytsa* in front of my orchestra. Bad enough you hired him, now you must feature him as well?"

"I'm sorry, but you left the Board. This decision was made with their full support."

"Of course--they support the money! No care for decency." Alexei shook his head, and I found his sharp eyes suddenly focused on me. It was disconcerting just how exactly his eyes were like Alexis's, and I fidgeted under his gaze. "And you, *dorogaya*, you don't mind sharing the stage with this man? You stand there with his hands on you, and I wonder if you know your danger."

"My danger." I glanced at Alexis, stony and impassive, and shook my head. "I mean no disrespect, but you are wrong. Alexis is no murderer."

I expected anger; I was braced for an attack. I was not prepared for the heart-wrenching way his face crumpled into sorrow. He turned from me then, back to Darren. "Many a maid has met her ruin, drawn in by a fair face. Darren, you must not allow this to continue. Stop this insanity, I am begging you."

Darren sighed and regarded his old friend sadly. "Alexei, I can't help you. I know what you believe, and I can't change you. But this concert will go on, with or without your support." He turned and left the stage without looking back.

I would have followed him, but Alexis stayed, so I stayed with him. Alexei heaved a broken sigh, and started slowly back up the aisle. I don't know which hurt more to watch; Alexei's slow, painful shuffle, or the way Alexis watched his father leave him standing there without ever even acknowledging he was there.

♫

Alexis and I were brought back out onto the stage four times to bow before the cheering, applauding crowd after the concert that night. The Green Room, when we finally made it back there, was filled with flowers.

Crowds of people poured in to congratulate us, and we stood shaking hands and smiling all around. Lots of people asked Alexis to autograph their programs---a few even asked me!

Darren somehow managed to shoulder his way through the crowd to us. "Brilliant performance, my boy," he said, clasping Alexis by the arm and shaking his hand, "simply brilliant. And Chrispen, my dear, you were sensational as well. Tell me, my girl, will you play the Mendelssohn with us? I know it's terribly short notice, but--"

"But she's been working on it already," Alexis said, putting his arm around me. "That shouldn't stop her, if she wants to do it."

I stared at Darren, a little slack-jawed. "Me? Play the tribute concert?" When I had told Darren we would find someone else, I have to confess that my name wasn't even on my mental list.

Darren smiled. "I can't think of anyone better."

"Nor I," Alexis said.

I turned to Alexis, suddenly anxious. "It wouldn't upset you? I mean--"

"Not at all," he replied, and he seemed to mean it. He squeezed my shoulders. "I think if you want to do it, you should go for it."

I smiled at both of them, at the room, at the world. "I'd love to, Darren."

Darren smiled back, pumping my hand in an enthusiastic handshake. "Wonderful. It's a date. The Trustees are going to love this, Chrispen. We'll talk details later--you kids get back to celebrating." He turned to leave, still shaking his head and muttering, "Brilliant."

We stood smiling and glad-handing for at least half an hour before Alexis took my arm, excused us politely but firmly to those around us, and led me back to the performer's lounge where we had left our violin cases before the concert.

"I thought you could use a break," he said, opening the door. "You look dead on your feet." He stood back to let me go first.

I stepped into the room, and felt the color drain from my face. "Oh--my God."

Alexis was right behind me. "What in the hell is this?"

The lounge had a little sofa and two chairs, arranged around a round coffee table. The coffee table presently held a huge bouquet of dead, black flowers.

I stood frozen by the doorway while Alexis went to pull the card off the thing. He read it, and grimaced. "Very nice." He crumpled the card in his hand and tried to smile at me. "I'm sure this has nothing to do with you," he said, but it sounded more like he was trying to convince me than reassure me.

I swallowed hard. "Actually, I think it does. I found one in my car the other day."

"Damn." He ran a hand through his hair, and laid his violin in its case. "You stay here, I'm going to get rid of this thing." He scooped it up and disappeared out the door.

I put away my own violin, then sank down on the sofa and leaned my head back against it, suddenly bone-tired. I closed my eyes.

"I'm sorry about that," said Alexis, suddenly right in front of me, "but maybe this will help make up for it."

I opened my eyes, and the table in front of me had a new bouquet on it--two-dozen yellow roses.

"Alexis," I gasped, "those are gorgeous! I love yellow roses, they're so sunny."

"That's why I chose them. They are for the sunshine of my life." He made a face and sat down next to me on the little couch. "I have to admit that sounded better in my head."

I laughed. "I think it sounded just fine."

"Well then," he said, "it served its purpose."

He leaned toward me, and my heart stopped. It was the Moment, take two, and Daniella wasn't anywhere around.

A sharp knock on the door startled us, and Officer Parker came into the lounge, wearing a suit instead of the uniform I was used to.

"Miss Marnett, I wonder if I might speak with you for a moment."

Alexis made a sound something like a growl. "I'll take your flowers to your car," he said, low and next to my ear, "but don't think you've gotten rid of me."

"Thank you," I told him. "The keys are in my violin case."

For the second time that evening, Alexis left the lounge with a bouquet of flowers. Officer Parker frowned after him.

"Please come in," I said, "have a seat. Did you enjoy the concert?"

"Very much," he said, and to my surprise it sounded like he was telling the truth. "I had never heard Alexis Brooks play before tonight. I wanted to see what all the fuss was about."

"And?"

He smiled, but it gave the impression of a grimace. "He's incredible. Really, really incredible. And you are, too. The way you played together was something else."

"Officer, I realize this isn't a social call. Please, say what's on your mind."

He laced his fingers together as though he missed having his hat to fidget with. "You haven't...reconsidered your position on prosecution, have you?"

"No."

He glanced at the door. "I could tell as much, but I had to ask." He sighed and looked at the floor. "This isn't an easy question, but I have to ask it anyway. Miss Marnett, what are your reasons for defending Mr. Brooks?"

I couldn't see where this was going. "He is innocent. I thought I had made that pretty clear."

"You did. But why do you think so?"

"I don't know how to answer that. Alexis is not a man capable of the things you ascribe to him. Could the performance you heard tonight have come from a soul as dark as that?"

Officer Parker shook his head. "I know that music is supposed to be the language of the soul. But I've seen too much of the dark side of the human soul to question what it is capable of. What I'm driving at is this--are you a danger junkie?"

"A...what?"

"You know the type. Women who are attracted to violent criminals, *because* they are violent criminals. They get a thrill from it. It's like the moth and the flame, and it's the danger that draws them. Is that what I'm dealing with here?"

I gaped at him. "No. No, not at all. Alexis is as dangerous as my grandmother."

"You really believe it's just coincidence that all this other stuff is happening to you?"

"I really do."

He sighed and stood up. "For your sake, I sincerely hope you are right. We got a call from Alexei Brooks this afternoon, very concerned about your safety. I told him I'd check on you."

"Thank you," I said, as graciously as I could manage. Officer Parker walked to the door, then turned around and regarded me sadly. "You really want to thank me? End this thing with Alexis Brooks before you get hurt. This is one time I don't want to be able to say I told you so."

He left, leaving me alone with the table, empty but for a few black flower petals.

♫

Alexis looked surprised when he came back into the lounge. "Done already? I thought that would take longer."

I shrugged, depressed by the whole exchange with Officer Parker. "I don't think he had much to say."

Alexis looked at me a long, quiet moment, but said nothing.

"It's getting pretty late," I said finally, standing up from the sofa and stretching.

"Yes. The Green Room is almost empty. I'll walk you to your car," he said, with a glance at the table that I figured was involuntary.

"Thank you," I said, relieved. There were creepier things than walking across a dark parking lot alone at night, but I couldn't think of any offhand.

Alexis seemed to understand, though. We gathered our violins and music folders and headed out of the lounge. The almost-empty Green Room was now completely empty, so we left the building without being bothered.

That dark parking lot was just as creepy in person as I had imagined it. I put my arm through his and tried not to let my imagination run away with me. His warmth was reassuring.

We got to my car, and I made sure to check the passenger seat and the back. Alexis patted my hand on his arm. "You seem a little worried," he said, which was probably an understatement. "Shall I follow you home?"

"Please do." All those dead flowers were beginning to feel less creepy and more threatening, and I was finding that the dark didn't help. I tried to suppress a shudder. "Isn't this silly--a grown woman afraid of the dark?"

"No," Alexis said seriously. "It's never silly to be afraid of the dark when there is something in it worth fearing."

Okay, so that didn't really help either. I felt like my eyes were bugging out, trying to see everywhere at once, as I got into my car and buckled in.

The drive back to my house seemed especially long. It was nice to see the Jaguar's headlights in the rearview mirror, and to know there was someone friendly behind them.

Of course everything looked normal when I pulled into the driveway. Well, except for the boarded-up front window, but that was only because they hadn't made it out to replace the glass yet.

Alexis pulled in the driveway behind me. I waited for him next to my car, looking at my boarded up window with a sense of foreboding.

"Here," said Alexis, "I'll carry your flowers in for you." He leaned into the car, and came back holding that impressive bouquet.

"Thank you," I said, surprised.

He grinned. "I know how to make myself useful."

"Yes," I mused, fumbling with the keys to unlock my front door, "you'd be surprised how many times I've heard that. When I told all my friends in Carolina that I was coming here to work with you, that's all any of them could say. 'Alexis Brooks! He's so useful!'"

He laughed dryly. "That's probably better than what they actually did say. Where do you want these flowers?"

I pointed to the left. "On the table in the kitchen would be great."

He went through the archway to the left, and I went through the one on the right of the entryway, to the living room.

I turned on the light, and I immediately wished I hadn't.

Various pictures of me--there was no earthly way to tell how many--had been carefully sliced apart, hideously but never randomly. I was always cut along the shoulders, the neck, the legs; precisely dissected, mixed with dead flower petals, and piled on the living room floor. In the middle of this was another note scrawled in heavy blue ink:

Stay away from him

I sank down onto my knees. It didn't feel like I could breathe. I thought I might be sick, but instead I was wracked with great, heaving sobs.

I buried my face in my hands and cried like a little girl. There just wasn't any way to win; there was nothing I could do to slow this guy down. He was always one step ahead of me, with something more horrible waiting around the next bend.

In this grotesque pile of my disembodied parts, there were no heads. This seemed to me more awful than everything else he had done combined. Where were they? What possible reason could he have for keeping them?

I just didn't even want to know.

A hand fell on my shoulder. "Oh, Chrispen--I'm so sorry."

I didn't know how to respond. I had forgotten, for a moment, that anyone else existed in that horrible moment. I sat back on my heels, wiping my cheeks with my hands.

Alexis moved past me to stare down at the horrific mess, and I could see the muscles of his jaw working silently in agitation. "Unbelievable," he finally said. "Just unbelievable."

He shook his head and left the room, only to reappear a moment later with the trashcan from the kitchen. He shoveled the pile of pictures and petals into the can, then turned and regarded me. "Are you okay?"

I took a shaky breath and nodded, struggling to get to my

feet. Alexis took my hand and helped me up. "I'm sorry," I said. "I just...I guess I wasn't prepared for that. That was so *horrible...*"

Alexis pulled me into a hug. "Don't you dare apologize. I can't imagine what this is like for you. Do you want me to leave?"

My arms tightened around him convulsively. "I can't stay here alone, Alexis. I just can't." My voice sounded pitiful and small, even to my own ears.

"Would you rather go somewhere else?"

"What are you suggesting?" I held very still.

Alexis sounded as though he was choosing his words carefully. "My house is only a few blocks away. You are welcome to stay there."

I raised my head suddenly to look at him, weighing the implications of this invitation. I was acutely aware of the warmth of his hand on my shoulder, of his arm around my waist. He smelled of woodsy aftershave mixed with the leather of his jacket, and just being near him was comforting. I needed that comfort, I really did.

How badly did I need it?

Alexis pulled his hands back as if I had burned him and turned away from me. "You don't have to sleep with me to stay at my house, Chrispen. I thought you knew me better than that. I have a guest room, and you are welcome to use it."

I willed myself not to blush. It was sort of like willing the tide not to come in. "I'm sorry, Alexis--you're right, of course. I don't think my brain is working right now. I would be honored to use your guest room, if you still want me."

He turned to look at me then, and instead of the smile I was expecting, his face was dead serious. "I'll always want you."

I stared at him, tears welling up in my eyes again. I had not been prepared for that, either.

And then he broke into a wide grin. "But you'd better get a

move on, because I'm not waiting here all night. In ten minutes the good ship Jaguar sets sail, with whoever is on board."

"Yes, sir!" I snapped him a mock salute and scurried back to my room to throw some things in an overnight bag. When we dealt in humor, we were in my element.

But one day soon, I figured, I wouldn't be able to hide behind humor any more. And what on earth was I going to do then?

♫

From the outside, you probably would have called the Brooks residence plain. It was dark red brick, well-maintained, solid and not ostentatious. It had a little windowed cupola on the garage, and trees all around so it seemed quite private. Driving by, you would never guess that an international icon lived there.

At least, not if the Jaguar was in the garage. That car was a local icon itself. The windows were tinted so dark they were almost black, probably for that very reason.

Alexis pulled the car into the garage and came around to help me out. He took my bag, opened the door, and I found that the view from outside was only half of the story.

From the garage we went through a little utility area, where he left my overnight bag on top of the washing machine for the moment.

In the kitchen, dark cherry wood cabinets gleamed in the low light, with green plants on top of them. The dining room beyond was elegant but stale somehow, with a layer of dust over everything that spoke of long disuse.

It was a sad room, and I was relieved that we did not go in there. Instead, Alexis went right out of the kitchen.

I followed him into the living room, which was, in a word, fabulous. The high, vaulted ceiling had polished cedar beams, and on the far wall a matching cedar mantel was built into a river rock fireplace and chimney. I stopped there in the entryway, gawking.

Alexis looked back at me and smiled. "I agree. That fireplace is what sold Madeleine and me on this house."

"It's gorgeous," I said, but even saying the words felt redundant.

"It's early yet," he said, glancing at the ornate grandfather clock ticking solemnly in the corner. "Would you like something to drink?"

My throat had that uncomfortable raw feeling that comes from crying. "I would love that. Whatever you're having is fine."

"Okay. I'll be right back." He went back into the kitchen, moving quietly on the thick ivory carpet. I could hear him humming in there as he worked, a tune that sounded suspiciously like the Bach Double.

The living room furniture was all light champagne colors. The sofa looked like I would probably sink two feet into it if I sat on it, and I intended to do just that, until something on the polished mantel caught my eye.

A crystal violin, an exact replica of a real violin, glittered on a dark mahogany base. There was no dust at all here. A small brass plaque on the base read

To Alexis with love

Happy anniversary,

Madeleine

"Your drink, madam," said Alexis at my elbow, and I think I must have jumped about three feet. He handed me a glass of sherry. He was smiling, but I felt like I had been caught snooping. "Did I startle you?"

"I'm sorry--I was just admiring your crystal violin. It's lovely."

Alexis gazed at it reflectively. "Yes. Madeleine bought that for me when we were on tour in Munich."

"Munich," I said dreamily, sipping at my wine. "Heck of a town."

He looked at me in surprise. "You've been there?"

"No, never. Tonight was the first solo I've played that wasn't a school thing or a competition. How would I have toured Munich?" I went and sat down on the sofa, and sank about as much as I had predicted. It felt wonderful.

Alexis laughed, and settled into the sofa beside me. "No professional solos before? What a waste of your talent. You were terrific tonight."

I would have liked to believe the blush on my face was only the wine, but I knew better. "It was a good concert. Officer Parker even seemed to enjoy it."

"Hmm." Alexis swirled the sherry around in the bottom of his glass, watching it as if he was unaware of me watching him. "He doesn't seem like much of a classical music fan. What made him decide to come?"

I sighed, looking down at my own glass. "Your father."

He abruptly stopped playing with the wine glass. "What?"

I couldn't look at him. After our experience at the police station, I knew how wounded Alexis really was. He could be better around me, more like the old Alexis who had charmed the world for years before the murder, but underneath it all he was still broken. And what had hurt him the very most was the way his father had turned on him.

"Alexei called the police after his visit to the concert hall today. Apparently he was very concerned for my safety, concerned enough that Officer Parker promised to check in on me after the performance."

It galled me, I have to admit it. I didn't know whether I felt like crying or screaming, but at that moment I was so intensely worked up my hands started shaking.

Alexis leaned over and gently lifted the sherry from my hands, setting the glass on the coffee table before I splashed it all over both of us. He parked his own glass right next to it and put his arms around me, pulling me to him, leaning his face into my hair. "Calm down."

"I don't know if I can. So many people--I've heard so many warnings, it's so unfair to you--but your own father?" He squeezed me tighter, but he couldn't stop the shaking. My voice shook too, with anger and frustration. "Don't tell me I have to forgive them for looking out for me, Alexis. I want a reason. Give me a reason why a father could refuse to see the truth about his own son."

There was a silence while he considered my impossible request.

"Okay," he said finally. "I can do that."

I leaned back and regarded him in surprise. "You can?"

"I can. But remember, you asked for it."

That sounded ominous. I leaned against him, my head on his chest in the quiet living room, and listened.

"You already know my father was born Alexei Bruskalov. What you may not know is that the Bruskalov family has been producing violin virtuosi for generations. My father's father, Aleksandr Bruskalov, founded the Maestri Soviet."

"Really? The Maestri Soviet? I had no idea. Isn't that the group Dmitri Kast usually tours with?"

Alexis nodded, stroking my hair. "Yes. There are no Bruskalovs associated with the Maestri Soviet anymore."

I wanted to ask why, but he sounded so sad. I just couldn't do it. This was a story he would have to tell, or not, on his own terms.

"By the time my father was twenty-three, he had a wife and a three year old daughter. Elena, his wife, took care of Natalya while my father toured with the Maestri. Aleksandr no longer performed with the group, but handled its administration.

"My father was on a three month tour of western Europe. He was at a hotel in Paris when a friend came to his room in the middle of the night. Aleksandr and Elena, he said, were dead.

"Based on his tour locations, hotels he had stayed in, the people visiting him--I don't even know what all they looked at--the government decided that my father was spying for the West, using the tour for his own purposes. Aleksandr had been tortured to death to find out what he knew. Elena had been placed in a forced labor camp for families of traitors--you'd call it the Gulag. By the time my father got this news, she was already dead."

"Oh, my God," I whispered. "And Natalya?"

"Well, that's the thing. This friend could not tell my father what had happened to Natalya. She had not been killed outright. She was not sent to the camp with Elena, nor was she placed in any of the state orphanages for children whose parents were in the camps. Natalya had been disappeared by the government.

"My father was certain she was alive. He could not openly return to Russia--he would have been a dead man. His friend and some connections in Paris helped him sneak back into the country to try to find her--he came back empty-handed, lucky to escape with his life.

"That's when he moved to the United States. Kolbi wasn't kidding about his high ideals for this place--he needs it to be perfect. My father has always believed Natalya lives and will one day come to find him. America was the safe place he could offer her to do that. Do you see? He lost his entire family to a police mistake in Russia. If the police make mistakes here too, what makes this any safer?"

I sat with that a moment, tried to feel Alexei's position. "In his mind, believing in you means he's got to give up on her."

Alexis nodded. His eyes were indescribably sad. "I think it

does, yes. Does it make sense now?"

"No. But I think I understand. The price is too high."

"Yes. The price of supporting me is more than he can pay. More than most people can pay."

I regarded him solemnly. "Not me, Alexis. The price will never be too high for me."

And before he could answer, before the door could open or the police could visit, I leaned forward and kissed him.

My heart was pounding in my ears--why should it feel like a risk to kiss a man who had already tried to kiss me twice? It didn't make sense. But it did feel like a risk and I couldn't imagine what I would do if he rejected me.

His hands went up and I thought he would push me away, but he laced his fingers into my hair and his mouth moved against mine and I sort of melted.

How can I describe the electricity, the heated rush, of that first kiss? I suppose I thought I would kiss him and it would be over and done, but I couldn't break away from him. Soft, urgent, caressing, demanding; his lips were all of that and more and it felt like a different lifetime when we finally released each other, wide-eyed, short of breath.

Neither of us spoke a word, but I looked at him in that moment, his hair mussed and his shirt rumpled, and I knew my fate was sealed. I could not have turned from him now. No matter the cost, I would stand beside him, against my stalker, against the police, against the world if necessary, from here to forever. Even my own life was forfeit for this.

No price was too high. I had said it, but until that moment I don't think I really felt the enormity of it. This was far beyond any question of choice.

My fate, in that moment, was sealed.

The grandfather clock in the corner struck eleven-thirty, and it was a jarring sound in the quiet room.

"Eleven-thirty already?" Alexis ran a hand through his hair, restoring it to relative order. "It isn't early anymore, is it? Pretty soon it will be early in the morning."

It didn't seem possible to me--how had it gotten so late? I laughed, but it sounded uncomfortable.

Alexis looked at me shrewdly. "I'll go get your bag. We should get you settled." He patted my thigh, got up and headed out of the room back toward the laundry room.

I leaned my head back into the sofa cushions and stared at the vaulted ceiling. It felt like I was in a different world than the one where I had found the pile of dissected pictures on my living room floor. In that world I had cried in shock and terror. In this world, the shock and the terror were so distant I couldn't feel them. I couldn't even *remember* them.

I sighed contentedly. I was dangerously close to falling asleep right there on the couch.

The phone rang.

I cracked an eye open. Alexis's phone played Mozart's Symphony Number 40. My favorite. It made me want to laugh, which made me realize I must have been even more tired than I thought.

"Do you think you could get that?" Alexis's voice floated in. "I don't have a phone in here."

"Sure," I called back. It amused me that he was so unconcerned about a strange woman answering his phone late at night.

I leaned over the arm of the sofa and grabbed the phone off the end table, yawning. "Hello?"

"I see you."

The world seemed to stop spinning. There was a click as he disconnected, but I was still sitting there, staring at the telephone in shock when Alexis came back in with my overnight bag over his shoulder.

"Okay, Miss Marnett, we can--" He stopped short, looking at me looking at the phone. "Chrispen, tell me that maniac did not just call you at my house."

I couldn't convince my mouth to make words. I looked from Alexis to the phone, and my hands started shaking.

"Ach. I'm sorry." He lifted the phone out of my hand and pulled me to my feet. "I should have known better than to ask you to get that--I should have guessed that might happen." He frowned. "Whoever this fellow is, he certainly knows who your friends are."

I nodded.

He took my hand and squeezed it. "Don't you worry. I am unplugging that phone--there won't be any more calls like that."

I smiled at him, making a concerted effort to shake off my mood. "Thank you. I'm sorry."

"Don't you apologize." He put an arm around my shoulders and started walking towards the small hall that opened on the other side of the room. "He got to you that time, but it won't happen again. Remember, I had to deal with paparazzi and worse...this house has had a few precautionary measures. If he tries to get in here, he'll be in jail by morning."

The little hallway opened into two bedrooms, with a bathroom between them. The bedroom on the left had been turned into Alexis's music room.

The bedroom on the right was the guest room. The room was all creams and tans, light and airy, with a window seat. I fell in love with the room as soon as I saw that. What the fireplace did for the living room, the window seat did for the bedroom.

Alexis put my bag on the bed, and looked around the room like he was forgetting something. "Here are your things...the bathroom is out in the hall..." He trailed off. "You look so upset,

I feel bad leaving you."

"I'll be fine." I went and sat down in the window seat, and my mood improved considerably. "It was only a phone call."

Alexis smiled at me. "I'm going to unplug that phone. My room is on the other side of the living room if you need anything." He leaned over and kissed my forehead, and left the room.

I discovered I was bone-tired. I dragged my bag into the bathroom, got ready for bed, and went back to the bedroom. The rest of the house was already dark.

The sheets and the comforter felt stiff and new--here was another room that didn't get used much. A young couple in a house with a fancy dining room and fully furnished guest room-- obviously they had intended to entertain. But all of that changed when Madeleine died, and now the rooms sat unused, filled with the ghosts of what should have been.

I shivered under the heavy covers. The past that held Alexis prisoner was almost tangible in this house; it surrounded me like a shroud.

What did he think about, alone in the dark room he once shared with another? Was I doing the right thing, inserting myself into his life? Was I just bringing him more stress, more problems than he already had?

Or could I really help heal him? Could I bring him peace? Could I free him from the chains of the past that held him, and make him happy again?

Only time could tell. It made me dizzy to consider it all, like looking down from a great height with no safety rails.

There were no safety rails here, and no nets.

I rolled over on my side, looking out the window over the seat. The trees swayed in the night wind, and broke the moonlight that came in. Only time could tell, I reminded myself, and waited for sleep.

Time passed, and kept its secrets.

♪

I awoke sitting up in the bed, in the dark, shaking. My throat was raw from screaming.

And Alexis had his arms around me.

All I wanted at that moment was for a giant hole to open up and swallow me. Since none did, I buried my face in my hands. "I'm sorry, Alexis." My voice sounded rough and hoarse. "I am so, so sorry."

"Don't apologize," he said, and seemed to mean it. He rocked me back and forth for a moment, murmuring soothing sounds to me. "Was it the nightmare Kolbi told me about?"

I nodded. "I can't seem to shake the thing."

"I know it doesn't help, but try not to get too upset about it. Stress can aggravate that kind of thing. Being in a strange place can be a problem too--sometimes it makes things better, but evidently not this time."

"Wow. You sound like you have some experience with this."

He nodded and looked away. "Madeleine used to have a lot of nightmares."

"Really?"

"Really. Why do you think I toured for two years straight? Anytime we stopped in one place for too long, the nightmares caught up with us."

"Was it the same one every time?"

He laced his fingers through mine, and regarded our intertwined hands. "Yes. Always the same."

"What were hers about?" It was a horrible, prying question; I knew that. But this unexpected similarity fascinated me, and I couldn't stop myself.

"Dwight," he said shortly. "Madeleine was always afraid of Dwight. Even after we left she always had nightmares about something that had happened between them."

"Oh." Good sense finally kicked in and I didn't press the matter farther. Then a thought occurred to me. "Is that why you warned me away from him?"

Alexis couldn't look at me. "Yes. I'm sorry, I know it was none of my business. I just--I couldn't forget those nightmares. And to see you getting involved with him, heading down the same path..." He shook his head.

I yawned. I couldn't help it. Some yawns won't be suppressed.

"I think I've kept you awake long enough," he said wryly, ruffling my hair as he stood up.

"I think it's actually the other way around."

He grinned at me. "You tell it your way and I'll tell it mine. Either way we should probably get some sleep."

"Yes," I sighed, "that is what I came here for."

He had already left, but his wicked laugh floated in from the hallway. "You tell it your way, my dear, and I'll tell it mine."

♪

I slept in fits and starts after that, but at least I didn't have that nightmare again. Waking up screaming was never fun, but waking up screaming in someone else's house--that was a whole new level of awful.

Finally I could see faint tendrils of light in the sky when I looked out the window, and I decided I'd had enough of this. I was getting up, and I didn't mind sitting quietly in the living room until Alexis was awake, too.

So I took myself to the bathroom and made myself presentable, then went back to the bedroom and stowed everything in the overnight bag. I made the bed and you couldn't tell anyone had ever been in the room, which was pretty much how it had looked to start with.

I left the overnight bag on the floor by the bed and tiptoed out into the living room. But I could see from there that the door to Alexis's room was already open. I moved a little closer and peeked around the corner--the bed was made and the room was dark. The kitchen and the dining room were dark, too.

It seemed I was alone in the house.

Well, if he wasn't in the house he must be outside. I went to the back of the living room, to the door that led out to the backyard. It was already unlocked.

Outside was a cobblestone terrace with a patio table and chairs, all presently empty. To the left sprawled a beautiful garden framed by high hedges. A white arch wound with climbing vines seemed to be the only way in, so I headed for that.

There was no way Alexis kept this garden up by himself. Just no way. The garden had narrow walkways framed by flowering plants and bushes, all healthy and trimmed.

In the center of the garden was a small fish pond and a stone bench.

And sitting on the bench with his elbows on his knees and his face hidden in his hands, was Alexis.

It tore at my heart, to see him look so unhappy. All of my doubts from the night before came crashing back down on me. Was this the best I could do for him?

I didn't have an answer for that. But I couldn't give up. If he asked me to leave, I would, but until then, he was stuck with me.

I sat down beside him on the bench, and tentatively laid my hand on his back. I wasn't sure what to do, and I wasn't sure what to expect.

He lowered a hand and gripped my knee. I could see the tendons standing out on the backs of his hands, could see his knuckles turn white.

And I understood--I didn't know what was going on but I did know my part.

Last night I had needed Alexis. Now, Alexis needed me.

"Oh, Alexis," I said, "what is it? What's wrong?"

"Nothing," he said, and his voice sounded strained. "Everything."

"Well," I said uncertainly, "that doesn't really narrow it down."

Alexis laughed, but it sounded like it hurt. He sat up and looked at me.

It looked like it hurt, too.

"How do you do that?" he asked. "How do you make me laugh when it feels like my soul is bleeding?"

I stared at him in horror. "Why is your soul bleeding? Did I do something?"

"No, no!" He let go of my leg and brushed his fingers across my face. "Of course not. You haven't done a thing wrong. It's me I don't understand."

He turned to watch the koi dart around in the little pond. "This was her garden, you know. Madeleine's."

I looked around in wonder. "She did all this?"

"Not quite. We hadn't been here long enough, when she...for her to do all this. She started it, though. And after she was gone I took her sketches to a professional and had it finished.

"But that koi pond," he gestured at it, "and this bench--these were the first things she put in. Just like they are now."

He watched the fish for a moment in a silence I did not have the heart to break.

"Two years," he said. "That's all we were married. We promised each other forever, and we got two years."

I looked down at my hands in my lap. "I'm so sorry. I can't even imagine what that must be like."

"I made a promise to love her forever. Forsaking all others. Till death do us part, and then it did. So how can I *need* you like this?"

I didn't know what to say to that. My heart had sort of stopped.

"What kind of man does that make me? How can I betray her like this?"

I reached out and took his hand, and held it in my lap, tracing my finger along the lines on it. "Alexis, I never knew Madeleine. I can't claim to know how she felt or what she thought about things. What I do know is this--she loved you. And when you love someone you want them to be happy, more than anything. I can't imagine she would have wanted you to be alone for the rest of your life. Not if it isn't making you happy."

I looked up and found him looking at me. "You are always so sure about things," he said. "How can you be so sure?"

I squeezed his hand. "I know what I would want. Think about the last five years. Is that how you would want her to live, if you were gone?"

Tears brimmed in his eyes. He looked away. "No. I would never wish that on her."

"Of course not. Knowing her as you did, I think you can guess better than anyone what she would want for you."

We sat in the early morning quiet for a moment, watching the fish, his hand in mine.

"Thank you," he said at last.

I cast him a sidelong glance. "Don't thank me. You can't trust my motives. I have a vested interest here. Maybe I'm just telling you what I want you to hear."

Alexis laughed, a normal, not-painful laugh. "Maybe so. It was still true, though."

He squeezed my hand and stood up, pulling me to my feet with him. "We should get some breakfast. Early rehearsal today, remember?"

In truth I had forgotten. "It seems cruel, early rehearsal right after a concert."

"No rest for the wicked," he teased, leading me out of the garden.

"Who's wicked?" I demanded. "Me or you?"

"Both," he said.

And the look he gave me over his shoulder really was wicked.

♫

We ate breakfast in the dining room. There was a china cabinet in there with a truly gorgeous set of dishes in it, and a chandelier that was small but fantastically beautiful. They were dusty, though, and there were cobwebs in there.

"You'll have to excuse the dust," Alexis said, looking around the room as if it was the first time he had seen it. "I don't ever use this room."

"What, you don't eat? That seems a shame; these omelets are terrific."

He shrugged. "I just usually eat something quick in the kitchen, or bring in takeout and eat on the couch. There's something uncomfortable about being in this room alone."

I could believe that, especially in its current condition. It was too obvious he had been avoiding the room. It made you want to keep right on avoiding it.

After breakfast, Alexis dropped me off at my house. He tried to convince me otherwise, even as I was getting out of the car.

"Are you sure?" he asked me for the fourteenth time, leaning across the seat to talk to me through the open passenger window. "You could just grab your violin, and I could drive you. I mean, I'm going there anyway."

I laughed. "I know. And I appreciate the offer, I really do. The sleepover was great. But if you drive me home from rehearsal, I am not going to let you leave, and I think you need some time alone."

He looked hurt. "Why? Have I been bad?"

He was joking, but I was serious. "Alexis, we had a real roller-coaster ride at your house. You were pretty upset this morning."

"But I thought we settled that."

"Me too. But how can you be sure if I'm around you every second, influencing you, feeding you my opinions? I'd feel better if you sat with your answers awhile on your own, and still felt like they were true."

"I suppose you're right," he said, but I couldn't tell if he really meant it or if he was just humoring me. "I guess I'll see you in a little bit then."

I stepped back from the car and waved at him. "I'll be right behind you."

He waited in the driveway until I was safely in the house. I turned on the light in the foyer, and I thanked my lucky stars I had insisted on taking myself to rehearsal.

The tile floor was littered with rose petals. Yellow rose petals. The glass vase had been smashed on the floor, and every petal, every leaf, had been ripped off the flowers and dumped in the wreckage.

The stripped stems had been broken and arranged into crude letters that formed words above and below the ruined mess of Alexis's flowers.

STAY AWAY
FROM HIM

♫

For some reason I didn't quite understand, I felt nervous walking into rehearsal, as though everyone knew where I had been all night, and were conjuring up their own judgments of me because of it. The symphony was large, and I knew everybody was too busy with their own lives to be worrying about me, but I couldn't shake the feeling that all eyes were on me. A direct look from anyone always made me blush.

So I just about lost it completely when Kolbi walked up to me and asked me point blank where I had been the previous night. "Your cell phone was off. I tried calling your house, but I got your machine. I must have left you half a dozen messages."

Kolbi's gaze was more scrutinizing than I would have liked. Obviously she could tell something was up. I could feel my face turning red before I even spoke.

"I--well, the truth is that I haven't checked my messages yet. I just stopped by the house long enough to grab my violin, and then I came straight over here. I'm sorry if I worried you."

"With all the trouble you've been having, I like to check in on you, I--wait a minute, you mean you weren't home at all? All night?"

"I tried calling you last night, too," Dwight said suddenly from behind me, startling me. How long had he been there? I had no idea. He came around to face me, and grimaced. "I hung up. I hate talking to those things. So the hang-up message--that was me. I confess."

"Sorry," I mumbled.

Dwight looked from Kolbi to me, and my blush deepened. He frowned. "Hey, are you all right? Did Kolbi say you were out all night?"

"Not 'out all night,' Dwight." Kolbi sounded exasperated, like he was being deliberately dense. "I don't think she partied all night or anything. She was just away from home."

Dwight folded his arms. "So you were at someone's house last night, just not your own. Care to tell us who?"

"No," I said immediately. "I don't care where you spent your night, and it's none of your concern where I spent mine."

Alexis walked around the corner from Darren's office, whistling a tune. He walked over to us, put him arm around my shoulders and kissed my forehead. "Good morning, sunshine."

My face was instantly bright red.

"I'm going out to the stage to warm up," Alexis said. "Come join me."

"Okay," I said, and he was gone.

Kolbi grinned and clapped me on the back, exactly as I had once imagined her doing, and I knew she had the answers that mattered to her.

Dwight, though...Dwight was steaming. "Okay? That's all? 'Okay?'"

"Dwight, it's Alexis Brooks," Kolbi pointed out. "How can she say no?"

Dwight frowned at her funny smile and glowered at me suspiciously. "How, indeed."

♫

I was relieved to walk away from that conversation. I carried my violin and bow in one hand and my music in the other and hopped down the stairs out to the stage.

Alexis was already out there, setting up a tall stand at the front of the stage. My stomach did a sickly little backflip when I saw it. "We're not--starting with the Mendelssohn, are we?"

He smiled. "Sure--why not get right to the good stuff?"

I put my music folder on our usual stand. "And that's exactly how Darren explained it, is it?"

"Well, not in those exact words. But I'm sure that was his general intent."

"If you say so." I looked at the stand doubtfully.

Alexis flipped open the music folder in front of me and pulled out my Mendelssohn part. "You know, you're going to have to get used to playing it onstage at some point."

"I know. Am I going to play your cadenza?"

"I don't see how you can honor me properly any other way."

He gave me a wicked grin and spread my music out on the tall stand.

"Oh, way to take the pressure off, Alexis!" I shook my head. "I don't think I feel up to this. Maybe I'll just sneak out."

"Ach, you don't want to do that. Darren's really excited about this. He called everyone this morning to remind them how important this rehearsal was. Of course, he couldn't get hold of you." He looked at me reflectively. "Or me."

Belatedly I remembered the monitors in the Green Room. I fervently hoped everyone in there had better things to do than eavesdrop on us. "I thought you said you were going to warm up."

"I am. Look, why don't you play some of the Mendelssohn now?"

"What?"

"Oh, you don't have to play the whole thing," he said soothingly. "Just get a feel for the stage--you've never played here alone."

I stared at him as though he had suggested I dive off into the front row.

"Please?" He put on his sweetest tone. "I'd really like to hear it."

"Oh, all right," I grumbled. "Honestly, Alexis, the trouble you get me into."

I shouldered my violin, took a few deep breaths, tried to focus, and dove in before I could think better of it.

The Mendelssohn Violin Concerto has such a haunting, soaring melody...it is instantly recognizable, and it always pulls me in before I know what's happening.

I was at the bottom of the first page before I realized Alexis wasn't standing beside me anymore.

I lowered my violin and turned around. "Alexis?"

He was sitting in his usual chair, leaning forward with his

hands on his knees. "No--please go on. It's beautiful," he said. But his face was white and his voice was strained.

I put my violin in a different chair and sat down next to him. "Tell me about it."

He swallowed hard and shook his head. "I don't know if I can, really. I haven't played that in so long...I didn't realize I had so many memories attached to it."

I understood--a familiar piece of music could bring back vividly the things you associated with it. I rubbed his shoulder. "What do you remember?"

"I think my heart stopped when you played that. I remembered hotel rooms in foreign countries, playing the Mendelssohn for Madeleine with a practice mute. I remembered playing it at the recital where I met her. I remembered how Dwight used to beg for a copy of my cadenza. The fundraiser Darren asked me to play the Mendelssohn for. I remembered playing it, wearing black, in the church..."

I didn't say anything. What could I say? I sat beside him, rubbing his shoulders, until he sat up straight again and turned to me. "Come on," he said. "Back to the music."

I looked at his suddenly determined face in surprise. "Are you sure?"

"Yes." He opened the violin case next to his chair. "I'm going to play it with you."

My jaw dropped. "Are you *really* sure?"

"I'm really sure." He was already up by the stand, waiting for me. "Memories are fine, Chrispen, but I have some ghosts to lay to rest."

I couldn't argue with that. His courage humbled me, and I joined him at the stand, nervous for him. I still half expected he wouldn't go through with it.

Then he shouldered his violin, dropped a couple of beats to cue us in, and we were off.

The sound of our two violins together was surprisingly loud. I had been regularly practicing this concerto, and he hadn't played it in five years, and he was still wiping the floor with me.

I didn't mind, though. This was a lifelong dream come true, and I was happy just to be here to take the whipping. I turned pages as we played, though we probably didn't need the music to play.

When we came to the cadenza I dropped out completely and let him take it. I sat down in his chair and watched.

There aren't words for it, there really aren't. All I can say is that many times before I had imagined the pain of Alexis's situation. That day, sitting there on the stage listening to him play the cadenza he'd written, I really *felt* it. I sat spellbound through a cadenza that outshone anything he had ever done before, and the perfect pain of it could have killed me, could have killed us both.

This was the Mendelssohn, the concerto he had owned for the past eight years.

It was also goodbye. When Alexis spoke of ghosts, he really meant *a* ghost, and the music conveyed his goodbye to her as clearly as if he had spoken it. He was entirely in his own world, and he didn't notice that I did not join back in after the cadenza was finished. I could not have; no one could have forced me. It was too personal, too painful, and it was all his. To join in would have seemed an imposition.

When he finished with a flourish, I was stunned by deafening applause, surrounding us.

The entire symphony was out there, hovering in both wings and backstage. They cheered and applauded, and I stood up from my chair and joined them. I was surprised to find tears on my face.

Alexis turned around and hugged me so hard he lifted me off my feet.

I was surprised to find tears on his face as well.

♫

We waited longer than usual to start rehearsal, because Dwight never showed up. Darren kept looking at his watch and looking at the empty chair, and finally announced that we would just have to go on without him.

After the incredible performance Alexis gave, my own rehearsal of the Mendelssohn seemed anti-climatic. The only saving grace was that I did not have to play the cadenza during rehearsal. That would have been downright embarrassing.

Still it was a nerve-wracking experience, playing the piece with Alexis in the orchestra behind me. I could finally understand why so many others had refused.

It was a relief to take my seat back in the orchestra when I was done.

Alexis reached over and patted my leg. "You are going to be phenomenal."

"I think you defined phenomenal before rehearsal even started."

He smiled at me, a brilliant, happy smile. His performance hadn't just been phenomenal, it had been cathartic as well.

I was glad. He had needed that for a very long time.

We were also doing Addinsell's *Warsaw Concerto* for piano at the tribute concert; Alexis had told some teeny-bopper magazine back when I was in college that it was his favorite piece for the piano. Kolbi was playing piano on that, and after the rehearsal I could see why Alexis liked it so much.

All in all it was a good rehearsal. When it was over I retreated to the Green Room to pack up, and it was there that Darren Johnson approached me.

"Chrispen," he said, "dear girl--forgive me, but did I hear you talking with Mr. Richards before rehearsal today?"

I nodded. "That's right. What happened to him?"

He pursed his lips. "I'm hanged if I know, my dear."

His tone alarmed me; I had never heard Darren sound so angry. "What are you going to do?"

"I had hoped," he said hesitantly, "that I might impose upon you to speak with him."

"Me?"

Darren sighed. "I do hate to ask, dear girl. The only reason I am asking you is because if I speak to him myself I will fire him."

"Fire him? Doesn't that seem a little excessive for a single missed rehearsal?"

"A single missed rehearsal that I expressly called to remind him of, for a concert whose importance to this symphony cannot be overstated?"

"Wow." I zipped up my case and turned to face Darren. "I had no idea you felt so strongly about it."

He sighed. "There is also the little matter of his attitude of late. I am not unaware of the confrontations between you two."

"Oh." I didn't know what else to say.

"But he will listen to you, Chrispen, and he will talk to you as he would not talk to me. If he has a good reason for his absence today, so be it. But if not--he is on his last chance with me."

I sighed and gathered up my things. "I'll let him know."

"Thank you, dear girl." He patted my shoulder and left.

I turned around, and there was Alexis. "Did I hear that right? Did he just ask you to go see Dwight?"

I nodded, looking at the floor.

He took me by the shoulders. "Don't do it. It isn't fair of Darren to ask. If he's aware of the confrontations, he should know that."

I shook my head. "It's Dwight's job on the line, Alexis. I can't let him get fired without doing anything. He would do the same for me."

Alexis sighed. "Don't go alone, then. Let me take you over

there."

I felt like laughing at that, but he looked so honestly upset I was afraid of hurting his feelings. "I can't. The way you two get along, what are the chances he'll tell me what's going on if you're there? What are the chances he'll talk to me at all?"

"You're right. I don't have to like it, though. Call me as soon as you get home, okay?"

I nodded and headed out the door with all the cheer of a person heading for the firing squad. As bad as I had already felt about this errand, that conversation had only made me feel worse.

♫

I had never been to Dwight's apartment before. He had given me his address once, though, and I had it in my cell phone. Thankfully my cell phone also had the GPS to tell me how to get there.

I sat in my car in the parking lot, trying to work up my courage to actually go in and find Dwight. It was a tall, brick building with ivy climbing the sides, and it seemed familiar even though I had never even seen it before. Just the sight of it seemed to be enough to render me spineless.

This was ridiculous, I knew that. Dwight would be thrilled to see me; he was always asking me to come over. I was doing him a favor, and he would know that.

I knew all that; it didn't help. I thought about the astounding courage Alexis had shown at the rehearsal earlier, and that finally got me out of my car and moving toward the building. This was nothing, nothing at all, next to what he had done.

Dwight's apartment was on the third floor. There was an elevator, but it was on the other side of the building. The stairs were right there, so I started up that way.

Right at the top of the stairs and around the corner, I found Dwight's apartment. I knocked on the door.

Nothing happened. I was just getting ready to knock again when the door opened.

Dwight stared at me blankly for a moment, then his whole face lit up. "Chris!" He leaned out into the walkway and dragged me into a sloppy hug.

The reek of alcohol hit me like a solid wall. What had he been drinking? What had he been swimming in?

"Dwight, hi." I disentangled myself. "May I come in?"

"Sure, sure." He stepped aside, but he kept one hand on my arm like he thought I was going to run for it.

That sounded like a good idea, actually. But I had promised Darren, so I needed to at least try to finish what I had come for.

I stepped into the living room, and turned back to Dwight, ready to ask him about rehearsal.

Dwight was locking the door.

Okay, so that gave me a bad feeling. I tried not to jump to any conclusions; maybe this was a really bad neighborhood.

He turned back to face me, and he didn't look like a psycho who would lock someone in his apartment. "What brings you here?"

I tore my eyes from the chain on the door, and tried to smile. I think I probably just looked ill. "Darren asked me to come check on you," I said, sugar-coating it as much as I could.

His expression turned sour. "Figured it was something like that. I hoped you might be here to apologize, but it seems to be beyond you."

I eyed him guardedly, trying to figure out what he meant. I was beginning to wish he wasn't between me and the door.

I went to the couch and sat down, trying to look casual. Maybe he would follow me and sit down too, instead of hanging there like a spider by the door. "I don't understand, Dwight. Apologize for what?"

He came over to the couch and knelt in front of me so his

face was level with mine. "You stayed at that bastard Alexis's house last night, didn't you?"

I stared at him. His words were all slurred together, and the venom in his voice shocked me.

"I knew it!" He stood up, pacing the room with short, savage strides. "What did you come here for? To rub it in? I heard you playing the Mendelssohn with him, practically screwing him right there on the stage. Is that why you're here? To rub my nose in it?"

I stood up, edging for the door. "I came here to save your damn job--but I can see that it doesn't matter to you. Forget about it--I'll just tell Darren you skipped rehearsal to get drunk."

"Sure, you tell him that," he mocked, and his hand shot out, quick as a snake, and grabbed my wrist. "You tell your precious conductor I went home and got wasted because you were out whoring with Alexis Brooks!"

"I was not!" I didn't know how to defuse the situation, and I couldn't pull my wrist out of his vise-like grip. "I told you before, I haven't done a thing with Alexis!"

I twisted my arm over and finally wrenched free. I could feel the bones in my wrist grinding together as he struggled to maintain his grip, but I was free.

I ran to the door and fumbled with the chain, but my hands were shaking and I couldn't get the thing loose.

Dwight caught my shoulders and forced me around to face him. "You are a lying whore," he told me, pushing my back against the door. "You are a lying slut and you are mine, no matter what Alexis thinks. I saw you first."

"Dwight," I said, and my voice trembled like a leaf in the wind, entirely out of my control, "you don't--"

"I saw you first!" he shouted in my face, and then his mouth was on mine, sour with alcohol, his tongue forcing its way between my clenched lips. His fingers dug like claws into my upper arms, pushing me back against the door so I couldn't move.

I struggled against him, but seemed unable to gain any leverage. I managed to get both hands into his hair and yanked backward as hard as I could, pulling his face off of mine.

"Dwight," I gasped, "damn you--"

And then he was on me again, in another kiss that was an assault. He released my arms, reaching instead for my blouse and jerking at the buttons.

I finally understood there was more at stake here than just my pride, more to lose here than just a fight. I brought my knee up into his crotch, as hard as I could manage with my limited range of movement.

It didn't stop him--he didn't drop like you always see in the movies, but he did pull his face back from mine in shock.

I balled up my fist and hit him for all I was worth, putting all of my rage, fear, and adrenaline into the side of his nose and his left eye. Another thing they don't show you in the movies is how much that can hurt an already damaged wrist.

But it worked, enough. He fell back, and I spun around and unlatched the locks. I could feel his grasping fingers brush my arm and then I was out, pounding down the stairs without looking back.

I huddled in my car, doors locked, cradling my injured arm until I stopped shaking enough to drive.

I didn't care what happened. I would never set foot in that building again. No matter who asked me. Wild horses couldn't drag me.

I made it back to my own driveway before I cried.

MOVEMENT THREE:
Prelude to Destruction

I leaned over the steering wheel in my car, my bruised arm curled up against my chest, and cried until I felt hollowed out inside. It was better than the anger, hurt, and shame that had been in there before.

I pulled a tissue out of the glovebox and scrubbed at my face, trying to pull myself together. What I needed to do was call the police, and I needed to be partway coherent when I did. I dried my face, blew my nose, and pawed through my purse for my cell phone.

It was ringing when I found it. The display said "Private."

Hell, my day couldn't get any worse. I answered it.

"Hello?"

"I have the evidence you seek."

I sat there slack-jawed. Even after everything that had happened, I was unprepared for this. The words were remarkable, but the voice, usually heavy with disguises, was bare.

The voice was Dwight's.

"I--I don't know what you mean."

"Yes, you do. You want evidence to exonerate your bastard lover. I have this. If you wish to have this evidence you will do exactly as I say."

I was too stunned to speak.

"Do you understand me?"

"Yes. Yes, I understand. What do I have to do?"

"You will not go to the police. If you involve them in this I will destroy the evidence. Do you believe me?"

I had no doubt. Dwight, I was discovering, was twisted and evil. "Yes."

"Good. You will not tell Darren Johnson anything that will cause me to lose my position. I don't care how you sell it, you will keep me in my job. Have we a deal?"

I swallowed hard. "Yes. How do I get the evidence?"

He chuckled, and my hair stood on end. "All in good time, my dear, all in good time. Right now I think you need to lick your wounds. Or you can have your bastard lover lick them for you."

There was a click as he disconnected the call, and I heard a car pull into my driveway.

It was the Jaguar. A chill crept up my spine. How had he known?

♫

Before I could really get my mind around this sucker-punch fate had just dealt me, Alexis was at the car, opening my door and kneeling down next to me. "My God--what happened to you?"

Tears welled up in my eyes, and I didn't trust myself to speak right then. I just shook my head. I had to look away from his shock and concern. I felt the same way. I was just realizing that I had let this person in my *house*. I could remember Dwight telling me I looked terrible, asking me what had happened--when all along he had been the one tormenting me! It made me want to curl up in the car and cry.

He frowned, looking at the way I cradled my right arm against my body. He reached out and gently pulled my arm toward him. "My God, Chrispen," he breathed.

My wrist and fingers were swollen and purple, and my wrist had lines around it that were almost black where Dwight's fingers had gripped it. Stretching my arm out hurt, and I found I had matching dark, blotchy bruises on my upper arms.

Alexis ran his fingers over my battered wrist, the touch as gentle as the merest whisper. A tear splashed on the back of his hand, and he looked up at me in surprise.

"I'm s-sorry," I stammered. I wiped at my face with my free hand.

Alexis saw the bruises higher up my arm, and his face hardened. "Come on," he said, helping me out of the car. He reached into the back and grabbed my violin. "Let's go inside and get you a bag packed."

"Why?" I followed him to my front door, carrying my keys in my uninjured left hand that wasn't good for much but playing the violin.

"Why?" he repeated incredulously. He turned on me in surprise and took the keys, opening the door. "You can't stay here. You just can't. Or do you want to wait here for whatever happens next?"

I shook my head.

"I didn't think so." Alexis was outraged, it was plain in his voice. "Show me where your things are and I'll pack. I don't want you lifting a finger."

We went back to my room and I pointed out everything I needed, and sat dejected on my bed watching him pack my things into my overnight bag. He talked to me the whole time, and even asked me questions, but I never heard any of it. I had but one thought, moving back and forth across my brain.

I understood now why Madeleine feared Dwight.

♪

I don't think my brain started working until we were back at Alexis's house again. It felt so peaceful, so safe, that it seemed the horrible chain of events at Dwight's apartment couldn't possibly have been real.

But I sat on the sofa in the living room with my arm in my lap, and the evidence was undeniable. It was so swollen it didn't even look like I *had* a wrist. A tear landed on my arm, and I brushed it away with my fingertips.

Alexis came in from the kitchen, carrying a bag of ice wrapped in a towel. He carefully arranged my arm on a throw pillow, and covered it with the ice.

"Chrispen," he said, kneeling in front of me, "you have to go to the police."

"No," I said reflexively. "This was an accident. I--I fell down the stairs at Dwight's apartment."

"Bullshit. I'll drive you to the police station right now."

"No! Alexis, if you take me in there like this they are going to think you did this to me."

He looked at me oddly. "That's why you are going to tell them the truth. And then we are going to Darren, and we are getting Dwight out of the symphony."

"No!" I fluttered my free hand at him in a wild gesture. "No, no, no--nobody can know about this!"

He eyed the ice pack doubtfully. "But Chrispen, I don't know about that wrist. You may need to go to the hospital."

"And if we do, we tell them I fell down the stairs. That's what we tell the symphony, too. Dwight was sick, that's why he left rehearsal. I fell down the stairs after I went to check on him."

Alexis sat back on his heels. "Why are you defending him? Dwight did this to you--why are you protecting him?"

I swallowed hard. This conversation galled me more than I had imagined possible; the very words were bitter in my mouth. But I remembered what I had promised, and why.

"It wasn't his fault. He was very drunk, Alexis--he didn't mean to do this."

Alexis stood up, and paced to the far end of the room and back. "Have you ever been drunk?"

I shook my head.

He folded his arms. "Well, I have. Not just a little drunk-- blind drunk, drunk off my ass, so drunk I couldn't find my way from this living room to that bedroom, so I slept right here on the floor. It doesn't magically change you, Chrispen. It doesn't make you capable of anything you weren't capable of already."

I couldn't look at him. "I see what you're saying, I do. But please, *please* let me do this, Alexis. I can't let anything happen to him right now. I just can't."

He sat down next to me, holding onto my free hand. "This is your decision--you don't have to ask me for anything. I know he's your friend. You had your reasons for standing up for me; I believe you have your reasons for standing up for him, too. Whatever you say, I'll go along with."

I pulled my arm out from under the ice and wrapped him in a tight embrace. I had no right to ask him to lie, for Dwight or myself, and his support meant the world to me.

I could only hope I was doing the right thing.

I sat on the couch with my arm under the ice, and between the quiet of the room and the ticking of the grandfather clock, I dozed off.

I don't know how long I slept there on the sofa before movement around my injured arm woke me up. I opened my eyes, and found Alexis leaning over me.

"I'm sorry," he said, kneeling down. "I didn't mean to wake you; I just figured it's about time we need to be checking that wrist."

The swelling had gone down, but my wrist was still turning scary colors. Looking at it brought back the fear and the pain, and I swallowed hard.

Alexis took my arm gently in his hands and looked it over, then he turned it over and inspected the underside, probing my wrist with tender fingers. His jaw was tight, but he didn't say anything.

"I don't think it's broken," he finally told me, releasing my arm. "Can you move it?"

That didn't sound like much fun at all. But if it would get me out of a trip to the hospital... I held my arm up in front of me, and slowly curled and straightened my fingers, then carefully flexed my wrist.

Every muscle screamed in protest, and I heard popping sounds that emphasized the point. I grimaced, but I didn't scream out loud, so I was doing better than I had expected.

"No," Alexis said, "not broken. But pretty messed up just the same."

I nodded. "How am I going to play like this?" I kept moving things around, and it started to hurt less.I wrapped my other hand around my wrist for support, and continued flexing it.

Alexis watched me thoughtfully. "Hmm. I bet we can work something out." He stood up. "I'll have to run to the store though. Do you want to come along?"

I shook my head. "No, I think I'd rather stay here if it's okay with you. This is still pretty sore, and it feels pretty conspicuous."

"That's fine--are you sure you will be okay here alone?"

I grinned at him. "Alexis, I never figured you as a worrier."

"Only about you," he said, and pushed my hair back so he could kiss my forehead. "Only about you. I'll have my cell phone if you need me. You have yours?"

I nodded. "In my pocket."

"Good then," he said. "Make yourself at home. I won't be long."

After Alexis left, I found that the beautiful living room felt lonely without him. I let myself out the back door, and stood briefly on the terraced patio. The breeze felt good and the sound of it moving through the big trees was peaceful. I still felt lonely, though.

So I left the patio and wandered through the garden, running my fingers over the fragrant blooms and eventually finding myself at the fish pond again.

Maybe they weren't human, but at least the fish were company. I lowered myself onto the stone bench, rested my arm in my lap, and watched them swim.

It was hard to believe I had sat there with Alexis that very morning. So much had happened, even though so little time had passed--it felt like everything had changed.

Was it true what they said, that what didn't kill you made you stronger? I flexed my sore wrist and hoped that it was. It felt like I was going to need a lot of strength to make it through this.

My cell phone rang. I pulled it out and looked at it-- Richards, Dwight.

Sure, why bother to hide it now? It wasn't a secret anymore. I knew exactly who had been terrorizing me--only now I found myself unable to do anything with the knowledge. Maybe I was crazy for humoring him at all. But he was the only lead I had; I certainly had nothing myself that would exonerate Alexis.

I flipped open the phone. "Good afternoon, Dwight."

"Don't you think Alexis should plug in his phone?"

"No," I said immediately. "He would never agree to that. He unplugged it to protect me."

"He would agree if you tell him to do it. And you will tell him to do it, if I tell you to do it."

"No," I insisted. "Dwight, Alexis is the only person other than Darren who knows where I went today. Darren won't be a problem; he doesn't know the truth. But Alexis does. I've barely managed to convince him to go along with my story to keep your job."

"But--"

"But nothing. I want to clear Alexis's name. You know that. But Alexis would never agree to this. I need him on my side, and that means there are things you can't ask me to do."

He considered it. "I suppose for now I will go along with that. Alexis's phone is not of much concern to me." He paused. "But you should check your email."

I sighed. "Okay."

He hung up the phone without another word.

I hated this new Dwight, hated him more than I had known I could hate anyone. Having to cooperate with him, however marginally, was incredibly galling.

I brought up the email application on my phone. The first one I found was from Kolbi:

where r u?

I emailed back--a laborious process on a cell phone, with a bum hand:

A's house.   long story.

Next was a message from Dwight. It was a single hyperlink, to YouTube.

If it came from Dwight, it had to be bad. I braced myself and opened the link, ready for anything.

Well, I had thought I was ready for anything, until the screen came up. The title of the video was "Alexis Brooks and his latest victim."

The video showed me, in my car, in my driveway, and Alexis holding my battered arm and pulling me from the car. There was no sound, the video was short and choppy, and gave the impression...well, look at the title. The video was obviously intended to give the impression that it did.

I had learned something about myself--I had learned exactly how many seconds it took me to go from zero to completely pissed off, and it wasn't very many. I flagged the video as inappropriate, and sent the YouTube team an email telling them exactly why.

Things had changed, but it wasn't over. I wasn't ready to give in to Dwight entirely; the phone conversation had been an important battle won. I was not going to mindlessly do everything he demanded of me.

But he was not giving up either. He obviously intended to terrorize me into complete submission. A webcam at my house-- who knew what other heart-warming snippets he had around, just waiting their turn?

I shivered and shoved my phone back into my pocket. I couldn't stop him from terrorizing me. But I was going to do my damnedest to protect Alexis. If Dwight wanted a fight, he would get it.

I just hoped I was capable of winning.

♬

I can't think of another place I have ever been that was as peaceful as Madeleine's garden. It was so easy to sit there and zone completely out, watching the fish; in fact that's what I did. I lost all sense of time in that beautiful garden.

So it could have been three minutes or three hours later when I first heard the footsteps and saw Alexis coming toward me.

"Aw, you found me," I said, smiling.

He grinned back at me. "You'll have to try harder than that to get rid of me." He sat down next to me on the bench, and we took in the quiet for a moment.

"Can you believe," he asked me, putting his arm around me, "that we sat here together just this morning?"

"I was just thinking about that," I said.

I remembered sitting there that morning, and the conversation we'd had then. I wondered if I had done the right thing, if the advice I had given him had been true. I wondered if Madeleine would forgive me, if she disagreed. I wondered what she would say to me, given the chance.

I shivered in a sudden chill.

Alexis looked at me in surprise. "Maybe we've been out here long enough. Should we go inside?"

"Oh, it's so nice out here--let's stay just a little longer," I begged.

Then my stomach growled, loud enough I swear it scared birds out of the flowering bushes.

Alexis laughed. "We've definitely been out here long enough. Let's get you some dinner."

I reluctantly agreed. I hadn't eaten a thing since breakfast, and it was after four.

We walked back into the house together, and Alexis nodded toward the couch. "Make yourself comfortable; I'll have something ready in a jiffy."

"Do I have to? Isn't there anything I can help with?"

He laughed and ruffled my hair with his hand. "I appreciate the offer, but I really don't see how, with that wrist the way it is."

"I thought you were going to fix that," I grumbled.

"Hey, I'm not a miracle-worker. These things take time. I'll show you what I'm thinking after dinner. In the meantime, if you want to have a seat, I'll bring something out to you."

I looked at the couch doubtfully. "I don't know, Alexis...the way this arm feels I don't think I trust myself to eat on the couch. Maybe we had better eat in the dining room."

He grinned at me. "Sure thing. I even dusted in there after rehearsal. Go ahead and wait in there for me, if you'd rather."

He wasn't kidding--it looked to me like he had done more than just dust. The room smelled fresh and clean, and every surface shone. When I turned on the light, the sparkle from the chandelier could have blinded me.

Alexis came in just a few minutes after me. He had cucumber sandwiches, and soup he ladled into stoneware bowls.

I wondered how well I would manage with a spoon. "Did you bring me a bib?"

"Silly," he said, placing a bowl in my hands. "We're not using spoons. I thought this might be easier on you."

I felt a rush of gratitude. The warmth of the bowl already felt good on my sore right hand. This simple, thoughtful gesture-- well, I hadn't been expecting it. "Thank you," I said, my throat suddenly dry.

He winked at me and reached for a sandwich.

"Alexis," I said, examining my soup bowl, trying to sound casual, "when the police investigated Madeleine's death...did they talk to Dwight?"

"Yes--they talked to everyone we knew."

"And he had an alibi, I assume. What was it, do you know?"

"He was playing a performance that night--a private party, I believe. Twenty of the most influential people in town could verify that he was there."

"Oh." I couldn't quite look at him.

Alexis set his sandwich down and regarded me shrewdly. "But just the fact that you ask....things must have been even worse today than I had imagined. Do you want to talk about it?"

I swallowed hard. I just couldn't even find a place to begin.

"It's okay--don't feel pressured. You don't have to say a word until you are ready. But...no one fell down the stairs."

I shook my head.

Alexis reached across the table and gave my good hand a squeeze. "It's okay," he repeated. "I know it may not seem like it now, but everything is going to be all right."

"Now who is too sure of things?" I grumbled.

Alexis laughed. But he looked at me, and I could see in his eyes he understood, only too well.

♫

After we ate, Alexis disappeared into the kitchen and brought out a bag from a local drugstore. He pulled out a blue sling and a little box.

"I thought you might like the sling when you aren't using your arm," he said, tossing it on the table and opening the box. It had a flesh-colored elastic bandage in it. "I was watching the way you held your wrist earlier, and I thought the same kind of support might help you when you play."

"I never thought of that," I said, holding my arm out. "It's sure worth a try."

Alexis wrapped the bandage around my arm, from the base of my thumb to about halfway up my lower arm. It wasn't tight; in fact I couldn't even feel it until I flexed my wrist.

"Wow," I said. "That really does feel better. Do you think it will help me play?"

He grinned. "There's only one way to find out, isn't there?"

My violin was in the guest room with my bag, so we left the dining room and headed that way. Alexis unpacked it for me, turning the instrument over in his hands before handing it to me.

"You know," he said, "I knew you had a nice violin, but I

don't think I ever realized how nice. Maggini, right?"

I nodded. "1610."

He whistled appreciatively. "Very nice. You'll have to be sure they put a note in the Mendelssohn program, that that's what you play."

"Hmm. You're right, I hadn't thought of that." I looked it over carefully, but didn't find anything that needed attention. "I am proud to have it. There's really only one violin in the world I would rather have."

"There's a violin you'd prefer to that Maggini? What is it? An Amati? Guarnieri?"

I laughed. "No, nothing like that. You would probably think it's silly."

He folded his arms. "Try me."

"All right. My grandmother played the violin. She did several recital series, and toured nationally a couple of times."

"Wow--was the Maggini hers, then?"

I sat down on the bed. "Well, no. My grandmother passed away when I was six. I didn't play at that time, but she left her violin to me anyway. She told everyone that she just had a feeling I'd make a fine violinist one day."

"Well, see, she was right." Alexis reached over and tousled my hair.

I smiled at him. "Thank you. But I had this aunt--this bossy, overbearing aunt, not that I am biased--and her boy was studying the violin. So she latched onto it and wouldn't give it up. It was only right, she said, that it should go to my cousin, since he was a real violinist like my grandmother, and I didn't even play."

"Bummer. What happened to your cousin?"

I laughed so I wouldn't cry. "He quit studying two years later. A year after that he pawned my grandmother's violin for drug money."

He stared at me. "No way."

"Way. It wasn't a fine old antique--it was a very good violin custom made for her by a talented contemporary maker. Probably worth a fraction of this one. But I would rather have it than any other violin in the world."

"I think that is the saddest story I have ever heard."

I gave him a wry smile. "I've heard sadder. Besides, mine has a silver lining. When I was nine, my mother was driving me home from school one afternoon when I saw a violin hanging in the window of a secondhand shop. Of course it wasn't the same fiddle, but it reminded me of it. I made her stop so I could look at it. I told my mother I was going to buy that violin. She kind of laughed me off--I don't think she really believed I would ever do it. But I saved up my allowance for nearly a year, and in the end I did buy that violin. My parents saw I was serious about it, and they agreed to get me lessons. The rest is pretty much history."

"That is pretty amazing, Chrispen."

I shrugged. "My mother must think so too; she loves to tell that story."

"I can see why. But right now, I'm beginning to wonder about another question."

"What's that?"

Alexis handed me my bow. "Are you stalling?"

"Yes," I said, standing up from the bed, "yes, I am." I took the bow with the best grip I could manage, and started tuning.

Alexis walked around me, watching my right hand closely. "Hmm. Not too bad. That's much better than I thought you would manage for a couple of days."

"You were right, the support really does help."

"Do you think you will be all right on your own for awhile, then? I was thinking of getting in some practice myself."

"Don't let me keep you from it," I grinned. "I think I'll survive."

"Okay. I'll just be across the hall if you need anything." He left the room, closing the door softly behind him.

So there I was, just me, my violin, and a wrist that felt oddly numb under the elastic bandages. I played through some warm-ups, concentrating on things requiring finger dexterity, but basic bow work. I worked through some of the trickier passages from our symphony program, and did some in-depth work on a few passages from Alexis's cadenza for the Mendelssohn.

By the time I finished that, my wrist felt less numb and more like someone was hammering on it with--well, a hammer. It seemed to me to be a pretty good indication that it was time to stop. I cleaned everything up and packed it away as well as I could manage.

I could hear Alexis working on something in his music room. It sounded experimental; he was stopping frequently, and playing short passages repeatedly, varying phrasings or making slight changes to the notes.

Whatever he was working on, it sounded intense. I didn't want to disturb him. I sat down in the window seat, trying to ignore my wrist, but it was throbbing. I carefully unwound the bandage, rolling it back up to use next time I decided to play.

Just having the bandage off felt better. But what it really needed was heat.

I decided I should be able to sneak out of the room without bothering Alexis. I eased open the door, and more or less tiptoed down the little hall into the bathroom. I soaked a hand towel in water as hot as the faucet would go, wrung it out, and wrapped it around my arm.

It was amazing how good that felt. I crept back into the guest room and sat down on the foot of the bed to eavesdrop on Alexis's practice across the hall. Between the warmth on my arm, the softness of the bed, and the violin in the other room, I could easily have fallen asleep. I struggled to stay awake, though--I was trying to figure out what Alexis was working on. I couldn't put a name to it, but it sounded naggingly familiar.

I shifted my position and concentrated on listening.

♫

Of course I fell asleep. It seemed like only a couple of minutes later when I jerked suddenly awake, in a silence notable for its lack of violin music.

It must have been more than a couple of minutes, though, because my towel was completely cold. I had slumped off to the side in my sleep, too, and made quite a formidable damp spot on the comforter.

I stumbled into the bathroom, trying to force myself to be more awake, and ran the towel under more hot water. I re-wrapped my arm in it, heading back out. The music room was dark.

I found Alexis in the living room. He had the top off of the big square ottoman, which was apparently full of compact discs.

"The lady wakes! Did you have a nice nap?"

"I'm sorry, I didn't mean to fall asleep. I was trying to figure out what you were working on."

He laughed. "And it was so exciting it put you to sleep, right? It sounds like I had better tear it out and do it over. I don't want the audience to snore."

I could feel my face redden, but Alexis waved a hand at me, still laughing. "No, don't apologize--I'm just picking on you. I'm working on writing a cadenza for the Brahms concerto."

"Ah. Well, that explains why it sounded sort of familiar, but I couldn't place it."

He looked back down into the box. "What's your favorite violin concerto?"

"What?" I hadn't been expecting that question. "The Sibelius, why?"

"Ah, yes, Sibelius. That's what you played for your NPSO

audition, right? I'm partial to that one myself." He plucked a CD out of the ottoman. "Prokofiev, too." He pulled out another. "Which Brandenburg?"

"Number six." I sat down on the couch.

He raised his eyebrows. "Viola fan, eh?"

"Well, no--I mean, I suppose. I just like the sound of that one best. Do you ever get tired of teasing me?"

"No," he laughed. "You just make it so easy--a violinist chooses the one Brandenburg with no violins in it at all."

I shrugged. "What can I say--I'm jealous of any good solo that isn't for the violin, like The Swan, or the Telemann Viola Concerto."

"I'm with you there." He picked out a few more CD's, then covered the ottoman back up and went over to the entertainment center on the wall.

"It's too quiet in here," he said over his shoulder to me. "I thought some music might be nice." He loaded up a disc changer and came to sit with me on the couch, propping his feet on the ottoman. "Here." He handed me a remote and leaned back, lacing his fingers behind his head.

"Um." I looked at the remote, then at him. "What's in there?"

"Oh, a bunch of stuff. Just pick anything--it's all good."

"Okay, if you say so." I hit the random-play button and sat back into the sofa cushions.

The changer picked the second movement of the Brandenburg Concerto Number Six.

"Ach," I said, "my favorite. But since we have a viola-hater in the room..." I pressed skip on the remote.

Alexis laughed and put his arm around me. The stereo picked another familiar tune.

"Wow, the Mendelssohn," I said. "This thing is really on a roll."

"Well, sure, anybody could recognize the Mendelssohn. But

can you name the soloist?"

"Name the soloist," I said, "now there's a game I've never even heard of. Hmm...too slow to be Heifetz, too fast to be Stern..." I listened for a moment. "Very clean, though. Nice precision. It's--it's you!" I poked him in the side. "You snuck a ringer in the mix!"

"Ringer?" he protested, laughing, trying to fend me off. "You never said there were *rules*. If you don't like the recording, you can always skip to something else!"

"No, I think your recording is my favorite." I sat back again. "Besides, I think I'd listen to the Mendelssohn no matter who was playing it. I love this third movement--it's so happy, especially after the angst of the first movement and the melancholy of the second. It's like, after all that, you deserve the happy ending."

"Yes," Alexis said, looking at me, abruptly serious, "everyone deserves a happy ending after angst and melancholy."

I tipped my face up and kissed him. It probably wasn't the best time, not with the aforementioned angst and melancholy swirling in the air around us, but it wasn't something I thought out logically.

Time stood still--my heart pounded and my pulse raced. Alexis leaned toward me, taking my face in both of his hands, and the world stopped spinning for me. There was nothing in that moment but him, and me, and the way our lips moved together in a harmony that far surpassed anything coming out of the stereo.

He trailed his fingertips down the side of my neck to my shoulder, raising goosebumps everywhere he touched me. I tensed, but I couldn't have said why. It seemed hard to breathe in that moment.

Then he moved both hands to the buttons on my blouse, and before I had any idea what was going to happen I was back in Dwight's apartment, with Dwight's hard mouth on mine and Dwight's rough hands on me.

It took me a minute to realize someone was screaming. It took me another minute to realize it was me.

Things came into focus slowly. I was huddled defensively on the couch, panting and shaking. Alexis sat against the other arm, as far away from me as he could get, watching me as though I might explode at any moment. It was probably a reasonable assumption.

I covered my face with my hands and wept. "I'm sorry."

I could feel the cushions of the sofa shift as he edged over towards me--cautiously, in case I flipped out on him again. He laid his arm gingerly across my back. "What did I do?"

"Nothing! You didn't do anything wrong at all, Alexis--this is all down to that damned Dwight."

I unwound the towel from around my arm. My purple wrist with its black stripes gave me something to focus on, and in a flat voice, like the whole thing happened to someone else, I told Alexis about my ill-fated visit to Dwight's apartment.

"Dear God," he breathed. "Chrispen, I am so sorry. I had no idea--I would never have--"

"Stop apologizing. This is not your fault. I should have told you earlier. I should never have gone over there at all."

He squeezed my shoulders. "I think it's time we got you to bed. It sounds like you've had a hard day."

I swallowed hard and nodded. I didn't think there was much I could add to that.

"You are safe here," he said, so quietly I could barely hear him. "I swear to you I will not touch you again. You don't need to worry."

I couldn't have said exactly why, but as I went to get ready for bed, that remark worried me more than anything else that had happened to me.

♪

I was in the same comfortable bed, in the same relaxing room, of the same peaceful house as the night before. The same gentle breeze stirred the same rustling trees, the same moonlight dappled the same soft carpet. And I was just as deathly tired as the last time I had been there.

So why couldn't I sleep?

I kept having flashbacks that scared me and made sleep impossible. Flashbacks that had nothing to do with Dwight. I kept seeing Alexis's haunted eyes, hearing the dead voice in which he had said, "I swear to you I will never touch you again."

It made me want to scream.

All in all not one of my better nights. I gave up on sleep and went to sit on the window seat in my nightgown.

The night air was cool but pleasant. In the moonlight, my skin looked so pale it almost glowed.

All except my wrist. In that other-worldly light, the dark purple was a shocking contrast. I looked at it, turning my arm in the moonlight, thinking about everything that had happened that day.

It occurred to me that what had happened with Alexis was fundamentally my fault. It was my fault for starting something with him before I had processed the business with Dwight.

That business at Dwight's had by no means been as bad as it could have been; I knew that. Still, it was scary and upsetting, and I had never really dealt with it, just sort of stuffed it all in a box and hid it away, where it could rattle at me when I least expected it.

I wondered if Dwight had been counting on this. Was he trying to drive a wedge between Alexis and me? Was that part of the reason he had assaulted me the way he did? He suddenly seemed a lot scarier.

But scarier still was the thought that Dwight had any control at all over my relationship with Alexis. This, I decided, would not be allowed to continue. From now on, I was banishing Dwight to his own compartment in my mind. No matter what he did or said, I would never permit it to affect my relationship with Alexis in any way.

But it already had. I knew that, and so I knew that somehow, I had to fix things. I had fixed me.

Now I had to fix us.

The grandfather clock was chiming midnight as I snuck across the living room in my bare feet in the dark. Of all the things that had confronted me in the last week, somehow this short walk was the most unnerving.

The master bedroom door was open, the room dark. I hesitated in the doorway, suddenly unsure. Should I really wake him? Couldn't this conversation wait until morning?

The sound of soft music finally registered. As my eyes adjusted I saw the dim light from an MP3 player reflected off his face, and realized I was not the only one in the house who could not sleep.

On with it, then. I swallowed hard. "Alexis?"

He sat up in the bed in evident surprise. "Chrispen? Are you okay? Do you need something?"

I shook my head. "No, I'm fine. I just--"

"Do you need me to take you home? I'm sorry, I know I upset you, I'm sorry, I--"

"No, Alexis, wait." I walked into the room, and sat on the edge of the bed next to him. "It's nothing like that. I just wanted to apologize for--you know, for earlier."

His eyes were impossible to read in the dim light. "That's not necessary."

"Of course it is. I didn't mean to hurt your feelings, Alexis. I certainly didn't mean to imply any similarity between you and Dwight by my reaction. I just--well, everything that happened at his apartment today really frightened me, and I hadn't dealt with any of that. It really didn't have anything to do with you."

He kept his hands tightly folded in his lap. "I don't want you to worry about that. This house is going to be a safe haven for you, for as long as you need it. Safe in *every* way."

"It already is." What was that thing Lady Macbeth said, about screwing your courage to the sticking-place? I did that, and then I leaned over and kissed him.

"Whoa, hang on." He caught me by the shoulders and held me a bit away from him. "Are you sure that's a good idea?"

I blinked at him in surprise. "Don't you want me?"

He winced. "Chrispen, that is not what I am talking about, you have to know that. I don't want you feeling forced to do anything, or to move faster than you are comfortable with. You were just screaming bloody murder a few hours ago."

"Yes. Weren't you listening to me? That had nothing to do with you, or with us." I lifted his hands from my shoulders and kissed his palms.

He shook his head. "Are you sure? Chrispen--this isn't what you came here for."

I laughed low in my throat and climbed up over him, pushing him back against the pillows. "You tell it your way, Mr. Brooks, and I'll tell it mine."

He might have had further protests, I don't know. Everything he had said so far centered around me not knowing what I wanted, and I'd had enough of that kind of talk. As soon as he opened his mouth to argue, I covered it with my own.

I caught his hands in mine, and I didn't let him up for air until he kissed me back.

"You know," he murmured against my neck, "you make yourself very hard to say no to."

I laughed again. "It's a gift." I tangled my fingers into his hair, and raised his face to mine again.

Alexis groaned and pulled me closer to him. I could feel the warmth of his hands through the fabric of my nightgown, on my shoulders, my back, my breasts. I pulled the gown over my head and tossed it to the floor.

"Chrispen," Alexis gasped, "if you're going to change your mind, please do it now."

"Why? Do you want me to change my mind?" I scattered little kisses along his jaw, down his neck.

"No." He gathered me up and laid me back against the bed. "I don't want you to change your mind now, or tomorrow, next week, or next year. I love you, Chrispen."

"And I love you, Alexis. I don't care what the police or the world have to say about it. I'm not changing my mind. Not now, not ever."

"Are you sure?" he whispered. Even in the dark I could see the intensity of his expression.

"Absolutely. I'm with you always. From here to forever." I pulled him down to me, and it seemed there was nothing in the world but me and him and this need for him that would never, ever be gone.

He moved over me in the dim light, and I moved with him. Our breath came in quick little gasps and when the fireworks exploded in my mind I could find no regret.

I laid awake that night next to Alexis in the tangled sheets, watching the faint light from the MP3 player shine on his sleeping face, listening to his deep, even breathing. I could still find no regret.

We seemed isolated now, bound to each other in our own private bubble, insulated from the rest of the world. It didn't matter what Dwight said or did to me; this was truth and he could never touch it.

The MP3 player shuffled to the Mendelssohn Concerto. It was Alexis's recording of the second movement, and it was like my own personal lullaby. I snuggled down into the bed with my arm over Alexis and let the music draw me toward sleep. Things couldn't have gotten much better in that moment.

It looked like we would get our happy ending after all.

♪

I stood in my kitchen, chopping up a potato. Diced fried potatoes with a little onion; that was my plan for dinner tonight. It was small, but it would do. I didn't need much; Alexis was at a benefit concert tonight, playing the Mendelssohn Violin Concerto to raise money for the youth symphony. There was always so much food at the receptions--I knew I didn't have to worry about cooking for him tonight.

It was my very favorite concerto, and nobody could play it like Alexis. I should have been there in the audience to hear it, but I was feeling a bit under the weather. Rather than make everyone at the concert sick, I had decided to stay safely home and eat fried potatoes by myself.

A knock startled me. It wasn't from the front door--this was someone knocking on the utility room door, the door that came in from the garage. Who would come around that way? Why not go to the front?

I went and opened the door, and to say I was surprised would have been a terrible understatement.

"Dwight!" I blurted, more out of shock than anything else. "What a--what a surprise."

"Hello, Madeleine." His eyes flicked from my face to the kitchen knife in my hand. "Do you think it would be okay if I came in for a few minutes? I'd like to talk to you."

In truth I didn't think it would be okay at all. The man had a nerve, I had to give him that. I had not spoken to him since our senior year of high school, when he--well, I don't like to talk about what Dwight did to me. I still carried the scars, inside. No children, the doctors had said. Ever.

But I had met Alexis because of him. And he probably wanted a chance to apologize, to clear the air between us.

I owed him that much. I stood aside and let him in.

He was wearing leather driving gloves, and he clapped me on the shoulder as he passed.

"Ah, fried potatoes," he said, taking in the skillet and the chopped vegetables. "Dinner of kings, that."

I smiled halfheartedly. "It'll do. It doesn't have to be fancy; it's just for me. I'm not really feeling well."

He took one of the potatoes out of the bag and played with it, tossing it up and catching it like a ball. "Is that why you're missing your favorite concerto?"

I nodded. "I thought you would be playing with the symphony tonight, though."

Dwight grinned, and it was a little unnerving. It was the smile of a predator. "Gig tonight. Private party. That's where I am right now," he winked at me, "if anyone asks."

I moved a little away from him and went back to chopping potatoes. It was quiet in the kitchen for a moment, which was a relief after that awkward conversation. I turned on the stove and poured a little olive oil into the skillet. Maybe the party was starting soon, and he would have to leave.

"I suppose I figured as much," he said quietly. "Nothing. Not a damn word."

"I beg your pardon?" I shook some seasonings onto the potatoes, shifting them around the cutting board with my knife.

He gave a sour laugh. "Well, you should, really. Look, Madeleine, do you have any idea why I came here tonight?"

"Not really." I dumped the potatoes into the skillet, guiding them off the cutting board with the backside of the knife.

He took a step closer to me. "To give you a chance to apologize."

My mouth fell open. "Me? Dwight, why on earth would I

apologize, when you were the one who--"

"You brought that on yourself," he snapped, cutting me off. "Whoring around with Alexis like that--then you meet me to show me his *ring?*"

I stared at him. "Whoring?"

His face was dark. He paced the kitchen in short, savage strides. You were mine, Madeleine. Mine! You had no right to leave with him the way you did, without a word, and now you come back."

"Dwight--"

"Shut up! You come slinking back into town, like you have any right to show your face here, and still not a word. Not a single apology."

"Dwight!"

He shook his head, stopping right in front of me. "You're a cancer, Madeleine. A cancer, and you are eating me alive. I can't be happy while you are with him."

I raised the knife in front of myself defensively. "Get out of my house!"

His face twisted. "And now you *threaten* me? You *dare?*" He grabbed my wrist, squeezing, digging his thumb into the center, until the knife clattered to the floor. He yanked me close to his face. "I'm going to kill you, Madeleine. You will never hurt me again."

I think I screamed. I grabbed for another knife out of the block, but as my fingers touched the handle he clouted me on the side of the head.

Everything swam before me. I was on the floor, dizzy and numb, and Dwight was pulling the big knife from the cutlery block.

I screamed again, scrabbling to my feet, and ran into the dining room. The door--I had to reach the door--had to get outside--

Dwight grabbed hold of my hair and yanked me savagely backwards. I hit my back on the big table and sprawled over it, in agony.

"Dwight, please," I begged. He looked entirely demented, standing there with a knife in one hand and a hank of my hair in the other. He leaned over me.

"Die!" he shrieked, and plunged the knife into my belly.

Agony--I had only thought I knew the meaning of it. How could he possibly stab me so many times--how could I possibly have so many places to stab? The brutal attack seemed as though it would never end.

Mercifully, though, I became gradually numb, and warm.

The last thing I saw was Dwight, pulling the hot potatoes off the stove, covered in my blood.

The first thing I was aware of was the screaming--long, painful, shrill, animal howls that rent my soul. I wished the screaming would stop.

The second thing I became aware of was that the screaming was coming from me.

I screamed until my breath was utterly spent, completely heedless of Alexis attempting to quiet me. When I was totally out of air I panted and choked, gathering up to scream again.

Alexis grabbed my shoulders and shook me briskly. "Chrispen! Chrispen, what is the matter?"

"Madeleine," I gasped. "Alexis, why didn't you tell me the real reason you don't use the dining room?"

Alexis dropped his hands and sat back, thunderstruck. "What?"

I wrapped my arms around my belly. I swear I could still feel the sharp bite of the knife, the warmth of my own blood spilling over me. I could still smell the potatoes in the hot oil. It turned my stomach.

"I swear," I panted, swallowing hard, "that I will never eat fried potatoes again."

He looked at me oddly, the way I might look at someone who woke me up with screaming in the middle of the night only to yammer about fried potatoes. "Chrispen, we didn't eat any potatoes today." He froze. "How did you know that's what Madeleine had for dinner on the night she...she..."

"Don't say it." I held up a hand in pleading, or warning, or both. I could still see the dining room, with Madeleine sprawled out on the table like it was a sacrificial altar. I shuddered. "Dear God, Alexis, how could anyone think you did that?"

He grabbed my shoulders again. "What is going on here? I thought you had your nightmare again."

I shook my head. "No. It was a murder, but not that one."

He stared at me. "No."

"Alexis, I'm sorry. I didn't mean to upset you." I backed away from him, toward the other edge of the bed. "I'll go back to the other room--I'm sorry--I didn't know--"

He caught my arm and pulled me back to him. "Don't you dare leave. I just--this is a bit of a shock, is all."

"Tell me about it." My voice was sarcastic and strong, but I clung to him as tightly as a child afraid of the dark.

If only it were that simple.

Alexis rubbed my back, but I couldn't tell if he was trying to calm me, himself, or both of us. "What did you see?"

"Dwight," I said shortly. "Dwight murdered her."

"No," he said reflexively.

"Alexis, I know what I saw. I already told you she was frying potatoes. You said that was right?"

He sighed. "Yes. That was right."

"You found her on the dining room table." I shuddered again, remembering. "The knife was in the kitchen."

"Yes." He didn't look at me; this conversation had to be just as horrible for him as it was for me.

"But they didn't find any fingerprints in the house except hers and yours."

"That's right."

I shook my head. "He was wearing gloves, leather gloves. Alexis, I saw him."

"I believe you. But he has an airtight alibi. Chrispen, I don't like him either. But there really isn't any reason to think that he did this."

"But--"

"I know it was upsetting, but it was just a dream. You had quite a scare today. Your subconscious probably just put the two things together."

I sighed. "If you say so." It didn't feel like my subconscious telling stories. I could still feel every wound Madeleine had sustained.

It felt real.

I could still feel the fear, could see the blood staining the house.

That felt real, too.

I could still see the dangerous glint in Dwight's eyes, could still hear the murderous rage in his voice when he shouted "Die!" in my face.

That felt most real of all.

I didn't really sleep after that. I finally gave up early that morning and quietly left the room, pulling my nightgown tighter around me against the chill. Right now, one of us couldn't sleep. If I kept fidgeting around in there, we would both be awake.

I wandered out towards the living room. There was

something sort of depressing about the thin, gray, pre-dawn light. I knew I should get to my room and get dressed. I could even just park myself on the couch and keep out of trouble. On no account should I go anywhere near the dining room. I knew that.

But I didn't go to the guest room, and I didn't sit down on the couch. I stood in the kitchen, staring around like I was lost. I had a weird sort of double-vision; I could see the room as it was now, as it had always been since I came to this house. But I could also see it as it was, as it had existed five years ago when Madeleine had cooked here while Alexis performed at the fundraiser.

The skillet--there. I ran my fingers over the burner on the glass-top stove where it had sat that evening. The cutting board had been just there, next to the stove on the counter. The knife...I reached my hand out where I remembered brushing my fingers against the handle. There was a block of knives there, but it was different.

Of course, it would be. Personally, I hoped never to see any of the knives from that particular set ever again.

I had stood...right here. Dwight--right there.

It was the creepiest thing I had ever done, walking through this room that I now knew to be a crime scene. I could walk the exact path Madeleine took in her flight, and without consciously meaning to, I did.

The dining room was essentially the same, but the furniture was different. This table was rectangular, with squarish, mission-style chairs. The other had been oval, darker, with Queen Anne chairs.

Still...I looked up at the chandelier. It was the same. Madeleine would have been right--there. I brushed my fingers against the table, and shuddered.

"Are you all right?" Alexis's voice was behind me, and it sounded like he didn't think I was very all right at all.

"This table is different." My voice sounded like it came from a great distance.

Alexis wrapped his arms around me from behind. "I was kind of hoping you had forgotten about that."

I laughed harshly. "It isn't really the sort of thing you forget."

"Tell me about it. That was the worst night of my life. You can't imagine what it was like."

I covered his hands on my belly with my own. "No, I can't."

There was a little silence while we regarded the room. "But Alexis," I finally said, "the table is different, right?"

He sighed. "Yes. The table is different. How did you know that?"

"Take a wild guess. There hasn't been a single thing in that dream that was wrong."

"Except for the most important part."

Now it was my turn to sigh. "Yeah."

But in the cold hollow in the pit of my stomach, I couldn't really believe it was wrong.

♫

Alexis drove me to rehearsal that day. As usual, we were some of the first people there. Today that suited me especially well. I had a job to finish.

As soon as we got in the Green Room, I headed down the hall toward Darren's office. Alexis was with me, which maybe wasn't ideal, but I didn't see any way around it. He spent half his time back there anyway.

I spent the walk planning exactly what I would say. As it turned out, I needn't have bothered. As soon as we opened the door, Alexis was on the attack.

"Darren, if you ever send her to that apartment again, I will personally--"

"Alexis!" I interrupted.

Darren's eyes were huge; obviously this verbal assault was not what he had expected when we barged into his office. "Well," he said uncertainly, "if it isn't my two favorite violinists. What--eh, what brings you in today?"

I gave Alexis a look strong enough to keep him quiet for the moment. He gestured me forward and folded his arms. "Be my guest."

"I went and talked to Dwight for you," I said, suddenly unable to look anyone in the eye.

"And?" Darren prompted. "Is it time to give him the sack?" He started shuffling through paper on his desk; evidently he had been working on just that.

"No. He was sick, that's why he left."

Alexis snorted and turned away from us.

Darren looked from him to me. "I don't understand why he came to the rehearsal at all, if he was sick?"

I shrugged. "It came on rather suddenly as I understand it-- food poisoning or something of that nature. I did go to see him, Darren, and he really was sick."

Darren looked at me a long moment, and I fidgeted uncomfortably under his gaze, crossing my arms in front of me. His eyes widened. "Dear girl, what happened to your arm?"

Damn. I had hoped, somewhat foolishly, that no one would notice the elastic bandage. "I fell down the stairs when I was leaving Dwight's apartment." My voice sounded a little hollow, but he didn't seem to notice.

"My goodness! Is it serious?"

"Oh, it's serious," Alexis said, turning back to us and giving me a dark look, "but she'll be able to play."

Darren looked thoroughly confused. "Well--that's good news, then, I suppose. Dwight had a reasonable explanation for his actions, and you will still be able to perform. All's well that ends well, right?"

I nodded. But I looked at the tension in Alexis's face, and thought about the story I wasn't telling Darren, and I wondered, how could any of this end well at all?

♫

I went back out to the Green Room as soon as I possibly could. Lying for Dwight was one of the most unpleasant things I had ever done, and I certainly didn't want to prolong the experience.

I warmed up just enough to loosen up my fingers, and then I went and sat down on the sofa in the back corner of the room. I didn't want to play enough to aggravate my wrist, and I sure didn't want anyone getting close enough to me to notice it. The room gradually filled up around me, but I went out of my way not to pay attention.

Alexis eventually came out of the back, and sat down next to me.

"That took awhile," I said. "Did you rat me out?"

He looked surprised. "No, of course not. Didn't I tell you it was your decision?" He sighed. "I did try to convince Darren to sack him anyway."

"Alexis, you didn't!"

"I did. I'm afraid I didn't get too far though. Darren values your opinion more than mine where Dwight is concerned."

"And a good thing, too," I said. "You wouldn't be doing me any favors if you got him fired."

"Speak of the devil," he muttered.

I looked towards the door. Dwight had just come into the Green Room, and even from where I was sitting I could tell he was three sheets to the wind. He lurched unsteadily into the room, a belligerent set to his jaw. His left eye was black, and his nose was swollen and bruised.

"Oh, man," I breathed. "This can't be good."

I tried to disappear into the sofa. Alexis slipped his arm around my shoulders. "Steady," he murmured. "You really decked him good, didn't you? His face is a mess. Good for you."

Dwight caught sight of us, and looked like he might lurch over in my direction, except that Darren had just emerged from the hallway and caught him. Whatever Darren had intended to say, though, was derailed by the sight of his face.

"Good Lord, boy, what happened to you?"

A general hush fell over the room in response to this outburst. I tensed up, fists clenched in my lap, waiting to hear how Dwight would respond.

"I got in a fight," he said thickly, "at a bar." Apparently Dwight wasn't any more eager to admit our altercation than I was.

"How simply atrocious. I--say, but are you drunk? At a *rehearsal?*"

Dwight clapped Darren heavily on the shoulder. "Shit, DJ, if your face looked like this, would you want to be sober?"

"Such language," Darren said stiffly, taking a step back from him, "will get you released from the services of this symphony." He glanced around the room; it was evident that every person there was listening to their conversation. He shook his head. "I hope the other fellow looks as bad as you do."

"The other fellow," Dwight said distinctly, "was a whore."

My nails bit into my palms. I felt Alexis's arm tighten around me a second before I heard his voice, low and close to my ear.

"Are you *sure* I wouldn't be doing you any favors?"

We did the Mendelssohn Concerto last that day. Sitting there in the orchestra with Alexis on one side of me and Dwight on the other was pretty tense. Fortunately I got to see the good side of his face--I felt sorry for the second chair second violin, who had to sit on his left.

So it was actually something of a relief to take my violin and move to the front of the stage for the Mendelssohn.

This was only our second rehearsal of the concerto, which meant there would probably be lots of stopping, lots of fixing things, and playing them over. For that reason, I took my music with me and grabbed a stand, so that when Darren called out a measure number I would be able to start with everyone else.

Kolbi, since we had finished the Warsaw Concerto and she had nothing else to do, brought up a chair and turned pages for me. I checked my tuning before we got started, and Kolbi frowned at the bandage she hadn't noticed before. "What happened to your arm?" She was giving me that scrutinizing look again, the one that had never bothered me until I had things to hide.

I couldn't look back at her. "Fell down the stairs," I said, sighting down the stick of my bow, pretending to check it for signs of warping.

"You don't have any stairs."

I sighed. "I fell down the stairs at Dwight's apartment."

She looked at me a long moment, frowning. She looked at Dwight's face, and her frown deepened. She didn't say anything, though.

Rehearsal went well, but there were naturally a few problem areas Darren wanted to work on. A few times he had me play passages alone so the orchestra could hear how I was phrasing or timing things.

All in all, by the time we finished my arm was throbbing. Alexis came up and helped me unwind the bandage, which was a big relief to my tired wrist.

I had forgotten Kolbi was there until she gasped. "My God, Chrispen!"

The bruises had green and yellow tinges to them. I had actually thought it was starting to look better.

She stared at my arm, then my face. "Fell down the stairs, right?"

I bit my lip and nodded.

"I see." She looked again at my wrist, at the long, narrow bruises that had clearly come from fingers, and she watched Dwight clear his things off the stage.

"You know," she said thoughtfully, "you and I should get together for a practice session sometime soon. You can tell me that long story you promised me."

I squirmed. That Kolbi--I couldn't hide anything from her. She was too perceptive.

"That sounds terrific," Alexis interjected before I could say a word. "You two should do that. Call her on her cell later, Kolbi. Or I'll remind her to call you."

I gaped at him, and he winked at me.

"Thanks, Alexis," Kolbi said. She slugged his arm and left the stage.

What was that all about? Obviously there was more going on here than I knew.

I figured I would find out, when Kolbi and I had our rehearsal.

♫

In the end it was another rehearsal I was glad just to walk away from. Alexis and I put our violins in the back of the car, and buckled ourselves in. I leaned back against the headrest and closed my eyes. I heard the Jaguar purr to life.

But the car did not move. I opened my eyes and found Alexis watching me, his hands folded in his lap. I couldn't identify his expression.

"What?"

"I need to talk to you," he said, "about what is in the backseat of this car."

"What, my violin?"

"No. Your overnight bag."

"Oh." I swallowed with some difficulty. "I'm sorry, Alexis, I know it's been an imposition--"

"Stop that--you know that's not what I mean. I assume that your bag in the car means you expect me to take you home now."

I stared at him.

"And to be honest," he continued, "I would really rather not do that."

"Really?"

"It can't have escaped your notice that your house is not safe for you."

My shoulders slumped; I had to admit that was not the explanation I had hoped for. "No, it hasn't."

Alexis grinned at me. "Besides, the house feels empty without you in it."

"Good," I said, "because after the last couple of days I feel more at home in your house than mine."

"Have you changed your mind yet?"

"No. Not tomorrow, not next week, not next year. Not ever."

"Good," he said, "because as empty as the house feels without you in it, I can't even imagine what my life would be like without you in it. You've given me my life back, and you've never asked for anything in return. And I've given you little but trouble, and now I'm about to ask even more of you."

I couldn't look away from him; I couldn't even breathe.

He pressed a small box into my hands. "Chrispen, will you marry me?"

I forced myself to inhale. "Yes."

Alexis laughed, but there was relief in it. "Aren't you even going to look at it?"

"Of course," I said, "but my decision is the same even if there is a cigar band in this box."

"There might be," he said, "there just might be. Seriously, Chrispen, I want you to take all the time you need. Think about this, make sure it's what you want, because you are not in for an easy ride. You know what the world thinks about me."

"I don't care. I've told you before it doesn't matter to me what the rest of the world thinks. I've given you the only answer I have in me, Alexis. It will be the same whether you ask me now, or two months from now, or two hundred years from now."

"It's a date, then," he laughed, lifting the box from my lap and opening it. "Mark it on your calendar, because I am going to ask you again, two hundred years from today." He slipped the ring onto my finger. It was a solitaire in a white gold band, as perfect as a single crystalline drop of dew in the morning sun's first ray.

"Oh, Alexis," I gasped, watching the sunlight play across it, "I don't know what to say."

Tears welled up in my eyes, and I looked up to find him watching me anxiously. "Say you haven't changed your mind."

"Never," I said, throwing my arms around him. "You'll have me forever, Alexis."

"Promise?"

I laughed. "I already did. I'm not taking it back. I promise. From here to forever."

♫

The police cruiser was in my driveway, right behind my little Toyota. It gave me a bad feeling as soon as I saw it, and I didn't even know why it was there.

Alexis parked the Jaguar on the street in front of my house.

"You'd better let me deal with this," I told him, climbing out of the car. "I don't like the look of it."

Alexis didn't say anything, but he didn't follow me either. I figured that was as close to agreement as I would get.

I walked up to the police car, and who should I find in the driver's seat but Officer Parker. I leaned in the passenger window. "You know, we have got to stop meeting like this."

He didn't even crack a smile. "Miss Marnett. Could you get in the car, please?"

"What? Why? Are we going somewhere?"

He glanced at me, a brief glance that seemed almost disappointed. "No, I don't think we are. Mr. Brooks and I may be, though."

I opened the door and slid into the passenger seat. "Okay, what is this all about?"

The radio gave a sharp crackle. "Parker, do we need to proceed?"

He grabbed the radio handset. "Negative. The victim has returned to the abode. Repeat: the victim has returned to the abode."

He turned back to me, and I'm pretty sure my surprise was evident. "Victim? Officer Parker, what is this all about?"

He glanced at my bruised arm in my lap, and alarm bells rang like crazy in my mind. There was just no way this could be anything good. "That," he said, "is what we are here to discuss." He glanced in the rearview mirror. "I would prefer that Mr. Brooks was not part of this conversation."

"He's not here," I pointed out. "What do you need?"

Officer Parker pulled out his cell phone and fiddled with the screen. "For starters, I would like your thoughts on this."

He turned the phone around and handed it to me. I recognized with horror the YouTube video "Alexis Brooks and his latest victim."

"I have no thoughts on that." In truth I had several, but none that were fit to be spoken in front of a law enforcement official.

"Chrispen?"

I jumped violently; it was Alexis and he was right behind me.

I turned the phone out of his line of sight, and looked at him as innocently as I could manage. "What do you need?"

"Nothing. I wanted to let you know I'm going to duck inside. I'm going to hunt up a suitcase and start throwing stuff in it for you till you come tell me to stop."

"Thank you." I watched him go into the house, and when I turned back to Officer Parker, I found him studying me speculatively. "What?"

"No thoughts at all?"

I sighed. "I flagged that video yesterday and asked them to remove it. It was filmed without my knowledge and I consider it a massive violation of my privacy. Does that count?"

He folded his arms. "Can I ask you why it scared you so much to find Mr. Brooks behind you?"

I gestured with the phone. "I was afraid he would see this!"

"Why, are you not allowed to watch it?"

"I don't know what you mean. I just don't want him to see it."

He frowned. "Wait a minute. Are you telling me he doesn't know this video exists?"

"That's what I am telling you. I only found out about it yesterday, and I haven't told him. There isn't much more I can say about this video."

"Miss Marnett, I should warn you; if I have reasonable cause to suspect domestic violence, I am required to arrest Alexis Brooks. With or without your support."

I stared at him. "Domestic...? Hold on a second. I know what the title says, but that video doesn't show anything like that. Alexis did not do this." I replayed the video, paused it, and handed the phone back to him. "My arm is already bruised when he reaches for it there. This happened well before that--Alexis wasn't anywhere around."

Officer Parker looked at his phone, and frowned. "If Alexis didn't do this, who did?"

I sighed and looked down at my wrist. "I've told all my friends I fell down the stairs."

"Roger that. That's the official story. What's the real story?"

"The real story." I sighed again. I seemed to be sighing a lot lately, and the thought for some absurd reason made me want to cry. "The real story is that the same person who posted that video did this to my arm."

"You're giving me riddles? Don't you want this guy brought to justice?"

I shook my head. "Not yet. Remember how you talked about giving a criminal enough rope? It's complicated."

"I don't like this." He stared grimly out the windshield. "This is a dangerous game you are playing."

"It is, but I don't have any choice."

Officer Parker looked at his phone again, and pursed his lips. "You say this video was recorded without your knowledge."

I nodded. "That's right."

"What about Mr. Brooks?"

"No, Alexis didn't know either."

He got suddenly out of the car. I did too, and hurried around to the other side to meet him. He was holding the phone in front of him, scanning the lawn. "It should be right...here."

He knelt in front of the hedges next to the driveway, and started reaching in, pushing leaves aside and looking in the branches.

It didn't take him long to uncover the wireless webcam. It gave me a chill, seeing it there. Was it the only one?

"These things aren't magic," Officer Parker said. "They've got to have a wireless network to transmit to."

I covered my face with my hands. "I have a wireless network. And I let him use my computer--I didn't know any reason not to, at the time."

He pulled the webcam out of the bushes. "I'm going to take

this with me if it's all the same to you."

I shuddered. "Please, take it."

"It may be useful as evidence if you ever actually let me arrest a criminal." He regarded me solemnly. "Please, please reconsider your course here. Crimes are for the police to handle, and attempting to deal with violent criminals on their own is how people get hurt." He gestured at my arm. "And whoever did that to you is a criminal."

I watched him get in the squad car and drive away. He was already on the police radio again.

I looked at the bushes; I could still clearly see the hole where Officer Parker had removed the webcam.

...and attempting to deal with violent criminals on their own is how people get hurt...

All at once, my wrist was throbbing.

♪

I expected to find Alexis in the back, playing stuff-the-suitcase. So I was a bit surprised when he opened the front door as soon as I stepped onto the front patio. His face told me clearly that something was very wrong.

I just didn't see how I could take much more. "What happened?"

He shook his head. "I'm sorry, Chrispen--I should have done something. I should have known what might happen."

I put a hand on his arm. "Alexis, what is it?"

He ran a hand through his hair. "Your collage..."

I pushed past him, into the living room. The bare spot on the wall jumped out at me, and it took my breath away.

Every single piece of decoration had been torn off the board. The fabrics were shredded, the ribbons destroyed, the lace nothing but tatters of string.

But the worst had to be the pictures. Every picture of Alexis had been ripped from the board and savagely defaced. Some had obscenities scrawled on them, some were torn into pieces too tiny to identify. Some of them had the eyes rubbed out with erasers, some were full of knife stabs. A few had the entire head completely burned away.

The board itself had been broken, chopped, and splintered into pieces.

I sank down into my armchair, suddenly lacking the strength to stand. A piece of art I had made when I was twenty years old was now suitable for nothing but kindling.

A hand fell on my shoulder. "I am so sorry, Chrispen."

I covered his hand with my own. "Did you manage to find a suitcase?"

"I did," Alexis said, "and it's stuffed full of clothes and things, but I'm not sure if I got everything you need."

"Grab it," I said, "and let's get out of here. There isn't a thing in the world I need bad enough to stay here another second."

He disappeared into the back, and came out carrying my flowered suitcase. "I don't understand. Who would do this to you?"

I sighed. "The same person who has done all the rest of it." I deliberately kept my eyes away from my wrist.

We walked slowly from the house like survivors of some terrible disaster. Alexis carried my suitcase, and had his other arm around me. I wrapped both my arms around him so tightly it was probably uncomfortable for him, but I couldn't help it. Losing the collage had been upsetting, but what upset me the most was the threat implicit in its violent destruction.

A threat that was not directed at me.

It was a quiet ride home. Alexis carried my suitcase into the guest room, then looked around uncomfortably. I wondered if he perceived the threat to himself as well, or if he thought the whole display was aimed at me.

"Are you okay?" he asked me.

I nodded. "It could have been a lot worse."

He hugged me hard, like maybe he had been thinking the same thing. "If it's okay with you, I'm going to give the Brahms cadenza a little more work, and then I'd like to play it for you a little later."

"I'd like that," I said, "but only if I get to hear the whole concerto."

"Deal," he said. "And I'll want to hear the Mendelssohn as well."

I grimaced.

"Don't be that way," Alexis laughed. "It's only fair." He kissed my forehead and left the room.

So there I was, alone in a quiet room with a violin and a stack of music I needed to learn, including a concerto I needed to know inside and out. It was pretty obvious what I needed to do.

What I actually did, though, was slip my cell phone into my pocket and leave the room. I could hear Alexis tuning and warming up, becoming gradually fainter as I walked across the living room to the back door. I had something to do first, something even more important than the Mendelssohn, at least to me.

I made my way to the familiar stone bench and pulled up the symphony directory on my cell phone. It was online and password protected, but it wasn't updated terribly often and out of date information was hardly ever removed. At times this had bugged me--both Jack Duncan and I were listed in the directory, and both of us showed our position as "assistant-concertmaster"-- but today I was counting on that.

I found the number I needed and added it to my contacts. That seemed to be as far as my nerve currently extended, though, and I couldn't seem to bring myself to actually dial the number. I stared at the fish instead, telling myself I was planning what I would say. But in truth I was trying very hard not to think about the phone call at all.

I was still sitting there pretending to think when the cell phone in my hand made an odd sort of chirp, alerting me to an incoming text message.

I sighed; the text was from Dwight.

`police, your house--explain`

I shook my head. "Geez, Dwight, how can that not be obvious?" I opened up a new message and texted him back.

`don't blame me, i didn't post vid on youtube`
The reply was almost immediate.

`how did they find that?`
I had spoken to people more exasperating that Dwight before, but I was having a hard time remembering any of them.

`u think only u + i use internet? i did not call them or give them link--we had a deal`
The reply was only a hair slower this time.

`good.`
I took that to mean we were done here. A good thing, too--I was sure I didn't have the patience for much more of that particular conversation.

I went back to my contacts screen, and before I could lose my nerve again, dialed the number I had been avoiding.

"Hello."

He sounded clipped and impatient, like the last thing he wanted right at that moment was to be talking to me. It made me want to throw the cell phone in the fish pond and run back into the house. But I was already in a bad mood. I took a deep, steadying breath. "Hello, Mr. Brooks. This is Chrispen Marnett. I'm sorry for the intrusion, but I wondered if there might be a time we could meet."

"Meet," he repeated, as though he had never heard the word before. "Marnett...are you the girl who played in the Bach Double the other night?"

"Yes."

"And you want to...meet? Why? You did not seem eager to listen to me before."

I sighed. "Please, I really feel I need to speak with you. It's very important."

There was a little pause. "Did that man make you do this thing?"

"If by 'that man' you mean Alexis, then no. He has no idea I am contacting you, in fact I imagine he would object rather strongly. And 'that man' is your son, Mr. Brooks."

"I have no son. Apologies, madam--I must go."

He hung up.

I sighed and put my phone away. Well, it wasn't as though I hadn't had a good idea of how that conversation was going to turn out. Still, it was depressing. Clearly this was not my day.

I kicked around the idea of asking Darren to arrange a meeting for me, but I had to admit it didn't seem likely to work. I had heard what good friends they had been in the past, but after the dress rehearsal it was clear that the situation was different now.

I started back towards the house, nursing a sudden feeling of defeat.

As much as I hated to do it, it looked like I was going to have to accept that there were some things I just couldn't fix.

♫

Alexis was waiting in the living room when I came in, holding his violin and wearing a knowing smile. "You really do like the garden, don't you?"

My face turned red. "I do."

"Me, too," he said, and shook his head. "And here I thought you would be practicing your fingers to the bone."

"I should have," I said, and the real irony was that it was true; my secret agenda had not worked out very well at all. "I just needed some time to settle my head."

"You picked the right place for it," he said. "I don't know any place more peaceful. I've actually taken my fiddle out there and played before."

"Really?" My mind was instantly taken with the notion of Alexis playing in the garden--that sounded as close to perfect as anything I could imagine.

Alexis nodded. "Oh, yes. The acoustics aren't great, but the fish are a very non-critical audience."

I laughed. "True."

"And speaking of critical audiences, I wonder if you have time to listen to the Brahms?"

I sat down on the couch. "You seem to have caught me at a lull in my super-busy schedule."

"Next time," he said, "I'll make an appointment." He leaned over and kissed me.

"Don't worry," I told him, "walk-ins are welcome." And this time I kissed him.

Finally I pulled away from him. "At this rate, you will never get to play."

"Oh right," he said, running a hand through his hair, "the Brahms."

And he shouldered his violin and just like that, he was off.

I could have listened all day. I had never heard Alexis play the Brahms Violin Concerto before, and it was an experience. He redefined it, and I didn't imagine I could ever be satisfied with any other rendition of it again.

"There aren't words," I told him when he finished. "There

just aren't words."

Alexis laughed, but I could tell he was pleased. "That's it? No helpful suggestions at all?"

"Hmm." I thought about it. "That double-stop you're hitting, right at the climax of your cadenza--it's such a powerful moment, and that's such a fantastic chord, I'd like to hear it held just a bit longer." I shrugged. "But that's all I got. If you want real criticism I'm afraid you'll have to go try the fish."

He laughed again and kissed me. "Your turn," he said in my ear.

"What?" I asked, disoriented.

"I thought you wanted an objective observer's opinion of your Mendelssohn."

I laughed out loud. *"Objective?"*

"Well," he grinned, "maybe not so objective, but definitely experienced."

"Sure. Give me just a minute to warm up?"

"Take all the time you need. Meet me in the music room when you're ready."

I saluted him and went back to the guest room and unpacked my violin. In truth I didn't think I would ever really be what you would call ready, but I did my best to get warmed up quickly. I wrapped my arm in the elastic bandage, took a deep breath, and went across the hall.

The music room had oak paneling and oak flooring, and an upright piano against one wall. Shelves covered almost all the available wall space, stuffed full of sheet music and music books. Alexis was in the far corner of the room, replacing a stack of music on one of the shelves.

"As if on cue," he said, grabbing the music book he had left out. "I just managed to turn up my piano part for the Mendelssohn." He spread the music on the piano and sat down on the bench.

"Wait a minute," I said. "You play piano too? Isn't that just adding insult to injury?" I'd had to become proficient on the piano at Juilliard. But there was no way I could have sat down and tossed off the piano part to the Mendelssohn.

He laughed. "My mother was a concert pianist. I started studying the piano only a couple of years after I started the violin."

"No way. And you started violin when you were...?"

"Three." He was suddenly very busy arranging the piano part just so.

"Wow," I said. "That's incredible. So piano at five, then? Are you as good on the piano as you are on the violin?"

He looked at me sidelong, fingers hovering over the keys. "Would you like to find out? Or would you prefer to keep stalling?"

I grimaced and shouldered my violin. "Whenever you are ready, maestro."

Was Alexis Brooks the pianist as good as Alexis Brooks the violinist? Well, no. But one must remember that it had been seriously proposed that Alexis was the single greatest violinist who had ever lived. Equaling that would be superhuman. But he would have given the pianists I had known at Juilliard a run for their money.

Still, I had a concerto to play. I tried not to pay so much attention to the piano that I missed my entrances. "Well," I said doubtfully when we finished, "what do you think?"

"It's beautiful, Chrispen. Really beautiful."

"But?"

Alexis peered at me from the piano. "Why does there have to be a 'but'?"

"Don't give me that. There was a 'but' on the end of that sentence and we both know it. So finish it. What is the difference between the way I play this concerto and the way you play it?

What do I need to do?"

He sighed. "You need to internalize it. Internalize everything--everything about the piece. Don't just internalize the beat, but the notes, the harmonies and counter-melodies, the slightest tempo change, the smallest dynamic variation, the composer's immortal soul--*everything*. You need a very clear picture of what the music means to you, what you are trying to say. For the audience, the music is a catharsis, but it's an externally triggered experience. For the musician, however, it's a completely internal experience, and how can that happen if you are relying every moment on Mendelssohn to tell you exactly how to play every note?"

I frowned, feeling like a conservatory student again. Then again, compared to Alexis I supposed I probably was. "Are you saying I need to memorize it?"

"Memorize it? You've already done that; anyone can tell. No, what I'm asking of you is much more than that. Memorization is the preparation for internalization. Memorize, then internalize. You've got to have more than just the notes, my dear; you've got to involve more than just your memory." He shook his head. "I'm trying to give you my basic approach to playing music here, and I don't think I'm making a very good job of it. Am I making any sense at all?"

I was still frowning, willing the light bulb to come on. "I think so. Let me work on it."

Alexis studied my face a moment. "Chrispen, my love, you are far too serious."

I looked at him, surprised. "What do you mean by that?"

He looked down at the piano keyboard and sighed.

"Just what I said. You've worked far too hard lately, worried too much, seen way too many horrible things. It's taken all the humor out of you."

I wasn't looking at Alexis anymore, but staring at the nearest bookshelf, wishing I could hide in it.

"Chrispen," he said, "you need to have some fun."

I laughed harshly, feeling somehow cornered by his assessment of me. "Oh, a violinist, a pianist, *and* a psychiatrist."

Alexis held his hands up in a gesture of surrender. *"Pax,* Chrispen. Tell me I'm wrong."

I couldn't argue. Instead I studied the tip of my bow very closely.

"Well, there you have it," Alexis said, standing up and closing the keyboard cover on his piano decisively. I studiously ignored him, until he lifted my violin and bow out of my hands and went across the hall.

"What are you doing?" I demanded, following him.

He raised his eyebrows. "I am putting your violin away for you," he said, doing just that, "since you seem disinclined to do it yourself. I assume you don't want to take it with you."

My eyes narrowed suspiciously. "Take it with me where?"

He smiled rather smugly, zipping my violin case. "That, my love, is for me to know and you to find out-- unless you would rather stay here with your violin."

I laughed, grabbing my purse and following him out to the car. "Alexis, you are insufferable."

He held the door open for me. "I've heard it said," he replied good-naturedly.

♫

We ended up at one of those Japanese restaurants where they cook everything on grills in front of you, where dinner is as much a show as a meal, where you usually must have reservations, but where for someone of Alexis's fame and tipping habits, such formalities could be overlooked.

It was all amazingly entertaining, and delicious to boot. "Do you realize," I said, toying with some fried rice I would have loved to eat, if I hadn't been so full, "we are engaged and this is the first time we have been on what you might call a date?"

"Wow--I never really thought about it that way." He snapped a shrimp off his plate and into his mouth with chopsticks, as if it was no big deal. I was using a fork. One of the first things we had discovered that evening was that I was truly abysmal with chopsticks. "Does that bother you?"

"Hmm. No, I don't think so. It just seems weird, doesn't it?"

Alexis reached out and squeezed my leg. "Sure, but so are we."

I laughed. "You're right, at that." I laid my napkin on the table. "If you'll excuse me, I have to visit the little girl's room."

In truth, I did not. I would have been fine. But the glances and stares of the other patrons--sometimes curious, sometimes downright hostile--were beginning to wear on me, and I decided I needed a break.

I took more time in the restroom than I really had to; dawdling over washing my hands, fussing with my hair in the mirror. I was kind of surprised at myself, that people could bother me so much. Alexis was right; something had taken all the humor out of me.

I breathed deep and splashed some cold water on my face, making a concerted effort to cheer up. One way or another, things would change. This impossible situation couldn't last forever.

I walked out of the restroom, and was completely disoriented for a moment. The restrooms in this place were way in the back of the building down a long and winding hallway. It took me a minute to figure out which way I had come.

"Well, well, if it isn't the whore in question."

I stiffened. This impossible situation had just gotten worse.

I turned slowly around. "Hello, Dwight."

He stood in the hallway like something in it had offended

him, clutching Daniella by the arm. They were both dressed pretty nicely, and his face had healed faster than my wrist, though the bruises were still visible.

I arched an eyebrow at them. "Having a nice date?" It looked to me like Daniella was as far away from him as she could get.

She shot me an apologetic look, and tugged on her arm. "Not so much, really--Dwight, *please!*" She yanked harder against him.

He gave her a dirty look and let go of her. "Whatever you say."

Her eyes were as round as saucers. She edged away from him and stepped over behind me in the hall.

"Run," I told her under my breath. "I'm serious. Get out of here. Don't look back."

She didn't need to be told twice. It seemed Daniella's infatuation with Dwight had abruptly soured. Looking at the bruised glower he was directing at me, I figured she was lucky.

I took a step backward.

"Oh no, you don't," he snapped, grabbing my arm, just as an older couple came around the corner, looking for the restrooms. "You are coming with me, my dear. We need to talk." He pushed my arm through his and pulled me farther down the hall, around the corner. The only thing back here was a janitor's closet that didn't look like it had been touched in weeks.

Several words passed through my mind right then, but none of them were very nice.

"Dwight--"

"Hush. You need to try to be civil."

"That wasn't part of the deal." I pulled myself away from him.

He gave me a smile I didn't really like the look of. "It is now."

"What? In that case you should try a little civility yourself, Dwight. Or have you forgotten my fall down your stairs?"

He waved that off. "You brought that on yourself. You

know that."

I snorted. "If you want civility, you had better wrap this up in a hurry. Alexis tells me my temper has been a bit short lately."

His expression twisted, darkened, when I said the name. In my mind I saw the mangled remains of my collage, and I shuddered.

"Funny you should mention that," he said, in a tone that made me wish he was here and I was somewhere across town. "Your bastard lover is exactly who I need to talk to you about."

I folded my arms. "What about him?"

Dwight grabbed my left wrist and jerked on it, pulling me right up in front of him and twisting my arm around so that my engagement ring was right in my face. "That. Tell me, Chris, does that mean what I think it does?"

"Dwight," I gasped, "please let go of my arm!"

He shook my hand in my face. "Answer me!"

"Yes! Yes, of course it does. It's an engagement ring!"

"Not," said a voice that stopped my heart, "that it's any concern of yours."

Dwight abruptly released me, and that's when I realized his left arm had disappeared up behind his back. His face was white, so it must have been way up behind his back. "Alexis--my arm..."

"Yes," Alexis said conversationally, "I imagine that smarts a bit. Rather like what you did to Chrispen's arm the other day, perhaps. Only you should still be able to use yours without much difficulty--providing that you back the hell off, *right now.*"

"Chris--" Dwight gasped.

"Chrispen defends you, for some reason I cannot fathom. She doesn't want to see you hurt. I myself have no such compunctions." He jerked savagely on Dwight's arm. "Ready to play nice?"

Dwight nodded, sweat beading on his forehead. "Y-- yes. Of course."

"Good." Alexis gave Dwight a shove away from us, releasing him. Dwight swung around, fists balled and mouth open, to respond, but Alexis simply held out a warning hand and stopped him in his tracks. "If you raise so much as your voice to me, you will never work in this town again. I am not as forgiving as Chrispen--I will take you to the police, I will see you out of the symphony. After, of course, I beat the holy hell out of you."

Dwight stared at him, slack-jawed.

"Now, you have asked the lady a question. She has given you an answer. Leave. Or I will be happy to help you go."

Dwight's jaw clenched. He gave me a dark look of warning, then turned on his heel and stomped away. I hoped Daniella had listened to me and gotten herself far away from here.

Alexis turned to me. "Chrispen, are you okay?"

I launched myself into his arms, hanging onto him like I thought he might disappear. "Oh, thank you, Alexis. Thank you, thank you, thank you!"

He leaned back and looked at me, smiling, but still anxious. "How is your arm?"

"It's fine," I said. "It's terrific. How did you know?"

"Daniella told me you needed some help."

"Really? But I told her to get away from here!"

Alexis pursed his lips and regarded me shrewdly.

"Don't worry, she beat it out of here as soon as she delivered the message. Did it ever occur to you that you would have been safer if she stayed?"

I blinked. "No. I just wanted her to get out of there before she got hurt."

He hugged me hard, burying his face in my hair. "Chrispen, I love you. I don't know what I would do without you. But you are completely mental, do you realize that?"

I laughed. "I've heard it said."

♫

Call me a prude, but I went to bed in the guest room that night. I couldn't sleep, though. I laid in the dark, and worried.

I worried about the situation with Dwight. How much longer could this go on? Would he be good for his word, and supply the evidence he had promised? Did he even have any evidence, or was that just a desperate ploy to dodge the consequences for what he had done?

I worried about the situation with Kolbi. How much longer could I keep her in the dark? It was plain she already understood far more about the situation than I would have wanted. And once she pieced it all together, how would I ever keep her from going to Alexis with what she knew? Would the promise of clearing Alexis be enough to buy her silence? Or would she decide my danger was too great? Alexis was right, I needed to talk to her, but not for the reasons he intended.

Somewhere in the middle of my fretting, I did fall asleep. But it was a nervous, fitful sleep, laced with the same anxieties.

I woke up in the middle of the night, facing the wall. Before it even really registered that I was awake, I fell back into my worries.

I worried about the situation with Alexei. I had so wanted to help, and it looked like I wasn't even going to get the chance to try. It was frustrating.

I sighed and rolled over to face the window. I looked for the big trees outside, swaying in their usual breeze, and my heart stopped.

There was someone sitting in the window seat.

A split second later, I realized it was Alexis, and my heart thudded to life again. I pushed up against the bed, sitting up.

"Alexis? What's wrong?" He was sitting there with his robe pulled around him, and it made him look somehow forlorn.

"I'm sorry," he said, regarding me somberly. "I didn't mean

to startle you."

I waved that off. "What's the matter?"

He lifted his shoulders in a helpless shrug. "I just...I just felt like I needed to check on you. I guess I had a pretty bad dream." He looked sheepish. "You can laugh if you want to."

"Are you kidding? How many people did you wake up with your screaming?"

"What?"

"Exactly." I scooted over in the bed towards the wall, and threw the covers back. "Get over here. There's no need to sit over there in the cold."

I didn't have to ask twice. He climbed into bed next to me, and pulled me into a crushing hug.

"Wow, it must have been a doozy," I said.

He shook his head. "I don't want to talk about it. You don't want to know." He buried his face in my hair.

"It's all right," I said. I could imagine well enough the sorts of things that might haunt his sleep, especially after what had happened earlier that evening. "You don't have a thing to worry about. Nothing is going to happen to me. I'm going to be fine."

"Really?"

"Really. I'm going to be fine, and you're going to be fine, and we are going to get married and live forever." I squeezed him hard. "I'm perfectly safe. I am going to stay perfectly safe."

Alexis leaned back to look at me. "Promise me," he said, searching my face. "Promise me you won't let anything happen to you."

"I promise," I told him, my voice full of confidence, wanting nothing in the world more than to reassure him.

But I wondered, even as I sought to comfort him, how hard would that promise be to keep?

♫

We had a morning rehearsal the next day. We walked in the Green Room, and Alexis immediately grabbed my hand and started towards Darren Johnson's office without a word. I didn't know what business he had back there, but I couldn't imagine it would be anything good.

"Well, if it isn't my two favorite violinists." Darren gave us his standard greeting. "What can I do for you two today?"

"You can fire Dwight Richards," Alexis snapped.

Darren looked from Alexis, to my surprised expression, and sat back in his chair. "Always one to get right to the point, Alexis. I thought we discussed this already?"

"We did," Alexis said, "but the situation has changed since then. If I had not intervened, you would have a violin soloist unable to use her left hand."

Darren looked at me in surprise. "Chrispen, my girl...is this true?"

They had me pretty neatly cornered. I hemmed and hawed, trying to find a way out that didn't involve a blatant lie. "Well...I--I guess there's no way to really know that."

Darren reached for a drawer in his desk, and I held out my hands in a desperate gesture. "But I don't think you should do anything hasty."

Darren sat back again. "It sounds like there is no consensus here." He looked at Alexis, which was more than I could do just then. "It is not my intent to upset either of you. In the end, I'll have to make my own decision about how to handle Mr. Richards. I thank you both for reporting this; I will definitely keep it in mind when making that decision." He looked back and forth between us. "Was there anything else?"

"No," Alexis said stiffly. "We'll see you at rehearsal." He went out of the office, and I followed him.

Halfway down the hall I realized he really didn't have any intention of slowing down to talk to me.

I lunged out and grabbed his arm, forcing him to stop. "Alexis, wait. I'm sorry."

He sighed, running a hand through his hair. "No, I should have talked to you first. I guess I just thought, after what happened yesterday, that you might have changed your mind."

"I'm sorry," I repeated. "I know you were trying to do the right thing. I wish I could, too--but I can't. It's important."

He studied me a moment, and it looked like he might press me. Then he shrugged. "If you say it, I believe you. But I don't like this situation. I don't think you are safe."

"I'm not," I admitted. "But firing Dwight won't fix that. In fact it would probably make it worse."

"Excuse me," said a tentative voice from behind Alexis. "I don't mean to interrupt..."

Alexis looked like he might like to sigh, but he didn't. "It's okay, Daniella," he said, turning to face her. "What did you need?"

She gave me an uncertain smile. "I wanted to talk to both of you, actually--Chrispen, I wanted to tell you thank you. And...I'm sorry. For everything."

I smiled back. "Thanks, Daniella. Don't mention it."

She turned back to Alexis, and it seemed like she was blushing. "Hey, Alexis...what do you call the cadenza in a viola concerto?"

Alexis stared at her like that was the last thing he had expected to hear her say. "What?"

Daniella was already walking away. "Comic relief," she said over her shoulder.

Alexis burst out laughing.

I stared at him, wide-eyed. "What was that all about?"

He put his arm around me. "That, I think, was Daniella's way of offering truce. She's very grateful to you." He leaned over and kissed the top of my head.

Kolbi leaned around the corner. "Alexis, I thought I heard you back here."

"Looking for me?" he asked.

"No, actually, I was looking for Chrispen, but it seems to have worked out either way. Chris, I wonder if I could borrow you after rehearsal for that practice we talked about."

"Works for me," I told her. "We can just grab a rehearsal room after this is over."

"Sounds good to me. I'll give you a ride home after," she said, disappearing around the corner. "Stay out of trouble."

And the way she said it, she sounded serious.

"Two days till the concert," Darren said, as we prepared to play the Mendelssohn. "Chrispen, let's hear that cadenza."

I had been sort of dreading that. During rehearsal, we usually just skipped over the cadenza, in the interest of time. As the performance got closer, though, Darren liked to rehearse the cadenza as well, so the orchestra could get a feel for it.

So when the time came, the orchestra dropped out and I dove into the full version of Alexis's cadenza. It was definitely different, standing on that big stage, with the orchestra silent around me, playing all by myself.

"Fantastic!" Darren said to me when rehearsal was over. "I know we haven't had as much rehearsal as usual, so I was thinking of adding a rehearsal this afternoon. Would that work for you?"

"I'll be there with bells on," I assured him.

"Wonderful." He turned to Alexis. "And you, dear boy?"

Alexis laughed. "Darren, if Chrispen is somewhere wearing only bells, you know I'm not going to be far behind."

I blushed beet red. "Alexis!"

Darren chuckled. "Very well, then--I'll go back to the Green

Room and make a formal announcement. Although," he said over his shoulder, "I think I shall omit the bit about the bells."

"Please do," I called after him, slugging Alexis, who seemed to find the whole thing hilarious. "Some people," I said airily, "have no shame."

"I know," Alexis said, "standing right here on stage talking about coming to a rehearsal in nothing but bells! To the conductor, no less! Honestly, Chrispen, you should be ashamed."

I tried my best to keep a straight face, but it was a losing battle. I held my nose high in the air and sailed off the stage, heading for the Green Room.

I never made it, though. As soon as I made it out into the wings where it was too dark to be seen from the stage, someone stepped in behind me. Before I had time to react, a hand clamped onto the back of my neck, the other over my mouth.

"You and I are going to have a talk," said Dwight's voice, low and right in my ear. He pushed me away from the stairs to the Green Room, towards the other, altogether creepier, staircase to our left.

I resisted, pushing hard to the right. I was counting on his furtiveness; it was pretty apparent he did not want a scene.

What I didn't count on was the immediate way he moved the hand that was over my mouth, keeping it covered but also pinching my nose between his thumb and the side of his hand.

I was suddenly completely unable to breathe, and that convinced me faster than any words. I went left with Dwight, through the narrow splintered wood door, into the concrete stairwell, lit by a single naked light bulb, that led down to the below-stage levels.

The wings, I loved. I loved backstage, and onstage, and the Green Room.

Below stage, though, I detested. It was dark, and full of old discarded sets and costumes, and it always smelled sort of damp.

Nobody ever went down there unless they absolutely had to.

If you stashed a body down there, it wouldn't be found for months.

This did not make me feel any better as I descended into the bowels of the concert hall with Dwight. He kept his hand clamped tight over my mouth and nose; a scream in the concrete stairwell would be heard all over the building.

I was starting to see tiny flashing specks in my vision when we finally left the stairwell and went into the first basement level below the stage, under the orchestra pit.

Dwight released me and pushed me towards an old piano bench. I stumbled toward it, gasping for air. It smelled just as bad down there as I remembered, and it felt even creepier. There were racks of old costumes on either side of us, and behind the bench I sat on was a beat-up upright piano who looked as though its spirit had departed this world long ago.

On top of the piano was a dusty little lamp. Dwight leaned over me and turned it on, instantly creating long shadows I did not like at all.

"This is charming," I said. I was going for sarcasm, but my voice shook in a way that gave me fear instead. "What do you want with me?"

Dwight gave me a twisted smile. "Lots of things, but for now I'll just talk to you. I heard an ugly rumor that you and your bastard lover went to see Darren before rehearsal. What was that about?"

"Alexis wanted you fired. I went to bat for you, and you obviously were not fired." I sighed. "Would you please stop calling him that?"

"I'll call him whatever the hell I feel like. Not everyone is as enamored of him as you are. Did you see how he turned Daniella against me? I told you so, but I don't expect you will admit it."

I shook my head. "You're crazy."

He slapped me, an open-handed pop on the cheek that stung my face and startled me. "Don't call me crazy."

I raised a hand to my face, shocked. I pulled my violin closer to me on my lap; his quick temper made me nervous. "Are we finished here?"

"Finished? We're just getting started. How did you get Alexis's Mendelssohn cadenza?"

"He gave it to me."

"Really? I have to admit I wasn't expecting that. Hmm. He must be serious about you after all."

I stared at him. "Serious? Dwight, we are engaged. Of course he's serious."

Dwight laughed at me. "Anybody can give a bitch a ring to get her to put out. The cadenza, though--that's different."

I stood up and tried to bull my way past him. "You are vile. I am not going to sit here and listen to this filth any longer."

He grabbed my face in both hands, so tightly it hurt. "You will stay here as long as I say you will." He seemed to be right, too--I couldn't move without hurting myself. And I was still holding my violin, so I couldn't even fight against him properly. "You must know I have no intention of allowing this wedding."

I could hear footsteps on the stairs. I spoke quickly to cover them. "You must know I have no intention of allowing you to interfere."

He chuckled. "It seems we understand each other, then."

Kolbi came bounding off the stairs into the room. "Chrispen? Dwight?" She paused. "What's going on?"

"Don't get your knickers in a twist," he told her, still holding my face. "Chrispen and I are just having a conversation."

"Must be a good one," she said doubtfully.

"I've had better," I said.

Dwight laughed, and kissed me on the mouth. I struggled and jerked away from his hands, beating on him with my free hand, until he released me. "We'll finish this later," he promised, and left.

I shivered, wiping my mouth with the back of my hand.

Kolbi raised her eyebrows. "What on earth was that?"

"That," I said, sitting down on the piano bench again, "was Dwight. He's completely mental. How did you know where I was?"

She shrugged. "I didn't. This was the only place in the building I hadn't looked. I knew you didn't leave with Alexis; he thought you were rehearsing with me."

"Yes," I said, "we should get to that."

"It can wait," she said, sitting down next to me on the bench. "You say he's mental like maybe you're joking, but I think you may be more right than you know."

I avoided her gaze. "Don't tell him that. Dwight doesn't like to be called crazy."

Kolbi looked at me seriously. "You owe me a story."

I fidgeted on the bench. "Are you sure you want to hear about all that? It's kind of long."

"I've got time," she said, and crossed her legs, watching me expectantly.

So I told her. I told her how Darren asked me to speak to Dwight for him, about my visit to his apartment and what ensued there. I told her about how he cornered me at dinner the previous night, and how Alexis had interrupted. I told her how I had come to be in the stage cellars with Dwight when she found us.

Kolbi listened to it all, and then she sighed. "Chrispen, you want to be careful. Dwight is dangerous."

"I see that now," I said wryly, turning my green and yellow wrist over in my lap.

"Do you? Because I have heard that Alexis is lobbying to have him released from the symphony, and you are taking his side. I have to admit I don't understand that."

I had carefully avoided telling her anything about the evidence and the blackmail; I had a hunch the situation was insane and I didn't relish the prospect of trying to sell someone else on it. But it looked like it was time.

"Well," I said slowly, "here's the thing--"

My cell phone rang shrilly. I dug it out of my pocket, expecting it to be Dwight, expecting to silence the ringer and go on. But before I did, I glanced at the screen.

Brooks, Alexei.

"Oh my gosh," I said, astonished. "Oh my gosh...Kolbi, forgive me--I have to take this call."

"Be my guest," she said, but she didn't seem upset.

I answered the phone. "Hello?"

"Is this Miss Marnett?" I recognized the heavily accented voice at once.

"Yes--yes, Mr. Brooks, hello. What can I do for you?"

There was a slight pause. "Actually I believe it is more the question of what I can do for you. If you are still wanting to talk, I will do that."

"Really? I would love that."

"Yes, but first let me warn you--I have decided to meet with you only for my conscience. If something were to happen to you, I would want to know that I had done for you all that I could."

"Oh. I see." Well, beggars can't be choosers. I decided I would take what I could get, and be glad for it. "When can I see you?"

"Right now is a convenient time." He gave me his address.

"Thank you," I said. "I will be there, right away." I put my cell phone away.

"Be where right away?" Kolbi said suspiciously.

"Kolbi...how would you feel about giving me a ride?" I tried to sound innocent, like I wasn't about to go stir up a giant ant's nest.

"I already promised," she said.

I had Kolbi drive me to my house. In theory, she didn't know where I was going or what I was up to. In actuality, she had gleaned enough from my side of the cell phone conversation to have a pretty good idea.

"Chrispen," she said, while I sat in the passenger seat of her car, digging through my purse for my keys, "I applaud what you are trying to do, I really do."

I didn't look up. "What on earth are you talking about?"

She sighed. "Just watch yourself, okay? It's a complicated situation. You don't want to make it worse."

I pulled my keys out of my purse and got out of the car, then leaned back in. "Kolbi," I said, "the man called the police because I played a solo with Alexis. I don't think it can get much worse."

♫

Alexei Brooks lived in an adobe villa, whitewashed, with a red Spanish tile roof. When I walked up the brick front walk, he had the door open before I reached it.

"Miss Marnett, I am so pleased you could make it. Please, come in."

I stepped into the foyer, and shook his hand. "Thank you, Mr. Brooks. I'm very glad you agreed to speak with me today."

I reached up with my free hand to push my hair out of my face, and he froze, gripping my hand tightly.

"What is it?" I asked, worried. "What's the matter?"

"Forgive me," he said, releasing me. "But this ring...you did not have this when I saw you last. Can you tell me--will you tell me whose this is?"

I had a bad feeling about this. "Your son's."

He turned from me suddenly, walking through an archway into the living room. "I can see this will not be easy," he said over his shoulder. "Please, come sit down."

I followed him into the room. Directly across from where I stood, a huge sliding door opened onto a little courtyard with a birdbath. It made it feel like the whole far wall was glass. The ceiling was low and white, and the room was light and airy. The only unfortunate thing was the variegated red shag carpet on the floor. I sat down on the couch, not sure what to do now. Alexei was right; this wasn't going to be easy.

The focal point of the room was a large oil painting of Alexei and Victoria Brooks, he with his violin and she at her piano. The same baby grand piano was still in the room, under where the painting hung. I already knew how much Alexis resembled his father; what I had not guessed was how easy it was to see his mother in him as well. Alexei's features were sharp and his coloring darker; it was Victoria who softened Alexis's features and gave him his sandy brown hair.

Those eyes, though--those piercing brown eyes were exactly the same, and Alexei was currently nailing me to the spot with his. "So you have decided to marry this man."

"Yes." I couldn't help it, my chin went up defiantly when I said it.

"I see. And you thought you needed to tell me this?"

"Mr. Brooks, you are going to be my father-in-law. I would rather you did not hate me. But Alexis is getting married. Your son is getting married. Don't you care?"

He sat down in a wing-back chair and looked away from me, out of the glass sliding door. "You keep calling him my son, as though you are reminding me. Do you think I have forgotten?"

"Yes. I think that you have forgotten, or are just choosing to ignore, the fact that you have a son. A son who is talented, and generous, and in trouble. He needs you."

"He needs me!" he exploded, in a fit of temper. "What *you* seem determined to forget is that this talented, generous man you speak of is also a cold-blooded murderer!"

"No." I spoke quietly. I would not engage him, but I would not allow slanders to stand as truth, either. "Alexis did not murder anyone."

He looked at me intently, like he was trying to detect a lie in my expression. "How can you be so certain of that?"

"The same way you could, if you wanted to. I love Alexis. I know Alexis, and I know he is not capable of that. I would need absolute proof before I would entertain such a notion."

"A dead woman is not proof enough for you?" he said sardonically.

"A dead woman merely proves that a woman was killed. It does not prove who killed her. The evidence for that is circumstantial at best. And it would take a lot more than circumstantial evidence to turn me against Alexis."

He waved a hand at me. "But you are in love, and you are blind. Madeleine herself would have defended him, once."

"Perhaps she still would. Look, you've known him since he was born. You raised him. Was the boy you knew capable of that?"

"No." It was a single word, but it carried indescribable anguish, as though it had been torn from his soul. "No, the boy I knew could not have harmed anyone in this way. But Alexis is a boy no longer. And fame, it changes people."

"Does it? Does it really? Because I've heard that Alexei Bruskalov used to be pretty famous, too. Did your fame change you, then, to make you capable of the things they said you did?"

If his eyes had been hard before, they were sharp enough to cut, now. "You are impertinent, young lady."

I shook my head. "I am sorry if it seems so. I am not here to upset you. I am here for you, and I am here for Alexis."

He glared at me, but he didn't throw me out, so I pressed on. "Impertinence aside, what do you think? Did your fame change you? Should I be refusing to visit the home of a traitor?"

Alexei leaned forward. "They were wrong." Each word was clipped, precise.

"Of course they were! What I am trying to tell you is that they were wrong this time as well."

"No." He was looking out into the courtyard again. "This place, it is different."

I sighed. The birdbath he was staring at depicted a little girl, a toddler, with a watering can. "I know that you want this place to be different. For her. But people are the same everywhere."

He shook his head. "She needs me."

"So does Alexis. Do you realize you are shutting out the child you still have, for the one who has been gone for thirty years?"

Alexei looked at me, stricken. Tears brimmed in his eyes. "What do you suggest I do? I cannot give up on her. She is an innocent."

"So is Alexis. Look, I'll leave. I've upset you enough." I stood up from the couch. "But you asked what I would suggest. I would suggest looking for a way that doesn't require you to give up on either of your children."

I started back to the foyer, but froze when I heard him speak.

"Victoria never believed Alexis was guilty. My wife, she died believing in his innocence. Believing a lie. It kills me, knowing this."

"What if," I said, "it wasn't a lie?"

I let myself out of the house without looking back.

♫

I was in a terrible mood when I got back to my car. All I had done was make an old man cry. I hadn't fixed a damned thing.

And to top it all off, now I was late for the rehearsal I had promised only just that morning to attend.

I flopped down into the driver's seat of my car, thoroughly disgruntled. I started the car, buckled my seat belt, and backed out of the driveway, concentrating on hurrying to rehearsal to minimize the damage.

I very nearly dropped dead when a voice addressed me.

"Very nice. Now to your house, if you please."

I looked fearfully into the rearview mirror, and there was Dwight, looming behind the driver's seat.

Damn. How had I not checked the backseat before I got into the car? I *always* did that.

Well, evidently today I had not.

I pulled my foot off the accelerator and turned the car toward the side of the road, preparing to bail out and run away on foot.

A hand clamped in a crushing grip on the back of my neck dissuaded me from that course of action.

"Now, now, Chrispen--be a good girl and do as you are told. Let's not make this any harder than it has to be." I guided the car back out onto the road, and his grip loosened a little.

"Cell phone on the seat where I can see it, please."

I dug my cell phone out of my pocket and tossed it onto the passenger seat.

"There now," he said, "isn't that better? See how much nicer things are when we cooperate?"

I swallowed a sarcastic response to that, figuring it would only get my neck crushed. "Dwight, I--"

"Tsk, tsk. No talking, if you please. I would like your attention on the road. It would be most regrettable if you were to take us the wrong way. I might decide you were being deliberately uncooperative." He squeezed my neck.

Because I didn't want the bones in my neck ground to pulp, I shut my mouth and drove straight to my house. My mind raced the whole way, trying to figure some way out of this, but I pulled into the driveway with nothing.

He finally released me and we got out of the car. I rubbed the back of my neck, but it didn't help. "Dwight," I said, "what's going on?"

He laughed, and for a moment he sounded like a normal person. "I just want to talk to you." He took hold of my arm and led me into my house as if it was his.

I gaped at him. "You're telling me you kidnapped me to talk to me?"

He shrugged. "I have to, don't I? Alexis keeps you under lock and key all the time."

Then he turned around and locked the front door behind us, and the resemblance to a normal person disappeared.

I stood in the foyer, feeling lost and out of place. This was my house, but there was not a room I could go into that didn't have an unpleasant stalker memory associated with it.

And now Mr. Stalker himself was making himself comfortable on my couch, leaning back against one arm and propping his feet up on the other.

"Chrispen," he called, "come talk to me."

"Do I have to?"

"Don't be that way. We used to be friends, before you shacked up with a murderer."

I sat down in my armchair, keeping my eyes away from the blank spot on the wall, the mess on the floor. "I think you know Alexis is not a murderer."

Dwight studied my face a moment. "So tell me, why were you at Alexei's place today?"

I frowned--hadn't seen that one coming. "I don't see where it's any business of yours, but I was hoping to patch things up between Alexis and his father."

He chuckled. "Everything you do is my business. The sooner you figure that out, the happier we're all going to be." He leaned back, staring up at the ceiling. "So you must have had a pretty good pitch, right, to get old man Brooks to change his mind?"

"No." I edged carefully over toward the phone. "Mostly I

just spouted off a lot about how I felt about things. I don't think I shook his resolve at all." Slowly, keeping one eye on Dwight, I reached out my hand toward the phone.

"Be my guest," he said suddenly. "This house does not have phone service anymore." He produced a toothpick from his shirt pocket, threw the wrapper on my floor, and started picking his teeth, staring at the ceiling, supremely uninterested in what I was doing.

I blinked at him, too surprised to do anything else. When I regained my wits, I grabbed up the phone and pressed the talk button.

Nothing. I wondered how long ago Dwight had cut the lines. I replaced the handset, thinking of the only working phone I now possessed--my cell phone, laying on the seat of my car. It may as well have been on the moon.

"So what did you and Kolbi talk about today?" he asked. It seemed a very casual question, very out of the blue, but I was immediately suspicious. These questions seemed innocent, but he had gone to great lengths to be able to ask them. Whatever his reasons for asking, I felt certain that my best interest lay in telling him nothing at all.

"Oh, you know, this and that. Not much, really. We were planning to rehearse together, but then Alexei called."

"Rehearse together," he echoed, and tossed his toothpick on the floor beside the wrapper. "That seems odd. You aren't playing any pieces together."

I shrugged. "We're friends, Dwight. We practice together a lot."

"Hmm." He sat up suddenly. "I don't think I like that."

I sensed another irrational demand coming on. "You know, Dwight, part of our deal was that you were going to give me this evidence that would help me clear Alexis."

He looked wounded. "Do you doubt me?"

I knew better than to step into that trap. "Of course not. I'm just wondering what the time-frame looks like."

"Ah, yes. Well, that's the tricky part, isn't it? Your wrist looks healed enough that chances of you going to the police now seem pretty slim." He regarded me thoughtfully. "I had intended to give it to you now, here...but then you showed up wearing that damned ring again...so I think we will have to wait. But don't worry. I'll let you know."

He started to say more, but a slight sound from the front door caught his attention. In the sudden silence we both clearly heard it again. He stood up, frowning.

The front door flew open, and Kolbi and Alexis burst in.

"Chrispen!" Alexis's voice dripped with relief. "Are you all right?"

"I haven't done anything to your precious fiancée," Dwight said sourly.

Alexis regarded him stonily, the muscles in his jaw working silently. "If you have a shred of sense," he said, "you will see that it stays that way."

They stared at each other a moment, and the longer that moment went on, the tenser I got.

Kolbi pushed past Alexis, jamming a hairpin and an ID card into her pocket. "Chris!" she said brightly, defusing the situation. "Had a hunch we might find you here."

"Yes," Dwight said conversationally, "how did you get in here, anyway?"

"Lock-picking is a hobby of mine. Everyone knows that." Her tone was dismissive.

Dwight's expression said pretty clearly that he hadn't known that, any more than I had.

"Lock-picking?" I said. "That seems a peculiar hobby."

She shrugged. "Maybe. It's like those puzzle games everyone likes, only more interesting. And occasionally even useful," she said with a broad wink.

I glanced cautiously at Dwight, and scuttled over to Alexis. He put his arm around me, but never looked away from Dwight, as though Dwight was a spider he was thinking about stepping on.

The look in Dwight's eyes didn't bear much contemplation. It chilled me; it reminded me that Dwight hated Alexis and everything he stood for. If my dream was to be trusted and Dwight had murdered Madeleine, he had certainly done it for the reasons he gave her.

But he had also done it to destroy Alexis, and he had almost succeeded.

I pulled at Alexis, suddenly agitated. "Let's go. Please, Alexis, let's just get out of here."

His eyes were dark and fixed on Dwight. I couldn't claim to know just what he was thinking, but it was pretty clear to me that without intervention, this would not end well.

"Problem, Alexis?" Dwight said, jutting his chin out.

"Yes." Alexis's voice was dark, too, and cold. I would not have believed it was him, if I hadn't heard it myself. "There is a very big problem here."

"And you think you're the man to do something about it?" Dwight challenged. He took a step toward us, his chest stuck out, arms flexed at his sides, ready. "Bring it."

"Alexis," Kolbi said, "I don't think this is the best time or place for this."

She may as well have not spoken. Alexis didn't even seem to hear her.

I let go of Alexis and stepped around in front of him, standing up on my tiptoes to get right up in his face. "Alexis, this is ridiculous. Just leave it. He's not worth this."

"You're right." His voice sounded strained, though, and whatever was going on in his head was obviously not easy to walk away from.

He did, though, taking my hand in a firm grip and turning for the door.

"Good man, Alexis," Kolbi said, clapping him on the shoulder.

"Is that so?" Dwight taunted. "Is that the kind of man you are, Alexis? The kind that walks away from a fight?"

Alexis stopped, and turned around. I watched with unspeakable dread. Was that all it took to turn him? A couple of insults from a jerk like Dwight?

"If the fight is a pointless one with you, then yes, I am. But I tell you this, Dwight. If I find you have harmed Chrispen again, I will not walk away from you."

He turned his back on Dwight and walked out of the house with Kolbi and me.

"What, is that supposed to be a threat?" Dwight yelled after us.

Nobody bothered to answer him. But I knew what Alexis had said was not a threat.

It was a promise.

♫

By the time we dropped Kolbi off at her house and got back to Alexis's, it was getting late in the afternoon. We walked into the living room, and I was surprised how much it really did feel like coming home.

"Chrispen," Alexis said, turning suddenly to me, "have you had a chance to look through your things? Do you know if I packed you anything sort of nice?"

"I'm sure there's something. It can't all be baggy rehearsal sweats. Why?"

"We've had a dinner invitation," he said. Something about his tone was odd, like maybe he meant to say root canal instead of dinner. But he wouldn't tell me any more about it, not even who had invited us.

So I gave up pushing him and went back to get ready.

I found a pair of slacks and a dressy blouse and decided that it would have to do, since I knew next to nothing about where we were going.

Alexis was waiting for me in the living room, wearing a navy blue suit and fidgeting. I had seen him on television, doing performances around the world since he was sixteen years old-- and had been backstage with him for the last six months--and I had never seen him as nervous as he seemed right then.

I stared at him, unable to make myself believe what I was seeing. "Are you sure this is a good idea?"

"No." He couldn't quite look at me. "Are you ready?"

"Ready as I can be, I suppose."

Alexis took my arm and walked me out to the car, and held the door for me. He seemed stiff, and formal, and unusually quiet. It gave me a bad feeling about the evening.

The ride was uncomfortable, and nobody spoke a word. In the fading light I didn't recognize the route we took until we pulled up in front of the villa.

"We were invited to dinner--at your father's house?"

Alexis nodded. His lips were a tight thin line, and his knuckles on the steering wheel were white.

I reached over and put my hand on his shoulder. The muscles were tense and knotted under my fingers. "Alexis, you don't have to do this. We can turn around and go straight home if it will make you happier."

He laughed harshly. "Oh, yes, I do have to. Do you realize the message inviting us to dinner was the first time he has spoken to me in five years? Or to my machine, I guess. I gave up trying years ago. If there is a chance that he is trying now...well, I have to take it."

I shook my head. "You are very brave."

"Am I? Because I have to tell you I don't feel very brave right now. The last time I saw him he was protesting our performance with the symphony. What could this be about?"

I should have told him this was about my meddling, but I was afraid to. I didn't know if it would only upset him more. And I couldn't bear to think about what would happen if it really did go badly.

He took a deep breath. "Nothing to it but to do it, right?" He climbed out of the car, and came around to my side.

He held my hand tighter than usual as we walked up to the door.

"Would you rather," I said hesitantly, "that I not be here? I don't mind waiting out here in the car if it will make things easier on you."

"God, no," he said, tightening his grip on me. "I don't think I could do this at all if you weren't here with me." He gave me an odd, sidelong glance. "Besides, he did specifically invite you as well. By name. I'm surprised that he remembered, really."

For once I recognized an appropriate moment to keep my big mouth shut.

Alexis reached out and pushed the doorbell. We could hear deep chimes from somewhere in the house.

It felt like forever that we stood there. I wondered if Alexei was being cruel, or if he was as nervous as we were.

"Is this where you grew up?" I asked, quietly, as though someone might be listening.

Alexis nodded.

It was hard to imagine him as a little boy, running around this place. Before I had managed to get my mind around it, the door opened.

I almost laughed out loud, but thankfully managed a wan smile instead. Alexei was also wearing a navy blue suit. They stood there nervously regarding each other, and they looked almost like age-distorted reflections of the same man.

"Please, come in," Alexei said, standing aside for us.

I followed Alexis into the foyer. Alexei nodded at him. "Good--good evening." Before Alexis could even respond, Alexei turned to me. "Chrispen, I am so very pleased you could come." He grabbed me by the shoulders and kissed my cheek.

I was pretty taken aback at this unexpected welcome. And Alexis looked totally floored.

"Thank you, Mr. Brooks," I said, recovering myself as quickly as I could manage. "We're thrilled to be here."

"Please, call me Alexei. If you say Mr. Brooks, I always look around me for my son." He laughed at his own joke and led us into the dining room.

I looked questioningly at Alexis but he just shrugged helplessly, evidently as lost as I was. What could have happened to change him so radically from the man I had visited earlier?

The dining room table had been laid out with baked chicken and rice with vegetables. Alexei held a chair out for me, and for a moment we all sat at the table, awkwardly avoiding eye contact with any of the others.

"Eat," Alexei encouraged, passing me the plate of chicken. "Please."

"Thank you," I said, not sure what else to do.

We passed dishes around, and started eating in a silence that was pretty uncomfortable. My stomach felt too tight to put any food in, so I pushed things around on my plate and sipped at my tea and tried to give the impression of eating without actually ingesting any food.

I glanced across the table to see how Alexis was faring. I found him doing exactly the same thing I was.

Alexei sat at the head of the table with his hands folded in his lap. Evidently we were all too nervous to eat.

"I heard," Alexei said, "that the Bach Double was a great success."

Alexis was staring into his plate as though he would have liked to hide under it. I set my fork down a little more eagerly than I probably should have.

"Yes, it was a terrific performance. One of the great things about playing with Alexis is the way he can blend with a less talented soloist, like me, so you aren't completely embarrassed."

Alexei smiled wryly. "Less talented? I have heard that Darren has engaged you for the Mendelssohn Violin Concerto. You must be very capable."

I fidgeted with my napkin, embarrassed. "I manage well enough. The audience seemed to think so, at any rate. It is a shame you missed it."

To my surprise, he nodded. "Yes. Perhaps I can attend the Mendelssohn performance."

I heard Alexis's fork clatter onto his plate. "You would do that? You would come to--to that concert?" It was the first thing I had heard him say since we had entered the house.

Alexei didn't look at either of us, keeping his focus carefully on something in the middle of the table. "I understand it is a tribute concert," he said, as if that explained everything.

We sat for a moment that felt like hours in another awkward silence.

Alexei cleared his throat. "I understand," he said to me, "that you are rather new in town. Have you had any experience with our youth symphony?"

Apparently coming at you way out of left field was a Brooks family talent. "No--our principal second violinist mentioned it to me once, or I wouldn't even know it existed."

Alexei laughed. "Ah, Dwight Richards. Interesting you should mention him. Alexis was the concertmaster of the youth symphony all four years of high school, but during their senior year Mr. Richards took particular exception to it."

I could not for the life of me see where this was going. Alexis stared at his father in open horror, as though he had just awakened from a nightmare to find it was real.

"Is that so?" I said, looking from one to the other of them, trying to figure out what was going on.

"Yes. It seems that young Mr. Richards felt that Alexis only secured his position in the youth symphony through...more inappropriate positions with the woman conducting the group at the time."

Alexis covered his face with his hand and slumped down in his chair.

My eyes bugged out as his meaning sank in. "You're joking."

"No, no--I am quite serious. He raised quite a fuss. There was an investigation, it was in all the papers. The publicity, it was not so nice. People seemed inclined to believe this story."

I laughed. "Well, you have to admit it's easy to see the attraction. Who could blame her?"

"I did not sleep with her," Alexis said from under his hand.

"Chrispen knows that," Alexei said gently, and turned back to me. "I knew it, too. I can't tell you how many times I had to speak about it, to the police, to officials, to the press..."

"It really was bad," Alexis said, finally looking at me. "They would have kicked me out just to quiet the scandal. I would have been assumed guilty if that happened. I would have lost everything without his support."

"But I did support you," Alexei pointed out. "There are things as a parent you do that are right, and things you do that are wrong. That was one time I did it right."

Alexis stared at him. I held my breath. The suspense was almost painful.

"More recently, I have done it wrong. I am a foolish old man and I cannot go back and make things right. All I can say is that I am here for you now, if you still want a foolish old man for your father."

Alexis went to him and wrapped him in an embrace. There were tears on both of their faces, and I dabbed at my own eyes with my napkin. I felt like an intruder in the room, so I just stayed quiet and out of the way. I couldn't imagine a better resolution for them.

It seemed even better, given how much reason I'd had to consider my own mortality lately.

♬

Alexis drove us home in a kind of dazed euphoria. Neither of us spoke a word.

It was late and we were tired, so when we got back into the living room, I started to go straight on through to the bathroom to get ready for bed. Alexis's quiet voice behind me stopped me.

"Thank you, Chrispen."

I turned back around, surprised. "For what?"

He was standing in the entryway from the kitchen, leaning against the wall with his arms crossed, looking at me the way he might look at a mischievous child. "For tonight."

My guard instantly went up. I had hoped my hand in this might go undetected. Had Alexei said something? I walked back over to Alexis, watching him carefully. "What do you mean?"

"Don't you think it's strange, how my father greeted you as an old friend, when he had never actually met you?" He smiled crookedly at me. "Or how you immediately recognized his house, even though you had supposedly never been there?"

My shoulders slumped. "The jig is up, I guess. I'm sorry, Alexis. I wasn't trying to interfere, honestly--I just, my father died when I was in high school, and I couldn't bear to see--"

He reached out and put his hands on my shoulders. "Why on earth are you apologizing? First you gave me my life back, now you've given me my father back." He shook his head. "I honestly thought he would never speak to me again. What would I do without you?"

"I don't know," I said seriously, wrapping my arms around his neck and kissing him. "I hope you never find out."

"Me, too," he said. It reminded me of my danger, and gave me a chill.

Then he scooped me up and carried me into the bedroom, and I forgot all about danger and fear.

♫

Alexis and I arrived in the Green Room the next day to the sound of drunken shouting. I froze just inside the door, unable to quite believe what I was seeing was actually real.

Darren stood in the center of the room, his arms folded, his expression stony. Standing as close as he could get, bellowing right up into his face, was Dwight.

"...and I'd like to know just who the hell you think you are! Seven years I've been with this goddamned symphony, and you think you can kick me out because my bitch ex-girlfriend comes crying to you with a goddamned story? I swear I--"

"Mr. Richards," Darren said firmly, cutting across the shouting, "this drunken rampage is doing nothing to improve your situation. My mind is made up. The Board has made their decision. You have your papers. Now leave this building, or I will summon the police."

Dwight stared at him a moment, fists clenching in impotent fury. He finally spun around to leave, saw me standing there, and grabbed my shoulders, pushing me back into the wall.

"You! I swear if I find out you had anything to do with this, I will make you wish you hadn't! I will--"

"I say, unhand her!" Darren shouted.

Alexis stepped up next to me and shoved Dwight off of me.

"You stay away from her, Dwight. She did her best to protect you. You brought this on yourself."

Dwight pulled back to swing at Alexis, but Darren caught his arm. Alexis grabbed his other arm, and between the two of them they dragged the flailing, swearing Dwight to the door and threw him out.

I sank into a chair. What on earth had just happened? I wasn't totally sure. The only thing I knew for certain was that my situation had just gotten a lot worse.

"Are you all right, dear girl?" Darren was right at my shoulder, but I didn't remember him getting there. I was seriously freaking out.

"I'm fine," I said, and I almost sounded like I was. "Just a little shook up."

Darren patted my shoulder. "We may be a bit late starting. I'm going to go call the police and report that man's behavior." He hurried off to his office.

Alexis knelt down in front of me. "You sure you're okay?"

I nodded. "He wasn't trying to hurt me--not that time." I drew a shaky breath. "Alexis, what happened? What was that all about?"

He sighed. "Apparently after you left yesterday, Kolbi went to Darren and told him about how she found you and Dwight in the cellars." He frowned at me. "I thought you were with Kolbi, I had no idea. Darren called me yesterday and asked for the truth about your wrist. I'm afraid I failed you. When he asked me directly like that--and after Kolbi stuck her neck out to protect you--well, I told him the truth. He had an emergency meeting with the Board last night. They fired him effective immediately."

I buried my face in my hands. "Oh, I wish that hadn't happened."

"You aren't angry at me, are you?" He sounded worried.

"No, of course not. It's just not a good turn of events. He

wasn't supposed to get sacked."

Untethered from the symphony, without his job to force him to behave like a halfway civil human being, I feared Dwight would be even more dangerous. It wouldn't matter whether I had actually helped fire him or not, if he decided I had. My safety was dependent on the whim of a madman.

But then, that was about usual these days.

♫

I was packing up after rehearsal when I heard Kolbi's voice behind me.

"I'm sorry about earlier, Chris. I was hiding out until the drama passed--I didn't know it would leave you to catch the brunt of it."

I turned around to face her. "I don't think you have anything to apologize for."

"You'd be surprised," she said darkly. "Alexis mentioned that you seemed upset that Dwight was fired?"

I looked away, suddenly uncomfortable. "It's complicated."

"Complicated." She looked at me, but I was volunteering nothing. "Look, Chris, do you think we could talk for a few minutes?"

I hemmed and hawed. "I don't know, Kolbi--Alexis drove me here, you know, and he'll be ready to leave, and--"

Kolbi grabbed my arm and pulled me toward the back hall. "Alexis isn't going to leave without you. Leave your violin out here; he won't mind if I kidnap you for a little while."

I gave up. Another thing about Kolbi; when she got her mind set on something, she was impossible to refuse.

She dragged me into a rehearsal room, and closed the door behind us. Then she leaned back against it, like she thought I was going to make a run for it.

"Chris," she said, in a tone that clearly indicated she would take no nonsense, "there is something you are not telling me about this business with Dwight. What is it? What has he promised you?"

"What makes you think he has promised me anything?" I asked, honestly curious.

She shook her head. "I know Dwight. I know the games he plays, the way he operates. And I have all day to stand in front of this door if I need to."

I sighed. "I guess it isn't like you won't figure it out on your own anyway." I couldn't help glancing around the room like I thought Dwight might be hiding in the corner. "He says he can give me evidence to exonerate Alexis in Madeleine's murder. I know, I'm crazy for believing that. I guess I'm just desperate enough to believe anything."

"Hmm." She stood considering for a moment. I figured she was trying to think of a polite way to tell me I was a moron. "No, I think he may actually be telling you the truth about that."

"Really?" I sat down in a chair; I felt almost faint. I had been hoping so hard that Dwight was telling me the truth--all the while believing that he was stringing me along-- I can't describe what a relief it was to hear that. "You really think he has evidence?"

"I do. You know there was a gig that night, a private party. The place had a video security system, backed up to CD's. When the police did their investigation, the security CD from that night was missing. I've always felt Dwight has it."

"That's great!" Then I realized what she was saying, and I abruptly deflated. "But--even if he gave me that, all it would do is prove his alibi. All of the guests at the party already did that. How does that help Alexis?"

Kolbi sighed. "Chrispen, you are my best friend. I seriously hoped we would never have to have this conversation. But I can see it really can't be avoided. How much do you know about that party?"

"Next to nothing. Alexis told me Dwight had a gig that night, that he thought it was a party for some important people."

"That's all he said?" She shook her head. "That Alexis--too much of a gentleman to name names. Violinists don't play gigs completely solo, Chris. He had to have a pianist to back him."

"You?" I said. "You were there too? And Alexis knew that?" It fell into place like a puzzle piece. "So that's why he wanted me to talk to you. He thought you could talk some sense into me--ever since Dwight attacked me I've been convinced that he murdered Madeleine."

Kolbi buried her face in her hands. "Oh, Chrispen, you are going to hate me. But I think so, too."

I stared at her. "I don't understand. You were there with him while he played. How could you think...?"

She swallowed hard. "You have got to understand something. I met Dwight after Alexis and Madeleine left, and before they came back. At that time he was a different man. Honestly, Chris, you wouldn't recognize him. You really wouldn't. He was so happy and bright, and caring...and he really seemed to adore me. I was crazy in love with him, with the man he was then."

"I never knew that," I said, trying to imagine it. "Dwight mentioned you had dated, but I didn't realize..."

"Of course you didn't. Who would? He is so different now..." She lowered herself awkwardly into a chair, as though everything hurt. "After they came back, he seemed so different--angry, depressed. I was distraught, trying to figure out how to help him, how to get my Dwight back. I didn't know it then, but as soon as Madeleine returned, I became basically just someone he could use."

I stared at her, unblinking. The tension weighed on me like a physical force.

"I thought it was odd that he booked a gig on the same night as the benefit concert, but we got excused easily enough. And then things got really odd. Dwight asked me for a favor. It was a pretty big favor, he said, but it was really important."

She took a deep, shuddering breath. "He said he wanted to marry me. But first, he needed to go put things to rights with Madeleine--make his apologies for the way they had left things, get closure--so that he could move forward with me with a clear conscience."

"But--the party..." I said numbly.

A tear tracked down her face. "I was such a fool, Chrispen-- such a lovesick fool, I believed him. And it had to be done while Alexis was gone, do you see? They couldn't have that conversation while Alexis was there. It had to be during the fundraiser."

"But--the party," I whispered, clinging to it like a talisman.

She shook her head. "Some of these fancy parties-- they're odd. They want the live music, but they don't want to actually deal with musicians. We had to come in a separate entrance, and we played behind a screen so we couldn't be seen. I don't know if the screen was their idea or Dwight's. Dwight did play the first part. But at the last--I played a piano sonata or two, and then a CD Dwight had given me to play, of the Mendelssohn Violin Concerto. I didn't realize it until I played it at the party that night, that the CD was a recording from Alexis's senior recital. That's why he stole the security disc. The cadenza alone would prove it wasn't Dwight playing. The security video may even show me playing the CD, I don't know. At the time I had absolutely no idea what was going to happen."

"But afterwards--Kolbi, why didn't you go to the police when you realized what he had done?"

"I should have--I should have! But I went to Dwight first, praying the murder was somehow unrelated to him. He never denied it...he told me how she had reacted badly, become irrational--she charged him with a kitchen knife, he said. He claimed he had acted in self-defense. And he had already given his statement about the party to the police; if I contradicted him now and told them the truth, I would be an accomplice.

"I should have done it anyway, should have taken whatever consequences came of it. But I was alone and I was scared--and I told Dwight's story, and saved my own neck."

She hid her face in her hands, weeping. "There is no one more despicable than me. I sacrificed Alexis to save myself. For the last five years I have watched him suffer and wither, change and die--and I've had to watch it knowing that if I had been a stronger, better person when it mattered, things would have been different. If you hate me I will understand. You can't hate me more than I hate myself."

"I don't hate you," I said, and I found that it was true. "You were used, Kolbi--you never signed on for this. The despicable one is the one who used you, who manipulated you, and who made everyone else suffer for his crime. And that is the person I have to bring down, now that I know the evidence is real."

She shook her head, wiping at her eyes. "I know what he promised, but he will never surrender that CD to you. The only way you will ever get it from him is to steal it."

My shoulders slumped. "That would have been easier before he was fired. At least then I could count on him being gone for symphony rehearsals. I'll figure something out, though. I have to."

She put her hand on my shoulder, and I looked at her in surprise. "It should be a bit easier with a best friend who picks locks."

"Are you sure you want to get involved in this?"

"Chris, whether I like it or not, I'm already involved up to my eyeballs. I've turned an innocent man's life into pure hell, from my own ignorance and fear. If Dwight catches you looking for that CD, I think he will kill you. And I can't let that happen to Alexis again."

I sighed. "Maybe we should turn him in to the police for everything he's done. They could arrest him, and we could search his apartment without worrying."

She shook her head. "It's too risky. As soon as there was any sign of trouble, he would destroy that disc."

"You're right. He's already threatened just that. What on earth are we going to do?"

"I can get in and toss the place. But he has to be away from the apartment. Is that something you can do?"

"I think so. After today, I think I even have the perfect excuse."

"I guess the only question, then, is when." She sounded like she dreaded this every bit as much as I did. "Can you think of a reason to wait?"

I shook my head. "Unfortunately I can't. The more time I have to consider it, the more time I have to lose my nerve. If I have to do something like this, then the sooner, the better."

Kolbi nodded. "I hear you. This evening, then. Before either of us can change our mind. I'll pick you up. You'll be at Alexis's?"

I nodded bleakly. "Yes. Are you sure this is a good idea?"

"No. But it's all we have. You need to clear Alexis, and I need to redeem myself. What other choice do we have?"

She was right, of course. And yet I couldn't shake a bad feeling about the whole thing. With any luck, I figured the bad feeling would fade by evening.

But then, it seemed luck had not been on my side for quite awhile.

♫

I was on pins and needles all afternoon. I should have been setting up some kind of story with Alexis so I wouldn't be leaving out of the blue, but I discovered I couldn't even bear to think about it, much less lie to Alexis about it. I fidgeted around in the living room until it started to get dark outside, and my anxiety suddenly got the best of me. I went to the guest room to hide and pretend this wasn't really going to happen.

I was huddling in the window seat, wrestling with an urge to hide under the bed, when there was a tap on the door, and Alexis came in.

"Chrispen, Kolbi is here for you."

I looked up at him in sudden, abject fear. "She is?"

"Yes. She said something about picking you up for a girls night out."

"That's right." I forced myself up from the window seat, and gathered my purse with fingers that were suddenly clumsy and numb. "I should have told you before--we talked about that at rehearsal today." I tried to sound casual about it.

He folded his arms and leaned against the door jamb, effectively blocking the doorway. "Did you, now?"

"Yes." I looked around the room a couple of times for my sweater before realizing I had it in my hand. "We thought it might be nice to get away for awhile, you know...what?"

Skepticism was evident in his expression before he spoke a word. "Chrispen, you are a terrible liar. What is going on?"

"I told you," I said, but I couldn't look at him. "I'm going out with Kolbi for awhile, no big deal. Are you going to let me out of here?"

"I don't know," he said seriously, standing straight and putting his hands on my shoulders. "I've never seen you so flustered. Whatever this is, it isn't 'no big deal.' What are you two up to?"

His eyes bored into me; I had to look away. "I'm sorry. I can't tell you any more."

"This is dangerous, isn't it? You two have cooked up some scheme, and you're going to wind up getting hurt."

"No. Alexis, I promise you we aren't taking any risks we don't absolutely have to take. Will that do?"

He ran a hand through his hair, agitated. "Not really. But I don't really have any choice, unless I want to try locking you up as though you don't have the right to make your own choices. Just please--whatever you're planning, be careful."

"I will." I stood up on my tiptoes and kissed him, and for a moment I forgot that I was supposed to be leaving.

"Promise?" he whispered, looking anxiously into my eyes.

"Promise." I scooted past him and met Kolbi in the foyer. She grabbed my arm and hauled me outside to her car.

"What's the matter?" she demanded, buckling in. "Alexis suspects something, doesn't he?"

"How could you tell?"

"You have tears in your eyes. Ach, I should have expected this. You are a terrible liar."

"That's what he said." I dabbed at the tears on my face.

"I bet he did." She shook her head. "This complicates things." She backed the car out of the driveway.

"Complicates things? How?"

"You may not have noticed, but Alexis is not the type to stand idly by if he thinks you are in trouble. However much time we thought we had for this, I think we have less now."

"Maybe we shouldn't try this at all," I said. "How can we possibly get away with it?"

"We might not," she said, and I looked at her in sudden shock. "Chris, it's possible I might not make it out of this. Whatever happens, you get yourself out of there, back to Alexis. I can't undo the damage I've done to him. All I can do is try to make some small part of it better." She glanced at me. "But I can't make you go with me. I don't even have the right to ask. Do you want out?"

"No," I said immediately. "If this is the only way to help

Alexis, I am in."

She sighed. "This is all going to work out. You'll see."

I tried to believe her, I really did. But before I quite managed it, we were pulling into the parking lot of Dwight's apartment building. I stared at it in a kind of terror. I thought I might start hyperventilating.

Kolbi seemed to think so too. "You are going to do fine. This is going to be easier than you think, you'll see. Dwight isn't expecting anything like this--he thinks he has got you caged pretty well with his blackmail. He has no idea you know what his evidence is. And he certainly expects that I will take my story with me to my grave." She reached over and patted my shoulder. "All you have to do is get him away from the apartment. After that, it's all me. Easy peasy."

"Easy peasy," I repeated. I let myself out of the car and started the walk towards Dwight's apartment. It felt like a bad dream.

Before I was ready I was standing at the door, with no real recollection of how I had gotten there. I raised my hand to knock, then hesitated. Had I already done that? I couldn't remember.

The door opened while I was still trying to decide, and there was Dwight.

"Well, hello, Chris. This is unexpected." He glanced at my raised fist, then back at my face. "Are you going to hit me?"

"What?" I looked at my own hand, and blushed, putting it away. "No, no, of course not. I couldn't remember whether I had knocked or not."

"Couldn't remember?" He frowned, leaning against the door. "Are you all right? Do you need to come in and sit down?"

"No!" All the color left my face in a rush, and I took a reflexive step backward. "I mean--that is, I was hoping we could go for a walk."

"A...walk? You want to go for a walk--with me?" He was

looking at me as if I were raving. Maybe I was. I felt sort of feverish with nerves, and I wasn't making a lot of sense even to myself.

"Yes. Yes, I--want to talk to you, Dwight, and--and I thought maybe...maybe it would be easier for me if we walked."

He stared at me a moment like he expected the hidden cameras to jump out. "Well--sure, Chris, whatever you say."

He locked up the apartment, then took my hand and together we walked down the stairs, and out onto the sidewalk. There was a city park maybe half a block away, so we headed that way.

"What was it you wanted to talk to me about?" he asked, and he sounded for a moment like the Dwight I had thought I knew before Evil Dwight turned my world upside down.

My hand was cold and clammy in his from nerves; I hoped he wouldn't notice but it seemed impossible to miss. "I wanted to apologize," I said, "about earlier."

"I do like a woman who knows when to apologize," he said, in a tone that made my skin crawl.

I tried to smile, like I thought that was a joke. "I didn't have anything to do with that. I tried my best to keep them from firing you."

"Is that so?" he asked, but he sounded distracted. We had made it into the park. The rustling of trees in the night air surrounded us.

"Oh, yes," I said with feeling, trying to keep his attention. "Alexis said the same thing. Would we lie to you?"

I had his complete attention now, and I wasn't sure I wanted it anymore. "I think he would, yes. I think you would too, in the right circumstances."

"The right circumstances?" I wasn't sure what to do; this conversation suddenly felt dangerous.

"Sure." He let go of my hand and turned to face me. "That's what this is, isn't it--this unexpected late visit, this sudden need for a walk, this fake apology--just setting up the right circumstances?"

I stared at him, suddenly afraid. "No, Dwight, of course not. I--"

He hit me then, right across the face. My nose made an odd crunching sound, and my lip split open against my teeth. I fell to my hands and knees in the grass. When I touched my nose my hand came away bloody, but I didn't think it was broken.

"How dare you lie to me!" he shouted.

My ears were ringing; it made him sound tinny somehow, distorted. "Dwight," I gasped, desperate. "I'm not lying to you!"

He swung his leg out, kicking me in the stomach, and I fell flat on the ground. I couldn't cry out, for a moment I couldn't even breathe.

"You are still lying to me! Do you think I am stupid? Do you think I don't know why Kolbi wanted to talk to you, what she has told you? Do you think I have any intention of letting you get away with this?" He leaned over and pulled my head up out of the grass by my hair to look at him. "I'll see you dead first. Do you hear me? I'll see you *dead!*"

In the sudden quiet we both heard a new sound--the ringing of my cell phone. Dwight dug it out of my purse, dropping my face back into the dirt.

"It's Alexis," he said coldly, tossing the phone down by my head. "I do not need to deal with him right now. You are going to take that call, and you are going to convince him that everything is fine, so that he will not come looking for you. If you do anything else, I will strangle you right here and he can listen to you die. Do you understand?"

"Yes," I gasped.

Somehow I managed to get the phone to my ear. "Hello, Alexis."

There was a short pause. "My God, Chrispen, you sound

terrible. Are you okay?"

"Sure," I said, "I'm fine."

"You don't sound fine. You sound awful. Has something happened?"

"Always so sure of things," I said, trying desperately to think of some way to say what I could not say. "It's been ages since I fell down the stairs. You worry too much."

"Fell down the...Chrispen, is Dwight there? Is that what you are trying to tell me?"

I tried to laugh. "Yes," I said, "not far at all."

He swore. "Are you in danger?"

"Sure. Absolutely. Like I told you, nothing to worry about." I paused, aware of Dwight watching me intently. "Right. I'll see you later then. I love you, Alexis."

"Chrispen, wait--"

I hung up the phone before Dwight could get any more suspicious. "Was that okay?"

"Very nice." He scooped my cell phone out of my hand, smashed it against a tree trunk, and stomped it into the ground. I watched in growing horror, thinking of Alexis trying in vain to reach me after that last incomprehensible phone call.

Well, if I had to choose my last words to him, "I love you, Alexis" summed it up pretty well.

"What are you going to do with me?" I wasn't sure I really wanted to know the answer.

"Hmm. That's a good question." He grabbed my arm and dragged me to my feet. "I don't think this weird little game of yours is about me at all. Isn't that right, Chris? Your lock-picking best friend is back at my place right now, isn't she?"

I looked at him in sudden fear, and hesitated a second too long. "No."

He shook me roughly. Blood from my face dripped onto my clothes, and now that I was sort of upright, onto my tennis shoes as well. "You are still lying to me! Do you think I am stupid?"

"Of course not, Dwight. I know you aren't stupid."

He laughed a truly demented laugh. "You know it now. I'm not going to do anything about you right now. You're in no shape to interfere, and I've got a meddling ex- girlfriend to deal with. I'll come back for you later. And when I do, remember this..." He leaned very close to my ear. "Never lie to me again!"

He let go of me suddenly, pulled back his fist and swung, right at my face.

A flash of light exploded in my brain and I fell over into the blackness.

♪

I woke up crumpled on the grass in the city park, stiff and sore from one end to the other. I had no idea how much time had passed.

But Dwight had left me to go after Kolbi, and I couldn't even call to warn her.

All I wanted was to curl up there on the ground and never move again. Instead I pushed myself onto my hands and knees, and lurched to my feet. I would never have believed it could hurt so much just to stand. I swayed unsteadily, and spit out a gob of something I dared not look at too closely.

I staggered a few steps toward the road, and my balance finally started to return. I found I was walking instead of staggering, then running instead of walking.

I was running, running as fast as I could, running for my life-- and for someone else's. Someone who had suffered enough, someone I had to save. Cold sweat pasted my clothes to me, my face and hair were caked in my own blood, and my feet screamed in painful protest. How had things gone so wrong? Kolbi had been so confident, had made so much sense. How had we screwed up so badly? My throat made ragged choking sounds as I struggled to pull in air.

But I knew it didn't matter. It didn't matter how hard I ran. If I had been out for even five minutes, I knew I was too late.

A building loomed up ahead, a brick building with climbing ivy, a building I had to get inside.

A building I'd vowed never to enter again. But that seemed like another lifetime now.

It was so close, and yet so impossibly far away. Still, it was in sight. I felt a doomed hope rush through me, and I did what I would have sworn couldn't be done--I ran even faster.

It couldn't be done, I knew that. We had miscalculated, and badly, and no power on earth could stop him now.

I was holding nothing back now, my muscles working so frantically there was no time for pain. One of my blood- spattered canvas tennis shoes worked itself completely off my foot on the stairs. I didn't slow down, didn't really notice. Once I had lied about falling down these stairs. If I missed a step and fell down them now, would it hurt as bad as the tension, the hopeless dread gripping me now? I didn't see how it could.

My attention was fixed on the third-floor landing, coming into view. Just around the corner now...I had to go faster...

I heard a woman scream, but I couldn't have told you if it was me or her. Had Madeleine screamed like that, the way I remembered screaming in my dream? Did he also think of Madeleine now? Did he even care?

The door was cracked open. But even as I pushed it open, I knew it was too late; even as I first saw her lying bleeding on the living room floor I knew I couldn't save her.

I fell on my knees beside her, crying hot tears. I fumbled for her hand. Her cell phone lay open on the floor beside her, but it was too late, even I could see that.

"Chrispen," she breathed, and she sounded so very, very weak. "Take these." She pressed a snub-nosed pistol and a key into my hand. "One to save you, one to save Alexis. I was...too slow."

"No, no, no," I whispered, a desperate, hopeless plea, "please don't die, you can't die!"

She turned her head in my direction and with her last breath managed to gasp a single word.

A name.

"Alexis," she gasped, and her mouth formed the words "forgive me," but no sound came.

Kolbi was gone. I stared at her body in shock and horror, unable to accept it. She was gone. I couldn't save her.

And then I heard the footsteps, and I knew I couldn't save myself. I had the little pistol in my hand--I hoped I would be able to use it.

I scrambled awkwardly around on my knees and there he was behind me, growing steadily closer, demented and spattered with my blood and Kolbi's.

"You aren't going to shoot me," he said. "Kolbi thought she would, too. But the only person that gun has killed is her."

I stared at him, frozen in horror, unable to will myself to move. Dwight was an apparition out of hell, and it looked like he was right.

He was wearing leather driving gloves.

The gun jumped in my hands before I consciously formed the intent to fire it. He looked at me, confused, astonished, as red blossomed and spread across the middle of the shirt.

It was too late, though, he was already on me. When he fell, he fell forward on to me, pushing me onto my back, his hands closing around my throat.

So this was it, then--this was how the story would end; Dwight would strangle me and bleed to death, and we would die together in this twisted embrace while I clawed ineffectually at his shoulders. "You will never have Madeleine," he panted. "She sings only for me!"

My lungs screamed for air, my muscles grew weak, and my vision dimmed.

All at once the pressure was gone. Kind arms helped me to sit up while I choked and gasped for air.

"Chrispen! Chrispen--my God, Chrispen, are you all right?"

The voice was Alexis's. I scrubbed at my eyes, and my fuzzy vision cleared enough to see him. "I will be." My voice was rough and hoarse, and talking made me cough. "I'm sorry, Alexis. You were right, we were stupid. He--he killed Kolbi..." I trailed off into disconsolate sobs.

"Shh," he said, pulling me to him, heedless of the gore all over me. For a long moment I could do nothing but cry.

"Alexis, help me up," I finally said. "I don't think I can stand on my own."

He looked at me like I had just asked him to hold my hand while I walked to the moon. "I don't know if that's such a good idea. You look like you're hurt pretty badly."

I looked down at my shirt. "Most of this isn't mine. This is important, Alexis--something Dwight said..."

Alexis took my hands and helped me carefully to my feet. "Just be careful. You look like you've had the devil beaten out of you."

"I sort of have," I said, and shuddered, which hurt more than it should have. "I need to find where he keeps his violins."

"Violins? I thought he only had the one."

I shook my head. "Just a hunch."

We found the familiar modern suspension case sitting on an armchair in the bedroom. But on the dresser--on the dresser was an old-style alligator violin case that I had not seen in almost twenty years.

I sank down on the bed, running my fingers across the case. "I don't believe it."

Alexis looked from the case to me. "You know this instrument?"

I flipped the latch and opened the case. "Did I ever tell you my grandmother's name?"

He shook his head. I lifted the violin from its case and placed it delicately in his hands.

"Her name was Madeleine. And this violin was custom made for her."

He turned the violin over, and we both clearly saw the design etched into the back.

MADELEINE

"Someone care to me tell what's going on here?"

The voice from the doorway startled us both. "Officer Parker," I said with feeling, "thank God you are here. There's been a murder--"

"I gathered that," he said dryly. "We got a 911 call from a Kolbi Edwards. That her?"

I nodded, but couldn't get any words past the sudden lump in my throat. I took the violin from Alexis and turned back to the case.

"The homicide team will be here shortly. I'm going to have to ask you to stay here until they arrive." Officer Parker stepped up behind me. "That yours?"

"It was supposed to be," I sighed. "My grandmother willed it to me."

He reached around me and pulled out a folded packet of paper that had been tucked into the lid of the case. He scanned over it, and frowned. "Your grandmother Madeleine Evans?"

I nodded.

"Well according to this it is yours," he said, handing me a notarized copy of the will my grandmother had apparently stored with the violin. "You don't want to leave it here. This is a crime scene."

I laid the violin back in the case, and my fingers brushed against something hard in the bottom.

The lining had been carefully slit, and hidden inside was a single CD in a paper envelope. When I opened the envelope, dozens of tiny pictures of my head, clipped from photographs, fell out.

Well, now I knew what he had done with them. I had to admit it was disturbing, though. I looked at the CD. It was hand labeled "Security" and had a date on it.

"What have you got there?" I could hear the frown in Officer Parker's voice even before I turned to face him.

"A security recording, I think," I said, handing it to him. "Kolbi told me she thought Dwight had hidden it."

"Did she." He turned the disc over in his hands, looking at it as if it might be venomous.

"Yes. She gave me this key, too." I handed him the little flat key.

"Did she tell you what the key is for?"

"No. She told me it would save Alexis. That sounds like your department to me."

Officer Parker gave me a sharp, penetrating look. "Miss Marnett, it sounds to me as though everything that happened tonight should have been my department."

"I'll second that," Alexis put in.

I sighed. "You're right, both of you. All I can say is that our intentions were good."

Officer Parker shook his head. "Come with me, you two. We need to get your depositions for the homicide team. It's time to piece together what happened here."

Between the pictures, the depositions, the recorded

statements, the bagging and labeling of evidence, the chalk line forms and the fingerprint dust, the night melted into a hellish blur that felt like it would never end.

When we weren't needed Alexis and I waited in the bedroom. When they weren't talking to one of us, they usually were talking to the other, so we didn't see each other much.

I sat on the bed at one such break, numb inside and out. I was so completely exhausted I was actually dozing off, even with all that was going on, when Officer Parker came into the room. I sat up suddenly straight, and he gave me a wry smile.

"I thought you would like to know that we are almost finished with you," he said.

"That's a relief. I never realized how much goes on with this type of thing."

He didn't respond to that. He leaned back against the door, crossing his arms. "I want you to know that we could arrest you, Miss Marnett."

I stared at him in horror. "But I only shot him because he was trying to kill me!"

Officer Parker shook his head. "That isn't what I'm talking about. Miss Edwards entered this domicile illegally. You knew about this--you distracted Mr. Richards to allow her time in which to accomplish this, correct?"

My shoulders slumped. "Yes. That's right."

"I see you understand what it means to be an accessory to a crime." He watched me squirm a moment, letting that sink in. "I think in this case you don't have much to worry about, though. The D.A. isn't likely to want to push this one."

"Isn't likely?" I echoed. "How much not likely?"

He chuckled. "Very much not likely. I just got off the phone with him. Unless our investigation turns up something you aren't telling us, when you leave this building, you are done with this case."

"Thank God," I breathed.

"I did try to warn you. This is exactly why police work should be left to the police."

I bowed my head. "I know."

"From the look of you, though, I'd say you have been punished enough. Go round up your fiancé and get out of here."

"Thank you," I said. As I passed him in the doorway, I paused. "You'll let me know what comes of the CD and the key?"

He nodded. "I'll check them out as soon as I can. Now you'd better get home and get cleaned up. Get some rest."

"Yes, sir." An order like that, I could obey.

It was early in the morning when Alexis and I left the apartment. I had my grandmother's violin over my shoulder, and I held onto Alexis's hand like it was a lifeline.

"I don't understand," Alexis said. "She did this--she chose to do this, knowing this might happen. Why?"

It hurt just to talk about Kolbi. "Guilt, Alexis. She never forgave herself for her part in Madeleine's murder, even though it was unknowing and unwilling. She wanted to redeem herself. She begged for your forgiveness with her last breath."

He shook his head. "I hope she knows she has it."

"Me, too." I stared up at the stars, feeling lost and adrift. "I don't know what we'll do without her."

"Remember her," he said simply. "Don't ever forget." He gazed up at the sky with me and together we remembered the ones we would never forget.

FINALE

A hot shower and a two-hour nap made me feel more human. I would have liked to have slept longer, but the dreams were too disturbing.

I awoke to the sound of the Warsaw Concerto from the music room across the hall. Last time I had heard that piece, Kolbi had played it. It didn't feel like it could be real. I listened to the familiar melody and fresh tears welled up in my eyes.

I got up and wandered across the hall, feeling like a helpless observer in my own body. I never made the decision to go into the music room, it just sort of happened, like someone else was at the wheel. I was just along for the ride.

I did not decide to sit down on the piano bench next to Alexis, either, but the next thing I knew I was sitting there, probably right in his way, watching him play while my tears fell in my lap.

"I didn't know you were awake," he said, continuing to play. "Feel better?"

I nodded. "What are you doing?"

He looked at me sidelong. "Last time I checked, I was playing the Warsaw Concerto."

I tried to laugh, but it came out more as a strangled sob. "Yes, I can tell that much. Why?"

He stopped, and turned to face me. "I spoke with Darren this morning. I'm going to play this tonight."

"At the tribute concert?" My brain was not at its quickest.

"Well, yes. It will be my tribute, do you see? To her."

I nodded. I didn't trust myself to speak right then. The doorbell rang into the sudden silence, startling us both. Not sure what else to do, I followed Alexis to the front door.

Officer Parker stood there, holding some papers and shifting his weight nervously from foot to foot. "Good morning, Mr. Brooks, Miss Marnett. May I come in?"

"Certainly." Alexis stood aside for him and looked questioningly to me, but I just shrugged, as lost as he was.

Alexis led us both into the living room. I sat on the couch next to him. Officer Parker seemed too uncomfortable to sit, and stood in front of us, shuffling through the few pages.

"I followed up on your CD this morning," he told me, "and the key Miss Edwards gave you."

I sat up straight. "And?"

Alexis reached over and took my hand. I could feel it shaking in his grasp; this was where we discovered if everything we had done had been for nothing. If Kolbi had died for nothing.

"And I don't know quite how to say it," Officer Parker said, "but Mr. Brooks, I feel this police department owes you a huge apology, and I would like to be the first to offer it to you."

We stared at him, both of us hardly daring to believe what we were hearing.

"The key fit a drawer in Miss Edwards's desk. She had left a letter there, detailing her account of the murder of Madeleine

Brooks. The CD that you found is the missing security video from that night, and it does back up the account she provided." He shook his head. "With this new data, the only conclusion we can draw is that Dwight Richards committed the murder. You, Mr. Brooks, have been officially cleared in this matter."

"Officially cleared," I echoed. They seemed to me like the two most beautiful words I had ever heard. Alexis turned to me and caught me up in a bear hug.

"Yes," Officer Parker said. "The department will be holding a press conference in a couple of hours to announce this. Would you like to attend?"

"Absolutely." We both said the word at the same time.

I discovered that carefully applied makeup--heavily applied, in places--could pretty much conceal the damage to my face. And a wide elastic bandage wrapped stoutly around my bruised ribs made it much less painful to move. I stood by Alexis on the conference room dais while the Newton Police Department announced to the world his innocence. Cameras rolled, and flashbulbs popped, and both of us had tears on our faces by the time it was over.

I spent the rest of the afternoon in the grip of the worst stage fright I had ever had. I couldn't keep anything down, and I couldn't stop shaking.

"I think," I told Alexis seriously, "that I am dying."

He smiled at me and shook his head. "You are only dying of anticipation. You'll see. When you get out onstage, you'll be fine."

I groaned. "Promise?"

Alexis laughed and kissed the top of my head. "Promise."

Of course he was right. As soon as I stepped out on the stage in front of the packed house, my physical distress was a distant memory. I carried my grandmother's violin to play the Mendelssohn Violin Concerto.

The first movement of the Mendelssohn is haunting, angsty,

full of drama. I certainly had plenty to draw from for that. The second movement--well, I didn't play the piano, so the second movement was my own personal tribute to my best friend. It is usually quietly, peacefully melancholy, but mine had an anguished sadness I had never played in it before.

But the third movement--the rollicking, exuberant third movement--embodied best the dominant emotion of the evening: joy. I could have played all night and never run short of joy to put into the Mendelssohn's happy ending.

Alexis caught me up and spun me around as I exited the stage. "That was unbelievable," he told me.

I grinned at him, high on a performer's rush. "Happy birthday."

He kissed me until I thought he would miss his entrance. "Best birthday present ever."

Immediately after the Mendelssohn came the Warsaw Concerto. While the stage crew moved the grand piano into position, Alexis stepped to the front of the stage in his tuxedo to address the audience.

"I know many of you came here tonight expecting to hear the Warsaw Concerto for piano played by Kolbi Edwards. It is my sad duty to inform you all that Kolbi passed away last night. Tonight I shall perform the Warsaw Concerto for you in honor of our friend Kolbi. She will not be forgotten."

No one could have surpassed the Warsaw Concerto Alexis played that night, in honor of the one who had given her life to give him back his. The orchestra got caught up in it with him, and together we gave a performance I have never heard equaled.

It was only a few short weeks later that Alexei walked with me out of the living room down a flower-lined path in the backyard, to the small ceremony Alexis and I had arranged in front of the garden, where I officially became Mrs. Alexis Brooks.

"Do you, Alexis," said the minister, "take this woman, to be your lawfully wedded wife, to have and to hold from this day forward, for better or for worse, for richer, for poorer, in sickness and in health, to love and to cherish, forsaking all others, till death do you part?"

"I do." Tears brimmed in Alexis's eyes as he looked at me.

"And do you, Chrispen, take this man to be your lawfully wedded husband, to have and to hold from this day forward, for better or worse, for richer, for poorer, in sickness and in health, to love and to cherish, forsaking all others, till death do you part?"

"I do," I said, aware of the tears in my own eyes. "From here to forever."

"From here to forever," Alexis echoed.

"Then by the power vested in me, I now pronounce you husband and wife. You may kiss the bride."

And he did.

An Excerpt from The Lost Concerto, Book Two in the Alexis Brooks Series

RITORNELLO:
The Nightmare

The dream started with a scream.

"He's got that poor girl! Somebody stop him!"

I reached into my purse and hauled out a silenced pistol, running out into the street, taking as careful aim as I could manage under the circumstances.

Snick, snick--two silenced shots in quick successions.

"It's just another day at the firing range," I muttered to myself.

--snick, snick--

"--just another few targets down at the range--"

--snick, snick--

"--just a group of targets that happen to be spinning, and moving away from you, and in uncomfortably close proximity to people." I lowered the pistol and wiped the sweat from my forehead.

Six shots fired, four tires blown out, no casualties. The car screeched and swerved to an undignified halt, sideways in the street like a toy car tossed aside by a giant child.

The back door flew open and a man came charging out, brandishing a weapon and cursing so quickly it was impossible to pick out individual words.

"You just cannot stop interfering, can you, woman? You could have left well enough alone and lived, but no--you keep making yourself a thorn in my side! No more, do you hear me? No more!"

He raised that big gun.

I was numb with fear, I couldn't feel my hands or my feet-- but I understood what I had to do. I pulled the pistol up and lined the sights up with that hateful, horrible man, squeezed the trigger--

--and heard the hollow click of an empty cartridge. I was out, and I was dead.

MOVEMENT ONE:
History Repeats

The first time I saw the Zwickauer Mulde, I wondered how it would feel to throw myself into a river like that one.

I suppose I should have accepted that as an omen, and demanded that we fly back to America that instant.

Instead I shrugged it off and turned away from the passenger-side window of the rented Mercedes. Jet lag could do strange things to a person. The midnight drive to the Dayton airport...the layover in Chicago...the seemingly endless flight to Leipzig...Alexis and I hadn't slept properly for far too long.

He glanced at me, then back at the road. "Are you okay over there?"

I smiled, but it felt kind of weak. "Didn't Robert Schumann

throw himself into this river?"

"No. That was the Rhine. He was born in Zwickau, remember?"

I nodded. I really *was* jet-lagged if I had forgotten that. Schumann's birth in 1810 in this town was the whole reason we were here, after all. One week from today--June eighth, Schumann's birthday, and coincidentally our first wedding anniversary--the Philharmoniker Zwickauer would have a special concert. In celebration of the one-hundredth anniversary of the great composer's birth, they had contracted Alexis to perform Schumann's Violin Concerto in D minor with them. The concert had been sold out for weeks.

I was along for the ride, but I didn't seem to be enjoying it very much. This was my very first trip outside the United States, and I had been impossible to live with for months, crazy with excitement.

And yet, since we had arrived in Germany, a pall had fallen over my mood. I was gripped by a peculiar melancholy, filled with an unspeakable dread. I wasn't afraid that something bad was going to happen.

I was certain of it.

"You aren't still thinking about that crazy phone call, are you?" Alexis's tone was deliberately, falsely light.

I glanced at him, then quickly turned back to the window. "No. No, of course not."

Of course I was, and he was, too, whether either of us would admit it or not.

"It didn't mean anything, you know," he said conversationally.

"I know."

"It was just a prank, or she was a couple sandwiches short of a picnic."

"I know," I repeated.

She hadn't sounded like a joker, though, and she hadn't

sounded crazy. She had sounded perfectly sincere, and she had begged us not to go to Germany. Alexis had answered the call, and what he'd heard upset him enough that he signaled me to pick up the extension.

"You could have your choice of venue, Mr. Brooks, any where in the world. Please, do not go to Germany. Not now. I beg this of you. Nothing good will come of this trip."

The voice was utterly unfamiliar. The woman had given no name. Caller information had been blocked.

There was not a single rational reason to take her seriously, or to give any thought to anything she said. At least, that was what I kept telling myself, pushing aside the memory of that dream. I mean, it was just a crazy dream. Right?

And yet, I couldn't seem to get that phone call out of my head.

Nothing good will come of this trip.

Maybe I could have better ignored it if I hadn't secretly agreed.

Enjoyed this excerpt? Look the *The Lost Concerto,* available now at Amazon, Barnes & Noble, iTunes, and many others!

Frequently Asked Questions

What do the chapter labels mean?

> The chapter labels are all music terms that fit the part of the book they are used for. A concerto is usually a solo piece for a single instrument, backed by an orchestra, although there are concertos for groups of instruments. If you're interested in these, check out the Bach Concerto for Two Violins, the Bach Brandenburg Concertos 1-6, and Concerti Grossi by any number of composers. Usually, a concerto will have three movements, which are the individual pieces that make up the whole concerto. There
> is usually a distinct break between the movements. As you can probably guess, Movements One, Two, and Three in the book are named for these.
>
> A concerto usually, but not always, includes an introduction at the beginning of the first movement, where the orchestra plays but the soloist does not. This is called a ritornello.
>
> Sometimes it is very short, sometimes quite long. The introduction to this book is named Ritornello after this.
>
> And finale...well, that one is probably self- explanatory. :)

Do orchestras really do deep-dive rehearsals?

> As you can imagine, not all orchestras rehearse the same way. But I have been with at least one student and one professional symphony who did do deep-dive rehearsals,

although none of

them used that term.

Is Alexis Brooks based on any real violinist?

Unfortunately, no.

Is Chrispen Marnett based on you?

Only inasmuch as we are both female, and we both play the violin. Past that, though—I never went to Juilliard, I don't play fulltime, and I hate iced tea. Next?

Is it true classical music is in crisis? What can I do?

Yes, it is undoubtedly true. The best way to help is to support it. Attend concerts, support the arts in your schools and your community. If you enjoy classical artists, buy their music.

How is a symphony laid out? How can Chrispen sit next to Alexis and Dwight?

There are variations. However the NPSO uses a very traditional layout, in a U shape around the stage. Closest to the audience on the left are the first violins. The first chair, first violin, sits on the outside. The second chair first violin sits on the inside. Next to the first violins are the second violins. The first chair second violin also sits on the side closest to the audience—so the first chair second violin does indeed sit next to the second chair first violin. Confused yet? :)

Is Maggini a real violin maker?

Absolutely. Giovanni Paolo Maggini was an Italian luthier who lived from 1580 to 1630. His violins, especially the later ones, are highly desired.

Does the Maggini Chrispen plays really exist?

It does, and as far as I am aware it is currently in a museum collection.

What is purfling?

If you look closely at a violin or picture of a violin, you will see a thin dark line that follows the edge of the body around the violin. This is an inlaid piece of wood called purfling. Maggini was well known for using double-purfling; two lines following the edge of the body.

What does it mean to play scales in thirds and octaves?

When you play a scale in any interval (thirds, fifths, and octaves are common on the violin) you play the scale as usual, plus the note that is the specified interval higher than whichever note you are currently playing. On the violin this means playing the scale in double-stops; on two strings at once for every note. It can be a tricky exercise.

What is concert ready position?

If you've ever seen an orchestra sit quietly ready before they play, then you've seen it. There are slight variations, but it usually involves holding the violin on your lap, with your right hand resting on the shoulder of the instrument, and your bow in your left hand, either across your lap, or straight up in the air.

What is a concertmaster?

The concertmaster is the first chair, first violin. It is the most important instrument position in the orchestra.

What is a cadenza?

A cadenza is a point in a concerto when the orchestra drops out, and the soloist plays freely, in a virtuosic style. A cadenza is usually provided with the sheet music when you buy a concerto. Some concertos have a cadenza in each movement, although the one in the first movement is generally the longest. Not all concertos have cadenzas.

Do violinists really write their own cadenzas?

Some certainly do. It used to be a much more common practice than it is today. For an excellent example of a cadenza written by the violinist, I recommend Joshua Bell's recording of the Mendelssohn Violin Concerto.

Do people really tell viola jokes?

> Absolutely! And violin jokes, and conductor jokes, and every other kind you can think of. Every viola joke in this book is real and circulating. I also have a couple dozen more of them that wouldn't fit. :)

More questions?   Connect with me online at www.sandra-miller.com